MERCY CLIFTON

PILGRIM GIRL

DEDICATION

To the courageous Pilgrims who came to America, and whose
faith in God enabled them to risk everything to obey His call.
And to the young men and women of today who are prepared
to take similar risks to follow Him.

ACKNOWLEDGMENTS

For their helpful research assistance, the authors are
especially indebted to two gracious ladies in Plymouth, Massachusetts:
Carolyn Travers, the Research Librarian at Plimoth Plantation;
and Peg Baker, the Director of the Pilgrim Hall Museum.

MERCY CLIFTON

PILGRIM GIRL

PETER MARSHALL AND **DAVID MANUEL**
AND **SHELDON MAXWELL**

PUBLISHING GROUP
Nashville, Tennessee

978-0-8054-4395-0

Published by B&H Publishing Group,
Nashville, Tennessee

Dewey Decimal Classification: F
Subject Heading: PILGRIMS (NEW PLYMOUTH COLONY)—
FICTION \ UNITED STATES—HISTORY—COLONIAL PERIOD,
CA. 1600–1775—FICTION \ HISTORICAL FICTION

This book is a work of fiction, intended to entertain and inspire.
Although it is based on actual historical events, some of the names,
characters, places, and incidents are the products of the authors'
imagination. In some cases, fictitious words or actions have been
attributed to real individuals; these, too, are imagined.

1 2 3 4 5 6 7 8 9 10   11 10 09 08 07

THE CHARACTERS

SAINTS

Mercy Clifton: Brown haired, brown eyed, and ready for adventure, she is sixteen in 1620, when the *Mayflower* sets sail for the New World.

James Clifton: Mercy's aged and loving father who sees this voyage as the fulfillment of his dream for his family.

Margaret Clifton: Mercy's mother, sickly and old before her time, has lost all her children except Mercy. For her the voyage is more a nightmare than a dream.

William Bradford: A committed Separatist since his youth, he has become one of their elders. He will soon be elected their governor, and his journal, *Of Plimoth Plantation,* will become the most valuable chronicle of the Pilgrims' settlement.

William Brewster: Another of the Pilgrim elders, his wisdom and kindness make him a father figure for them all, as well as their spiritual teacher.

John Carver: The Pilgrims' elected Governor for the voyage and for their first few months in the New World. Like so many others, he will not live to see their first summer.

Edward Winslow: The youngest of the Pilgrim elders. Gifted as an emissary to the Indians, he, too, kept a chronicle of their adventures, second only to that of Bradford.

Priscilla Mullins: Mercy's level-headed friend, who would one day marry John Alden.

Elizabeth Tilley: The more excitable of Mercy's girlfriends, she would later marry John Howland.

STRANGERS

Jack Billington: Seventeen and darkly handsome, he avidly courts Mercy who, though attracted to him, finds him mysteriously disturbing.

Francis Billington: Jack's mischievous, eleven-year-old brother, who seems a born troublemaker, but Mercy detects that what he really craves is someone to care for him.

John Billington: The head of the Billington family, he cannot stand anyone telling him what to do and is continually at odds with the Pilgrim leadership.

Miles Standish: A skilled and capable professional soldier, he is hired to be the settlement's military commander.

John Alden: He signed on as the cooper (barrel-maker) for this voyage, never dreaming that it would forever change his life and brighten his heart.

Stephen Hopkins: The Stranger with a strange past, he is faced with the choice of siding with the Billingtons or the Pilgrims.

John Howland: Saved from drowning by a miracle, he is the first Stranger to join the Saints in heart and deed.

INDIANS

Squanto: The lone surviving member of the Patuxet tribe, he becomes "a special instrument of God" to help the Pilgrims.

Massasoit: He is the chief of the Wampanoag Indians and also the Great Sachem (chief among chiefs) of other neighboring tribes.

Amie: Massasoit's daughter, who becomes Mercy's "blood sister," and helps to save the colony.

ANIMALS

Loyal: John Goodman's English Springer Spaniel, who becomes attached to Mercy.

Cromwell: John Goodman's large Bull Mastiff, who has more bravery than wisdom.

Charlemagne: More than just Captain Jones' cat, she sees herself as the rightful queen of the *Mayflower*.

1

LIMES

Puckered lips reluctantly kissed the sour green fruit. Stung by its bitter flavor, they curled back tightly against clenched teeth. Two soft brown eyes squinted. A slender nose wrinkled. The stale salty air hung so heavily throughout the small merchant ship that she could barely breathe.

The ship was packed with passengers, cargo, and livestock—everything needed to start a new life in a strange New World. Animal pens filled the under-deck spaces around the anchor rope and the capstan that hoisted it up. The stench of sheep, goat, chicken, and pig droppings was suffocating and certainly didn't match the fragrance of the ship's lovely name, the *Mayflower*.

"Limes!" gasped Mercy Clifton, plucking the offending fruit from her mouth. "Sucking them on empty bellies is awful," she moaned, grimacing at her two best friends.

"I'm hiding mine," Elizabeth Tilley whispered, blue eyes flashing. The girls snuggled together for warmth around Elizabeth's tin foot-warmer box, lined with embers from the cook's brick furnace on the main deck above them. "Limes are not much for eating, but rubbing them on one's nose fades freckles!"

"For the love of heaven!" exclaimed Mercy. "What a careless vanity if one dies of whatever they're supposed to cure!"

The third girl spoke more prudently. "We'd best eat these nasty limes. Dr. Fuller prescribes them to save our lives, not our faces."

"Just because *you* don't have any freckles, Miss Priss," protested Elizabeth.

Poking her nose in the air, Priscilla replied, "Pris–cil–la."

"Priscilla Mullins, not everyone has the face of a goddess, like you," Elizabeth shot back, sticking out her tongue. Priscilla returned the gesture, and their sour mood dissolved into quiet giggles.

The bed they were sitting on was a crude table Mercy's father had hammered together from scrap wood. For privacy he had hung a curtain over some twine. This makeshift space they called their "cabin" was wedged among many others in the cramped quarters along the bulkheads, the sides of the ship.

The girls huddled together on a canvas mattress stuffed with straw. Mercy didn't like the stubble poking through but was grateful to lie on anything soft at all. Less fortunate souls had already disposed of their bedding, ruined by mildew from water seeping through the upper deck, as storm after storm swept their ship.

Mercy counted five weeks since they'd put out to sea from Plimoth, England. For the first two, they'd enjoyed fair sailing, but the last three were spent in misery, confined below decks.

She sighed, as she thought back to the times she had stood at the railing on a sunny afternoon, watching the next storm approach. The blue horizon would change to an ominous gray. The rising wind would drive the green waters into towering dark waves. Beneath her feet the deck would begin to pitch and roll, and she would tighten her grip on the lifeline strung along the railing. Craving every last breath of fresh air, she would wait until the captain, Master Jones, ordered the passengers to go below and the crew to fasten down the hatches after them.

Once again confined to the crowded "tween decks," she would watch the *Mayflower*'s helmsman at the aft end of the ship, as he struggled to hold the tiller steady against heavy waves. Through a small hatch near the captain's cabin above, the first mate, Mr. Clark, called down course corrections. But battering winds shook the little ship; and the helmsman, his eye ever on the compass, could barely keep them on course. How terribly he cursed! With sails furled for fear of having them torn away, they would be forced to ride out the storm under bare masts.

"She can't bear a knot of sail!" the helmsman would mutter. "We'll be hundreds of miles off course by tomorrow!"

Days wore on into what seemed like an eternity. Coughing spells and the wailing of children echoed through the vessel, day and night. But Mercy's father had taught her to find something to be grateful for in everything.

She was grateful for these two friends. After long days at sea, they had become as dear as sisters. They shared their deepest secrets, made up new verses to old songs, and challenged one another with memory verses from the Bible, seeing who could remember them best.

Priscilla Mullins poked wisps of flaxen hair back under her tight cap. Sitting up, she closed the thin curtain. Though it offered little privacy, at least it cut the bone-chilling drafts from the hatch above their heads.

Priscilla noticed Elizabeth trying to find a place to hide her lime. "Don't let Dr. Fuller catch you!"

"Priss is right," scolded Mercy, swatting at tiny black bugs that skittered out of the straw mattress. Peeking through the curtain to see where Dr. Fuller was, Mercy spotted him soothing a small boy who was throwing up into a clay pot. The weary doctor was surrounded by miserable passengers, young and old, just as seasick.

Elizabeth tucked the lime into a pocket under her apron. "I'm almost sixteen! Soon I shall decide for myself about such things as sucking limes."

"If they catch you," Priscilla retorted, "they'll decide for all of us! 'Tis for the good of all," she continued in her grown-up way. "You want to get scurvy and die like Dr. Fuller's assistant, poor old Butten? He served each of us our daily lime but refused to eat them himself."

Mercy shuddered. She'd watched him succumb to the dread disease, feared by all on long Atlantic voyages. Yesterday they'd slid his bloated body overboard before the latest storm locked them below.

"What I *want*," replied an unrepentant Elizabeth, "is not to throw up anymore today." She shook her head. "My skirt's so soiled now, I'll have to throw it away when we land . . . *if* we land."

"Hush that talk!" Mercy hissed. She pulled her knees up to her chin, wrapping her long blue skirt and petticoats tightly around her ankles. But even that didn't warm her body, which had been chilled for weeks.

She turned to Elizabeth. "Don't say, *if* we land. Where's your faith?"

"Back in Leiden, swept away by a Dutch windmill, I guess" Elizabeth sighed. "Can't say I've had much since."

"That's silliness!" snapped Priscilla. "We wouldn't be on this journey if we didn't have faith."

"My father has enough faith for our whole family," retorted Elizabeth. "I had no choice but to come along. Besides, look at those Strangers among us that came on board at Southampton, when we got to England. They don't read the Bible or pray. What faith do *they* have? It's just an adventure for them."

"We'll see how it comes out for each of us, won't we?" Mercy warned. "Papa says, 'A man will only live to the end of his vision.' So you'd better get one."

"And *you* have one?" Elizabeth answered back. She was on the verge of saying more, when she suddenly grimaced and reached for the slop bucket beneath the bed.

Clutching it at the ready, she gazed out through the parted curtain at the murky shadows between decks, where it was sometimes so drafty that no unprotected candle could stay lit.

"Look," she murmured, pointing up to the grating over the hatch above. "Moonlight. We haven't seen sun or moon in a week! What I wouldn't give for one ray of sunshine through those horrid leaking cracks!"

As if to mock her distress, the moon disappeared. Howling cross-winds were soon roaring outside, as rain lashed the main deck above. The *Mayflower* rolled even farther than usual, causing rainwater to stream down through a crack in the deck, soaking Elizabeth's linen coif cap.

Galumph!

Something pounced from the darkness into their cabin. The invader, two feet of black-and-white fur, sprang wildly about, finally jumping up to put two paws in Mercy's lap. A wet tongue slurped her chin.

"Ugh!" She squealed into a face marked like a bandit with two black spots that covered both eyes. "Mr. Goodman's dirty little dog!"

"Scoot, Loyal!" Elizabeth rebuked the intruder. "You're getting the covers filthy!"

The spaniel avoided Elizabeth's swat and circled back to jump up on Mercy again.

"Let her be, poor thing," said Priscilla softly. "Her master's terrible sick over there." She pointed out through the parted curtain at a young man on a mat, tossing with a high fever and chills. "He's been delirious for days. Maybe she's worried about him. And she's probably starved," she mused. "There's barely enough food for us!"

"Sorry, Loyal." Mercy stroked her silky coat and floppy ears, which is what the dog wanted. She settled quietly at Mercy's feet and fell asleep.

Her companions were dozing off, too, when Mercy felt the dog tense. Loyal was staring intently at something.

Peering through the gloom to see what had caught her attention, Mercy noted that the hatch above was ajar. She heard a creak on the steps of the ladder beneath it.

Was someone going up there? Surely not! Didn't everyone know that only members of the ship's crew were allowed topside in storms? Mercy's eyes darted about. Just about every passenger was sick in bed. Then who . . . ?

Suddenly the hatch was thrown wide open. A bolt of lightning lit up the figure of a man leaping up the ladder and out on deck.

At that instant Loyal sprang up and raced up the ladder after whomever it was. Mercy jumped up after the dog. If Loyal got out on deck, the crashing waves would sweep her overboard in an instant!

2

MAN OVERBOARD!

Skirts tangling her legs, Mercy Clifton struggled up the ladder after the spaniel. "Loyal! Come back!" she cried. But the dog ignored her, bent on great adventure topside.

Mercy popped her head above the hatch just as a gigantic wave crashed over the deck. Making a desperate lunge for the dog, she somehow managed to grab her tail and pulled as hard as she could.

Loyal yelped, falling backward into Mercy, who would have fallen herself were it not for someone's strong grip on her shoulder.

"The ship's reeling!" declared her rescuer, tugging her and Loyal off the ladder. "Get down here before you break your bones!"

"He's gone!" she gasped, referring to the man who had opened the hatch.

"Blamed fool," muttered the young man holding her. Seeing she was safe, he raced up the ladder, crying, "Man overboard!"

The crew picked up the cry. "Man overboard! Man overboard!"

Elizabeth hurried to Mercy's side, followed closely by Priscilla. People were peering out of their cabins to see what was happening. Lanterns were lit, and children awakened by the commotion began wailing.

Priscilla smoothed Mercy's wet hair back into its tight bun, straightening her cap over it.

"What happened?" asked Elizabeth.

Taking a deep breath, Mercy tried to remember. "Someone, a man, I think, went out on deck. There was lightning. I caught a glimpse of him just before I caught Loyal." She paused. "A wave took him over the side." She started to cry.

The sound of boots clomping down the ladder's steps drew their attention to the open hatch. A husky sailor and then a lanky youth behind him carried a limp man halfway down the ladder. Outstretched hands of passengers reached to receive him and carry him to the nearest bunk.

Calmly closing the hatch, Mercy's rescuer slumped down on a step of the ladder just above her shoulder. Catching his breath, he exhaled, "He's near drowned, more dead than alive."

By a flash of lightning through the grating of the hatch, Mercy could see that he was drenched. Yet he shrugged off his shivers as if they were nothing. It was Jack Billington. A year older than she, he and his family were among the Strangers who'd joined their company just before they sailed.

"That Howland's a lucky man," Jack reflected. "The first mate said he was swept into the sea and was going under when a rope from the rigging, trailing in the water, wrapped around his arm. He grabbed it, and when the ship rolled the other way, the crew was able to haul him out like a hooked fish."

Mercy was trembling. "Thank you for catching hold of me at the ladder."

"Can't have *everyone* washed over the side," said Jack with a chuckle. "'Specially one as pretty as you."

Mercy blushed, and in the next lightning flash she thought she noted mischief in the dark eyes, set deep beneath heavy brows. He had sharp, clean features that included a strong chin covered by a first beard. The commotion around her faded away as she studied his fine-looking face.

"Mercy!" Priscilla whispered. "Stop staring!"

Elizabeth threw her own blanket over Mercy's shoulders and dried her briskly. As her friends hurried her back to their cabin, Mercy scolded herself. She should not be noticing such things, particularly about someone not in their group. Her father would never approve of her or any Separatist being attracted to a Stranger.

Still, she could not resist a look back over her shoulder, just as Jack joined the men around Howland. For the briefest of moments, he turned back, smiled, and winked.

Elizabeth was scandalized. "Mercy! He *winked* at you!"

"Despicable!" hissed Priscilla, referring to from Psalm 35: "Let not mine enemies wink with the eye."

Mercy knew the verse, and not from just hearing it; she had actually read it. And reading was something Priscilla Mullins in all her pride could not do. Reading for women was frowned upon as a frivolous waste of time. But Mercy's elderly father loved his large Geneva Bible more than anything he possessed. Determined that his daughter should cherish it, too, he'd taught her to read. It was their secret, and Mercy could not be outquoted by anyone.

"What's wrong with you, Priss?" Mercy scolded her. "He may be a Stranger, but he's no enemy. Did he not save me from a fate akin to Mr. Howland's? And does God's Word not also say, 'Love thy neighbor as thyself'? We should at least let him know we are grateful."

Priscilla continued to frown. "Well, there's something about him. . . . I just don't know what it is yet." Scooping up Loyal, she carried the wet dog over to Mr. Goodman's cot.

Mercy watched her friend. "Overly suspicious," she murmured, sadly shaking her head.

Elizabeth pursed her lips. "No, she knows better than to think the whole world's against us." Then she smiled. "Maybe she's a wee bit jealous. She can't have all the stares, now can she!"

A robust man in a gray cloak and stocking feet wobbled past them, trying to tug on a shoe as he hurried along. He stopped and turned to Mercy. "Tell me, lass, what exactly *did* you see?"

It was William Bradford, one of the senior men of their group. She did her best to relate the incident, adding what Jack Billington had told her.

He listened carefully, tapping the tips of his fingers together. "John Howland was mightily favored by God this night," he mused. "But it will be a miracle if he survives."

Jack, approaching them, heard this last. "Blamed lucky, if you ask me!" he muttered.

"Nay! Luck had nothing to do with it," stated another arrival. Mercy turned to see Elder Brewster, the most senior of their leading men. The white-bearded, smiling gentleman added, "The Lord God Almighty spared him."

Just then the ship's bow plunged into a wave, shaking the entire vessel. Personal belongings tore lose from their bindings and putrid slop pans spilled over, sending rivulets of vomit running down the deck. Even the livestock in their cages were affected, chickens squawking and pigs toppling on top of one another.

Elder Brewster was pitched against the starboard bulkhead but was kept from falling by a sturdy middle-aged man—John Carver, who was working his way along the wall, hand over hand. "Steady as she goes, Mr. Brewster," he said with a smile.

Violently the ship pitched again, knocking everybody down. When Master Carver got to his feet and pushed through the crowd surrounding the stricken man's bunk, he found Dr. Fuller already tending him. Carver's eyes widened. "It's my manservant, John Howland. God be praised, he's alive!" Elected Governor by the Leiden group, Carver spoke with an authority in his voice that calmed Mercy's fears.

Dr. Fuller mopped the stricken man's brow, and he groaned. "The rope," he murmured, over and over, eyes still closed, "the rope . . . the rope . . ."

The hatch opened briefly and down it came the ship's Captain, striding angrily toward them. The tempest outside held no fury compared to the wrath on Master Jones's face.

3

"FOR THE LIKES OF ME"

Master Jones addressed Governor Carver: "This being *your* manservant who disobeyed my order, and you being the leader of the passengers, hear me carefully." He raised his voice so that all might hear. "Mark my words: landlubbers must not be on deck in heavy weather!" He glanced at John Howland. "He'd be fifteen fathoms deep by now, were it not for the halyard that happened to wrap round his arm!"

"We know," replied Elder Brewster with a disarming smile, "and we thank the Almighty for that rope! It was, sir, a miracle."

"One most undeserved, if you ask me," retorted Master Jones. "In a storm like this, the *last* thing I need is to have my crew distracted by such folly. He put the entire ship at risk!" He turned to Elder Brewster. "Perhaps the rope *was* an act of God," he said more softly, "for there was no way we could have turned back for him."

Mercy heard the hatch open again. "Master Jones!" yelled the first mate from the main deck, "you're needed topside!"

As the captain turned to leave, he had a final word for Governor Carver. "We must make harbor before winter. No more distractions, sir; I'm holding you personally responsible."

Master Carver nodded. "You have my word on it."

"Good." The captain left, rapidly ascending the ladder.

No one moved. All eyes were on Master Carver, awaiting his rebuke. But there was none. Mercy watched as their leader simply knelt by the young man's side in silent prayer. Only the creaking of the ship was louder than the labored breathing of John Howland.

The Strangers among them were impressed; this wayward servant had received his master's love, not his wrath.

Now Dr. Fuller began to revive Howland. He thumped the man between his shoulder blades, until he gagged and started coughing up the seawater he'd swallowed.

Dr. Fuller chuckled. "He's got enough salt water in him to pickle his liver, but he'll live—*if* we can warm him up."

Gazing down on poor John Howland, Priscilla turned to Mercy and Elizabeth. "He's blue," she whispered. "We'd best get blankets on him in a hurry."

Elizabeth nodded and, hoisting up her skirts, hurried off to their cabin. She soon returned with a dry blanket and bent down to tuck it around the still form. Then she observed softly, "It would be a fine face if it had some color in it."

To that, Mercy smiled. "Weren't you just scolding *me* for staring?"

Elizabeth blushed but didn't take her eyes off him.

Another man—a Stranger like Jack, not from Leiden—came forward and knelt by Howland's side. From a cloth bag he produced a luxurious cloak lined with rich dark pelts of beaver, which he put over the stricken man. The girls looked at one another. Who could afford such a cloak?

"Maybe he's a furrier," Mercy mused. Their financial backers in London were expecting them to send back pelts by the boatload, and soon. But none of the Saints could ever hope to own such a cloak.

One of the onlookers, William Bradford's wife Dorothy, felt the edge of the cloak. "Mr. Hopkins, how odd of you to bring such an elegant garment into the wilderness."

"I trapped the animals for it the last time I was in the New World."

"You've been to America before?" inquired Mr. Carver.

"To Jamestown," the rugged stranger replied, tucking the cloak around Howland, whose teeth were chattering uncontrollably.

"Why did you leave, sir?"

Mercy turned at this new voice. It was another of their Elders, Edward Winslow. Tall and stately in bearing, he was younger than the others but still had a full mustache and beard. What Mercy liked best about him was that though well educated, he was reserved, never forcing his opinion on others. Waiting patiently for Mr. Hopkins' reply, his serene hazel eyes searched the Stranger's face.

The latter smiled. "I left, so that I could return."

What did that mean? Mercy wondered, looking at the faces of their senior men. As Mr. Hopkins bent to finish securing the cloak around John Howland, he missed the looks that were exchanged. But Mercy didn't. She saw the concern that passed between Brewster, Bradford, Carver, and Winslow.

Why did Mr. Hopkins' words trouble them?

Waving for silence, Dr. Fuller leaned into the chest of the still shivering Howland and listened. He scowled. "That hatch up there is too drafty. We've got to move him away from it. If he catches pneumonia, that's a death sentence that would spread through the ship."

"He can have our cabin," said Master Carver, who now directed his other servants, Roger, William, and a boy named Jasper, to help him carry Howland to the Carvers' berth.

Standing up, Mr. Hopkins ordered his own servants, Dody and Leister, to fetch their iron braziers—trays filled with sand and glowing charcoals used by the passengers to ward off the ship's chill. They placed them next to Howland.

Looking down at Howland's ashen face and trembling blue lips, Mercy doubted he would survive. She dreaded the thought of another burial at sea, like poor Butten's. The body encased in old sailcloth on a plank by the railing, the words by Elder Brewster, a psalm sung, a farewell prayer. The plank would be tilted, and John Howland's body would slide into the sea, committed forever to the deep.

She shuddered. Please, God, don't let it happen again!

Dr. Fuller asked for someone to fetch brandy, liquor kept for such emergencies. "The heat outside of him is not enough; we've got to warm him up on the inside."

When it arrived, he spooned it into Howland's mouth, a swallow at a time.

Mercy looked up at Elder Brewster. "What else can we do?"

"Pray," he softly replied. Then he bent near Howland's ear and said in a low voice, "Your Creator gave you back your life today, lad. You should be thinking about how you will live it."

No response.

Mercy stared intently at Howland's face. Was he slipping away?

Elder Brewster continued, as if certain John was hearing him. "We do not make vows lightly, but you should make Him one, one that you intend to keep."

John's eyes did not open, but his lips parted, and in a hoarse whisper he croaked out, "I am but a Stranger among you Saints, and now such a great sinner. You need not care for the likes of me."

"No, sir," Mercy gently assured him, "we are all but sinners in need of our Lord's forgiveness."

Elizabeth agreed, adding, "The Almighty wouldn't have saved you from the deep, John Howland, to condemn your soul."

Seeing Howland feebly smile, Brewster added, "Young man, hear and *heed* the words of Holy Scripture: 'If we confess our sins, He is faithful and just to forgive us our sins and to cleanse us from all unrighteousness.'"

John's face relaxed, and a hint of a smile came to his lips.

Mercy glanced around: all of the Leiden group were smiling, and the Strangers did not know what to make of what just happened. Could Howland have truly been completely pardoned by God?

Apparently Elder Brewster thought so. Looking at Stephen Hopkins, Jack Billington, and the other Strangers, he declared, "Saints and Strangers we may be on this ship, but an unsettled land awaits us, and in it we shall *all* be strangers together." He smiled. "May we all become saints in it, as well."

A wild New World, thought Mercy. What would it hold for them? She and her friends had tried to imagine a place with no cities, no roads, no houses. Nothing but wilderness.

And savages.

4

LOYAL'S LEAP

John Howland was not out of danger. His brow was hot with fever, and his skin was cold and clammy. Tenderly Mercy wiped his forehead. She was the only one left to tend him. Elizabeth had fallen asleep, sitting beside him, and Priscilla had to be helped back to her cabin.

She looked down at her fitfully sleeping patient. He'd just gone a little crazy in this confinement and done what every one of them would have liked to do—dashed up the ladder for one breath of fresh air.

Closing her eyes, Mercy tried to remember Holland, especially the town of Leiden where she'd grown up. In the spring a vast field of yellow tulips bloomed near their stone cottage. Windmills on high stone towers dotted the landscape, their white canvas paddles, wide as both her arms outstretched, turning slowly in the air.

Dikes held back the seawater from the Low Countries or Netherlands, as Holland was sometimes known, while barges moved sedately along canals that spread like a checkered maze over the countryside. The canals also irrigated the soil, making it rich and fertile, like the dirt in her mother's lovely herb garden.

Years before, Leiden had become a place of refuge for her parents and their friends, fleeing from persecution in England. They had originally lived in the mid-England town of Scrooby; and when she was just a baby, they had separated from the Church of England—what some called the King's Church. They had started a new church and had begun to strictly follow the Bible's teachings about living as Christians. However, neither the King nor his Church would simply let them alone to worship God as they chose. They'd tried to close down their church and chased them around the countryside, till the Separatists finally had to flee to Holland. And even there they were caught up in the religious fights and arguments.

One afternoon last year some young rogues had thrown stones at her and her elderly father, chasing them all the way home. Why? Simply because they had been mistaken for followers of the controversial Jacobus Arminius, a local pastor. The stoning incident made up her father's mind. He and his wife and daughter would join the others about to make a new start in the New World.

A soft slurp on her cheek roused her from her daydreaming. It was Loyal, wanting attention. She wagged her tail, and Mercy smiled to recall how she'd joined their company.

It had been a sunny, bright blue morning. The whole congregation had gathered at the Leiden dock to see them off. As they had bid their final farewells to lifelong friends and Mercy said good-bye to her only cousin, she had begun to cry. Her tears increased as they sang one of their favorite hymns together for the last time.

We sing of community, now in the making
In every far continent, region and land;
With those of all races,
All times, names, and places,
We pledge ourselves in covenant—firmly to stand!

They had vowed to blend their voices again in Heaven or the New World, whichever brought them together first.

Mercy brushed away tears as Loyal squirmed in her arms, reminding her how the dog happened to be there.

The barge had been so packed with goats, chickens, and belongings that the bargemen had allowed Goodman to bring only one of his two dogs. Mercy had watched him make the heartbreaking decision to leave Loyal with John, Edward Winslow's younger brother, and instead take his other dog, Cromwell. The large mastiff would be a better choice for hunting and guard duty in the wilderness.

John Winslow was a kind young man, not much older than she was, and he had always been sweet on her since they'd played together as children. The picture of him standing on a low bridge above their barge that morning holding Loyal was etched in her memory.

Then the bargeman on the bank had cracked his whip, and his team of mules leaned into their harnesses. With a long pole his assistant on the barge pushed the vessel away from the canal bank, and they began the first part of their journey—to the ocean port of Delfthaven.

But Loyal hated being left behind. As the barge passed beneath the bridge, suddenly the spaniel leaped out of John's grasp and launched herself down toward the barge, and into any outstretched arms that would catch her.

They happened to be Mercy's.

Now, looking down at the dog's big round eyes, she smiled. "You got to come, didn't you," she whispered. "But just you remember who you belong to, because when Mr. Goodman gets better, he'll want you back."

Loyal licked her again, but Mercy's smile faded. There was no telling if Mr. Goodman or John Howland would recover. When they'd left Leiden, everyone assumed it would be a fairly short and smooth summer crossing. They'd get to their new home in time to put up shelter well before it turned cold.

No one had any idea of the endless troubles they would have to overcome, which had turned a pleasant passage into a nightmare. Nor could anyone have known that their problems would test their determination to settle in the New World, and create a Christian haven for all those thinking of leaving Europe.

Stiffly Mercy rose to her feet and wrung out her rag, then settled back down to resume her lonely vigil and her thoughts, mopping John Howland's sweaty brow.

Can the faith of our small number light a candle for God in the wilderness? Mercy wondered. Can we create a place for people to live together with Christ at their center, loving Him and their neighbors?

Our pastor, John Robinson, thought so. So did the Elders. We'll even try to share that love with the natives.

At that thought she frowned, recalling that some had been brought back to Europe by French and English slave hunters, to be sold on auction blocks.

What if we do find savages in America? Can we repair the damage done by the slave hunters? It was a mission—a worthy one, she resolved. As she drifted into a daydream, the rag fell out of her hand.

5

PERIL AT SEA

In her half-awake reverie she was topside on the *Speedwell,* on a clear sunny day. Taking full advantage of a following wind, the small ship on which they'd departed Holland had all its sails up. Every inch of canvas was stretched taut. From the peak of the mainmast, a red pennant streamed out in the direction of England, where they were heading across the North Sea. They were moving fast; the wake behind them was foaming. The sun was so bright on the wave curling away from the bow that it hurt her eyes to look at it.

To Mercy it seemed that the little ship itself was flying like the seagulls escorting them on either side. All the children were up on deck, an adult beside each one. They were throwing bits of stale bread to the gulls and then squealing with glee as the gulls swooped down to fight over them. How she loved the sound of children's laughter; it had been weeks since she'd heard it.

Her long brown hair blew in the breeze, something she'd rarely experienced before under their strict dress code. She'd tried to keep her cap on, but it just wouldn't stay, so rather than risk losing it, she'd tucked it in a pocket. She could hear the wind humming in the ship's rigging, and she hummed along with it, licking her lips to taste the tangy salt air.

Mercy smiled at the memory of carefully balancing a drawing slate on the railing, then taking a piece of chalk and sketching the beautiful scene in front of her. Papa had taught her how. He had taken her to the studio of a talented red-haired young lad, not even as old as she was, who had dropped out of the University of Leiden to devote his full time to painting. Her father was himself enough of an artist to recognize the extraordinary gift of young Rembrandt, predicting that he would soon be relocating to Amsterdam.

Mercy loved Rembrandt's sketches, done with a red pencil. She marveled at the care he took with the tiniest detail, which never detracted from the overall mood of each study. That was when she realized that she would love to become an artist.

In her daydream her father now came up behind her and critiqued her rendering, showing her how with a little effort she could get it exactly right—like Rembrandt.

Turning the slate over, she prepared to do a fresh study and looked up at her father. What to draw?

He suggested she focus on the masts and rigging, as sailors not much older than she was scurried up and down the ship's ratlines every time the ship changed course, shifting sails to take full advantage of the following wind. It was a challenge, but Mercy took it on to impress Papa, her dearly beloved admirer.

They'd tried to understand exactly what the men were doing, but the terms they shouted to one another were puzzling, and they dared not interrupt or ask what they meant.

A couple of the sailors did notice her sketching, though, and now and then took a peek before she would wipe the slate clean and start again. *If only I could use fine paper and red pencils like Rembrandt,* she thought, but paper had been mighty hard to come by in Holland. John Winslow, Edward's younger brother, had occasionally bought some for her in exchange for a drawing. She wished she didn't have to erase these sketches, her best yet. He would never see them.

Now in her daydream a sailor cried, "Land ho!" There was no mistaking the meaning of that, and all eyes looked to where he was pointing, the welcoming shores of Southampton.

"There she is!" called William Bradford, as their companion ship, the *Mayflower*, came into view. Mercy was excited. It was about the size of a barn; and unlike the smaller *Speedwell*, the *Mayflower* had proper tall masts and large square sails. It even had a small spar sticking out from the bow, which the sailors called a bowsprit. Underneath it, at the center of the bow, Mercy could see the carved petals of a mayflower, proudly proclaiming the ship's name.

In Southampton they met the "Strangers" who would be coming with them and loaded their belongings on the two ships.

The smile on Mercy's lips faded. If only the story could have ended there, when everything was joyful!

Her brow knitted as the reverie began to become a nightmare. After delay upon delay, just as they were ready to sail, Squire Weston, representing the London investors backing their expedition, demanded more money from them. They were forced to sell some of their precious provisions to pay him.

Finally they were able to leave Southampton, but hardly had they gotten into the English Channel when the *Speedwell* began to leak. After several attempts to caulk its hull had failed, the Elders were forced to abandon the ship and crowd everyone on board the *Mayflower*. They had used up a third of their provisions; and worst of all, summer had turned to fall, the season of great storms on the Atlantic.

Half asleep, Mercy groaned as she relived the debate of the Elders over whether to risk a crossing so late in the year. Their plan, to sail with two ships during summer's good weather, had been ruined. But after much talk and prayer, they felt God would have them go anyway. Now, come what may, there was no turning back.

She fondly recalled that when the *Mayflower* had finally departed Plimoth, setting sail for the New World, she had watched her father open his Bible and record the date, September 6, on the inside cover. Then he had added the Elders' declaration: *"We are part of a Great Design."*

In her reverie he thumbed the pages till he came to the blank one that separated the Old Testament from the New. "You have no paper, Mercy, on which to paint or draw, and you will have none until another ship comes. In the meantime there may be a scene which should be captured. When that time comes, you are to use this page."

"But Father, that's Holy Writ!"

"No, child, the printer chose to leave this page blank." He paused. "Use it wisely. You'll know the scene."

As he closed the pewter clasp on the large wooden cover, overlaid with hand-tooled leather, he said solemnly, "One other thing: promise me you'll teach your children to read it, just as I am teaching you, young lady."

She gave him her word.

"If anything happens to me, you will keep up your reading and writing, won't you? Even if others think it folly?"

"It is *not* folly, Father! It's what you love most. And that makes it a treasure to me."

"No, child, what I love *most* is to hear you greet the morning with a song."

Mercy smiled.

Father put the Bible back in its protective oilcloth covering.

She daydreamed on until a great rogue wave caught the *Mayflower* amidships, rolling the ship over, further and still further. The passengers had begun to wonder if she was about to roll over completely, but then she slowly began to come back upright. No sooner had they started to breathe a sigh of relief when a great *boom* echoed through the ship.

Mercy shook herself awake. Had she imagined that? No!

The terrible sound was real!

In an instant the hatch cover was off, and Master Jones flew down the ladder to survey the damage, which was visible to all. The crossbeam supporting the mainmast had cracked. The captain stared at it, his eyes widening. "Mother of God!" he exhaled, under his breath. "If that beam lets go. . . ."

He didn't finish; he didn't have to. And Mercy saw something in his face that none of them had ever seen before.

Fear.

6

JOHN ALDEN TO THE RESCUE

Shivers ran down Mercy's spine as the dreadful sound of splintering wood echoed through the ship. Frozen with terror, she sat on the floor right where she had awakened from her daydream, next to John Howland's berth.

Run! she urged herself. But where? Am I trapped in the belly of this ship? Are we going down?

Master Jones raised a lantern to the overhead beam under the deck above as crewmen and Elders strained to inspect the damage. "If that beam lets go," murmured the first mate, "there'll be nothing to support that mainmast!" Mercy knew that without the mast and its mainsail they were doomed.

As they watched, the deck overhead began to sag ever so slightly, allowing seawater in, and groaning each time the ship rolled and the crossbeam split further. Behind John Howland's berth, frightened pigs and goats bleated and kicked at their stalls. Feathers flew as hens beat their wings against wicker cages.

John Howland thrashed about in his bed. "The sea is swallowing me," he moaned. "It's swallowing me."

Trembling, Mercy gave in to her darkest fears. Convinced they were going down, she sprang up to go and be with her parents, just as they arrived at the beam amidships.

"Mercy!" James Clifton dropped the cane he was leaning on to reach out a bony hand to his daughter and scoop her into his embrace. His other arm held her hysterical mother in nightgown and cap, so ill she could barely stand.

"Margaret," her father said soothingly, "calm down. I've found her." The woman wept as she laid eyes on her daughter.

Nearby Mercy saw Elizabeth clinging to her own father. The tormented girl was twisting her beautiful auburn hair into knots, sobbing uncontrollably.

Mercy went over to her. "Elizabeth! What's *happening* to you?"

"Lord," she mumbled, "I didn't want to die like this! Not in this horrid dark tomb! I wanted to see the sun, and now we're about to go to the bottom forever!"

"Talking out of our heads, are we?" murmured Priscilla, coming up behind them. She was putting on a brave face; but as she stared up at the growing crack, her eyes grew wide, and her cheeks were pale as chalk.

This can't be happening to us, thought Mercy. Somebody do something!

Elders Carver, Brewster, and Winslow hovered close to the captain. Silhouetted in his lantern's candlelight, they shook their heads. Even William Bradford, always the most confident, appeared to be losing hope. "Maybe we should turn back," he mused, "if we can repair her enough to take us."

Governor Carver glared at him. "What are you saying, William? After all we've come through? The Almighty tries our hearts this night, and His enemy, our resolve."

Though William Bradford seemed chastened, their words had been heard by all, and Mercy could feel alarm and uncertainty rising among them. If even their leaders could not agree. . . .

Just then a well-built, stocky young man in his early twenties came up. To keep his blond hair out of his eyes, he'd slapped on a woolen cap.

"Ah, Master Jones," said Governor Carver, "allow me to present our carpenter, John Alden. Let him have a look. We hired him in England."

John Alden yawned, and stumbled forward as the ship pitched again.

Christopher Jones slapped the young man's shoulder. "Know him well, sir. Your carpenter? My cousin."

Mercy's mouth fell open. She didn't know that!

"Gentlemen," replied the lad humbly, "knocking these crude cabins together hardly qualifies me as a carpenter." He smiled. "But give me a barrel to mend, and I'll own up to being a fair cooper."

Master Jones asked his cousin, "Can you mend this buckled beam? If you can, we can make land, under small sail, to ease her in."

"Aye, sir, I think we can. We'll shore up the beam with the jackscrew they brought from Holland for raising houses, when they get where they're going."

Master Jones, arms crossed over his broad chest, rubbed the gold ring in his earlobe and pondered. As he did, the *Mayflower*'s next roll caused the beam to groan and the split to widen further.

"Fetch the jackscrew from the hold," commanded the captain. "Right now!"

His crew, looking at one another, balked. The first mate spoke for the others. "Sir, that screw is buried at the bottom of the cargo. If we move those crates in this storm, the load could become so unbalanced she'll turn turtle and take us down. "

Hearing this, the pilot called from the tiller, "I won't be able to hold her on course if she's listing! Captain, we ought to turn back. There'll be no shipwright waiting for us in the wilderness to repair her. We're way north of our course, as it is. If we go any farther, we may never see home again!"

Master Jones glared at him, then turned back to the first mate, his face purple with rage. "I said, 'Fetch the blasted screw!' Now open the lower hatch and get down there, ye scurvy knaves, or you'll be shark-bait soon enough!"

No one moved.

"I said, *Now!*" bellowed the captain.

The women gasped, Mercy's mother fainted, and the chastened crew leaped to do his bidding.

Watching the fearful crewmen descend below, Elder Brewster called the others to prayer. "Lord, it is not with us as with others. Small things cannot discourage us. Small discontents cannot cause us to wish ourselves home again. We believe and trust You are with us."

As they prayed, they could hear and feel large crates below them being moved. The *Mayflower* took on a dangerous list to starboard, just as the first mate had warned.

Everyone clung together now. The ship rolled farther and then pitched, throwing them off-balance till some were vomiting on their stockings and shoes.

Elder Brewster stood in the midst of them, searching for some sign of hope. His eyes fell on the three girls, huddled together as always.

"Mercy, Priscilla, Elizabeth—our singing angels! Lead us now in Psalm 107."

Bravely Priscilla began the simple chant. Elizabeth caught it, and Mercy joined in, singing the words they knew by heart:

> *They that go down to the sea in ships,*
> *that do business in great waters;*
> *these see the works of the Lord,*
> *and His wonders in the deep.*

Mistress Carver and Mistress Winslow and others now joined the singing. Susana White and Mary Allerton, both expectant mothers, gaunt and sick, weakly gave it a try.

> *They mount up to the heaven,*
> *they go down again to the depths:*
> *their soul is melted because of trouble.*

Sarah Eaton rocked her wailing baby and picked up the tune in a strong, courageous voice. One of the Strangers, Mistress Hopkins, also great with child, attempted to hum along.

> *Then they cry unto the Lord in their trouble,*
> *and He bringeth them out of their distresses. . . .*
> *He maketh the storm a calm,*
> *so that the waves thereof are still.*

When the comforting psalm ended, Mercy's mother rallied and sang an old refrain: "Yet, Lord, Thou canst save."

Gradually Mercy sensed a presence of peace she'd never known. It seemed to enfold them like a blanket. Was this the calm before death? Or was it a hug from Heaven, the Lord saying that He would deliver them?

At last, three of the crewmen brought the screw up from below. The screw was as tall as they were and as big around as a man's leg. Under John Alden's direction, Jack, Stephen Hopkins, and others positioned it under the cracked crossbeam. Then several men working together began to turn the great iron screw. With each turn came another terrifying sound of tortured wood.

Mercy held her breath. Would the beam ease back into position, without splitting apart? Would it hold the mainmast?

Then she noted that the seawater had stopped seeping down through the deck. Maybe . . . maybe . . . maybe it *was* going to hold!

Four more turns of the screw and the beam was back in place, so tight that the crack was barely visible! Master Jones just shook his head and smiled.

Everyone—Saints, Strangers, and crew—gave a great cheer of triumph, slapping one another on the back, as the *Mayflower* regained an even keel.

Elder Bradford exclaimed, "Let our children say, 'Our fathers were Englishmen who were ready to perish in this great ocean, but they cried unto the Lord, and He heard their voice.'"

Nodding, Master Jones shook Governor Carver's hand. "She's firm in the hull below and under the waterline. As long as we don't overpress her now with too much sail, we'll make it." Pausing at the ladder, before returning topside, he added, "Say your prayers for an early landfall, gentlemen; we don't know how strong our repair job will prove to be."

7

SADNESS AND SUNLIGHT

When Mercy's father had taken them back to their berth, he asked her to look after her mother while he went over to sit under the lantern and read by its light for a while.

Mercy propped her mother up on pillows in the wet bedding. As she listened to her feebly trying to cough up phlegm, the girl knew in her heart of hearts that it was only a matter of time before the worsening sickness would take her.

Fishing around in the family trunk for something dry that her mother could change into, she pulled out a woolen shawl. Her mother had been saving it for the winter cold on land, but she needed it now, and was too cold to protest. She just kept singing over and over, "Yet, Lord, Thou canst save."

Then she surprised her daughter with a moment of clarity. "That was our cry twelve years ago, as we fled England to Holland. They even arrested *us,* the women and children! Your brothers and sisters were snatched away from me and given away to Church of England families. I was able to save you only because you were a baby in my arms." Her voice broke. "You're all I have, Mercy."

Old before her time, Margaret Clifton's constant self-pity usually wore her daughter down. But now she felt only compassion; and while her mother rambled on, Mercy held her dearly. Her mother had kept her alive, had kept them together, and she had something to tell her daughter.

"I don't expect to live through this, Mercy. But when I'm gone, you must marry a man who has the means to provide well for you, like that handsome Billington boy who rescued your dog."

"Loyal's not mine; she belongs to Mr. Goodman."

Her mother weakly waved away Mercy's evasion. "Eleanor Billington tells me her son will inherit his uncle's fortune back home. She hopes he'll return to claim it when he's old enough. He'll have to share it with his little brother, Francis, of course; but a fortune's a fortune, any way you look at it."

Mercy's mouth fell open. How did Mama know of her interest in Jack?

To cover her embarrassment, she dug out a piece of cold beef, some cheese, and a hardtack biscuit to feed them. "Why, Mama," she said with a smile, handing it to her, "the Billingtons aren't Separatists; they're not even Puritans. They're nothing like us. Papa would never approve."

Her mother muttered, "What does it matter anymore, what we are? God has taken everything from me. He has forgotten us in this foul-smelling ship, like Jonah in the belly of the whale."

Mercy, shocked at her bitterness, tried to close their privacy curtains tighter. Mama had always grieved but had never been bitter. She'd never given up before.

Margaret Clifton started to take a bite, then shuddered and dropped it on the blanket. With a low moan she rolled over and turned her face to the bulkhead. Mercy waited for her to say something, but hearing only soft sobbing, she decided just to let her fall asleep.

She tried to collect the precious ration of food off the damp blanket, but the biscuit broke into pieces, and crawling out of it were *weevils*!

"*Yechh!*" she cried aloud, spitting her own mouthful into her apron.

Just then a very pregnant Mistress Hopkins parted the half-open curtain and reached down to rest a comforting hand on Margaret's shoulder. "Please, don't give up, Goodwife Clifton. That song you were singing lifted my spirits, too. We need each other."

Mama shook off the gentle hand, but Mercy silently thanked her for the attempt and whispered, "I'll help you however I can."

"Mercy, you are a kind girl," replied Mistress Hopkins, hugging her. About to close the curtain and go to her cabin, she turned back. "I thought I'd be in my own cottage by now, with midwives to attend me in our new village with that patent we were promised near the Hudson River." She looked around. "I never dreamed I'd be delivering a baby in the wilderness or, God forbid, on this ship, if we don't make land soon!"

Mercy watched Mistress Hopkins draw a blanket tighter around her shoulders and waddle off slowly, cradling her protruding belly with both hands. The woman's labor would be dangerous at sea or on land if the winter was harsh with no heat. What had Mr. Hopkins been thinking of, bringing her in that condition?

She frowned. He was a mysterious one, wasn't he? Refused to tell the Elders anything about how he'd been to America before and why he'd left, only to return again. What was he up to?

Sunlight? Were those really rays of sun shining through the grating of the hatch? Mercy rubbed the sleep from her eyes in disbelief. *Yes!* That beast of a storm had finally stopped! She could hear the gulls again, swooping down over the upper deck, shrieking at the sailors for scraps of food.

Oh, joyful morning! She felt like dancing! She climbed off her lumpy mattress, only to discover that in spite of the brilliant blue sky the sea was still rough. She could barely keep her balance, and with a grunt sank back down on the mildewed covers. Splotches of stinking black mold covered them, but there was also something she hadn't seen for weeks—sunspots danced over the hand-sewn patchwork quilts!

She looked around to see if anyone else had noticed the sun yet, but they were all still asleep, exhausted from the night before.

Deciding to see how John Howland was, she passed under the hatch and paused at the ladder to enjoy the glorious sunshine streaming through. If only they would open the hatch, she would run up and smell the fresh air and feel the breeze!

Rubbing the smooth-worn step of the ladder with her forefinger, she yearned to raise the hatch herself. But Master Jones and Governor Carver had agreed, and their rule could not be broken. At least now she understood John Howland's temptation.

With a sigh she worked her way past the clutter of jammed-together cabin cubicles to John Howland's, and was surprised to see him propped up on pillows, sipping hot peas porridge from a wooden spoon served by none other than Elizabeth Tilley.

Seeing her friend approach, the girl smiled sheepishly. "He's come back to the living."

"So I see," Mercy replied. Then, while the young man was intent on the porridge, she mouthed silent words to her friend: *What are you doing here, tending him by yourself?*

Elizabeth blushed and mouthed back, *I'm not alone! See?* She swept her full skirt aside to reveal Dr. Fuller behind them, bent over the braziers, poking embers to keep them going. "He's been here most of the night," she told Mercy, "keeping a watch on Mr. Howland."

The doctor looked worn out, and Mercy felt pity for the poor man, while Elizabeth nattered on. "I woke up a little while ago. Did you see that wondrous sun shining down this morning? I just had to see if it affected John, too, and it did!"

John? The smitten girl had slipped and called this Stranger by his first name and not even realized she'd done it.

But as his dashing face turned toward Mercy, and he flashed a winning smile, she laughed inside. He's obviously more grateful this morning for his ardent nurse than his would-be rescuer. Probably doesn't even know that it was Loyal and me and Jack who sounded the alarm. Well, he's alive; that's all that counts.

"It is indeed a miracle, ladies," croaked John Howland. "Last night, as the sea was about to swallow me, my whole life passed before me—my childhood, my family, everything." He shook his head. "And this morning? I'm not dead! I'm *here*!"

He gazed up at the shafts of sunlight coming down through the grating. "And the glories of Heaven shine on us!" He paused. "You want to know what happened to me last night?"

"Yes!" responded Mercy, sitting down next to Elizabeth.

Pushing the proffered spoon aside, John Howland raised up on an elbow. "I could not take one more minute of being confined like a hog bound for slaughter. Next thing I knew, I was out on deck. Out of prison! Free to stand up straight and stretch my legs! I started toward the rail and found myself staring up at a mountain of water towering over us. I suddenly thought, *Perhaps this wasn't such a good idea after all!*"

His audience hung on every word.

"Just then a crewman came running up, cursing and yelling at me to get back below where I belonged. Had a rope around him, tying him to the mast; but he came at me, waving and cursing.

"I was about to go back down when the wave broke on me and swept me over the side."

"We fished you out, you big fool!" snarled a voice nearby.

The girls turned. It was one of the crewmen who had balked at Master Jones's order to fetch the screw. John Howland stared at him. "It was you! You're the sailor who cursed me!" He raised half out of his bed.

"Aw, you're crazy! Out of your head!" retorted the sailor. Dr. Fuller stepped between them, and John Howland, gripped by a sudden deep coughing spell, fell back on his pillows.

The sailor stomped off, muttering terrible profanities.

"That's Bart," Dr. Fuller said quietly, shaking his head. "You girls stay well clear of him. He's dangerous."

Spent, John Howland sank back into a deep sleep. The girls took turns watching over him so Dr. Fuller could attend other sick folks.

8

THE MOCKER

Shortly before sundown the ocean had finally calmed sufficiently for Master Jones to invite everyone up on deck. Though the ship had ceased its heeling from side to side and Dr. Fuller prescribed the fresh air as good medicine for all of them, many were still queasy. But all who could manage the climb up the ladder were quick to take advantage of the last rays of sun.

Mercy, Elizabeth, and Priscilla were assigned the care of the younger children to give their worn-out mothers a brief rest. The little ones scampered about at the end of safety ropes tied around their waists, the other ends tightly held by the girls. As the three girls gazed at the red-orange orb slowly sinking out of sight on the western horizon, while watching the little ones play, John Alden strolled by.

"Red sky at night, sailor's delight," he offered, quoting the mariners' proverb to the girls.

"Then, sir, let us pray that the sky changes tonight, lest we have 'red sky at morning, sailors take warning,'" responded Priscilla.

His face lit up with pleasure at Priscilla's quick wit. "My sentiments precisely, ladies," he said, tipping his cap.

"Thank you for saving our ship, sir," murmured Priscilla with a coy smile.

"It was the jackscrew, not I," he assured her humbly.

Suddenly he stared to starboard.

The girls' eyes turned to where he was pointing. "See that waterspout? That's a whale! Master Jones informs me there's good money in whaling. Who knows, perhaps I'll have a whaling ship of my own someday."

With a smile he bade them good evening and went on his way.

"He's not the hero you think he is," Elizabeth scolded Priscilla. "He only did what he's paid to do, fix things. It was Divine Providence that saved us."

"Well, now, Tilley," Mercy chided her, "so you *do* have faith in God's providence, after all?"

"After what we went through last night, who wouldn't?" retorted Elizabeth, smiling and taking deep breaths of the fresh air.

Priscilla, eager to change the subject, exclaimed, "Having the children play Hunt the Slipper was a smart idea. They're enjoying it."

"As we did at their age," agreed Mercy.

"Look at the color coming back into their cheeks," observed Priscilla. Reaching into her pocket, she handed each one a little cake of sugar and gum-dragon mixed with a fragrant spice of cinnamon and ginger. Squealing with delight, the children devoured them, never suspecting they contained Dr. Fuller's medicine to settle their stomachs.

Mercy handed little Damaris Hopkins a thimble to hide, but the child fumbled the thimble in her small hands and dropped it.

"Be more careful, Damaris," Mercy warned, rescuing it in the nick of time before it bounced overboard. "Now you get to be the guesser, instead. Let's close our eyes, and leave the circle until the others hide something from us, and then you can guess who's got it."

The little tyke happily skipped along by Mercy's side while Mercy replaced the precious thimble in her sewing kit. They carefully crossed the deck toward what Mercy thought was a group of passengers. As she opened her eyes, to her shock, vulgar sailors stood in front of her. Flustered, she backed away—but not before one of them jumped in front of her. Little Damaris pushed hard against his legs, but he stood like stone in their path.

"Glib-glabbety-puke-stocking-psalm-singers! That's what ye are!" It was Bart, the same sailor who had cursed John Howland!

Leaning into her face with foul breath, he grabbed Mercy's waist. With the other hand he yanked her pouch off its string belt, dangling it above her head. "What pretty treasures have ye in here, wench?" The sailors laughed crudely.

Mercy recoiled at his rudeness while Damaris beat his legs with her tiny fists. Mercy's eyes darted around the deck, looking for help. She cried out, but the ugly fellows behind them drowned her out. "Bart, she's a pretty catch, but you'd best throw her back."

The sailor only tightened his grip until Damaris suddenly bit the brute's knee!

He was about to whack the child into the railing when someone strode up to them. "Give the lady back her pouch," Jack Billington quietly demanded, as tall and imposing a figure as the surly sailor.

But Bart tossed it overboard with a coarse laugh. "That's what I'll do with all of you 'fore this journey ends. One dead body after another sinking to the bottom! And I'll make merry with all your treasures, too!"

Mercy's heart sank as she watched her precious sewing kit and the last of her drawing chalks splash into the sea.

Swinging his fist as hard as he could, Jack caught Bart on the chin. Releasing Mercy, he staggered back.

"Go below, Mercy!" Jack commanded, and she fled with Damaris in her arms as a scuffle broke out behind them. It caught the attention of a stocky short fellow carrying a musket; and as she started down the ladder, she paused to watch Miles Standish, the military captain they'd hired to protect them, walk briskly to the scene. He was not about to allow Jack to stand alone. With a fierce expression he raised his weapon, and was soon followed by the ship's boatswain, who had his whip out, ready to discipline the unruly crewman.

Disappearing below deck, Mercy collided with Priscilla and Elizabeth, who were shooing their children below with the help of Desire Minter, another young woman on board.

Elizabeth calmed Mercy. "That sailor's just a bully blowing wind, a coward, if you ask me. Foolish enough to get himself shot!"

"Jack came to my rescue," Mercy blurted out.

"Again?" Priscilla gasped, her eyes dancing. "Uh-oh, I think he's got eyes for you."

"Dark and beautiful ones!" added Elizabeth as she untied the rope from her waist, sending her charge back to his mother.

"Mama thinks he'd be a fine catch," confided Mercy, trying to set Damaris down; but the frightened child would have none of that, scrambling back into her arms.

Desire Minter came up behind them. "I'd have him in a heartbeat if he looked my way."

They all turned disapprovingly toward her.

"That is, if he proposed properly," she added, flushed.

"Well, not me," declared Priscilla. "He's not one of us. Mercy, your father and the Elders wouldn't approve of your becoming betrothed to a Stranger, would they?"

Mercy sadly shook her head.

At that moment Mistress Hopkins, the Stranger who had befriended her last night, stepped up and took her trembling child from Mercy's arms.

"Just depends how everything turns out," said Mercy with a smile, "when we're *all* strangers in the New World."

A moment later Jack descended the ladder, sporting a bruised cheek-bone and a bleeding lip.

The girls rushed to help.

Mercy hurried to Dr. Fuller's work area and found some vinegar and rags. She'd doctor him herself, not them. Besides, she had to show her gratitude, didn't she?

Returning to the cluster of young ladies gathered around him, she held out the rag to Jack.

"Only if you'll tend it for me," he requested, with a painful wink. Mercy wished he hadn't done that, not with Elizabeth and Miss Priss watching—the wink patrol!

Priscilla tossed her bossy head and tapped her foot. But Elizabeth had become a little more fond of the hero; she didn't point out his transgression this time. Instead, she winked back her approval, just to annoy Priscilla.

Mercy felt encouraged by that. She was not about to let someone else fix him up, especially with Desire Minter hovering at his side. As she tenderly dabbed the rag to his bruised cheek, he started to smile but then grimaced; his split lip hurt too much.

Nursing him, Mercy confided, "I was terrified! Mr. Howland said that sailor ran at him, yelling and cursing, just before the wave washed him overboard."

"I don't doubt it," agreed Jack. "He's got the strength of ten devils in him. It's like he's under a spell of mischief, that one."

"Whatever's the matter with him, you've now rescued me *twice*. And I am eternally grateful," Mercy assured him.

"Then this," he gingerly fingered his bruise, "was well worth it, to rescue a damsel in distress." His striking dark eyes told the rest; her gratitude was exactly what he'd wished for.

9

"I FORGIVE YOU"

Jack, Jack, Jack. Mercy could not get the Billington boy off her mind. Had Divine Providence set him in her path twice to be a hero? Or was it all just coincidence? Should she seriously consider the prodding of her mother? No! The future could wait for later—much later!

Yet all she thought about, as she did her chores, was Jack. The storms had passed. She could walk upright without wobbling. Many were still ill though, and she was collecting their chamber pots from behind their curtains. It was a labor of love that her father had suggested she do, one that few others would care to do. But he was always teaching Mercy to serve others—and even do good to those who did evil to you.

She sighed. That meant she'd have to forgive the sailor who'd grabbed her and viciously mocked them. She didn't want to. Nor did she feel like forgiving the Strangers who'd snubbed them because they had broken the King's laws by not attending the Anglican Church. So how was it that this Billington boy had eyes for her? Why wasn't he like all the other Strangers?

She heard something and jumped. That was his voice behind one of the curtains. Oh no! She'd thought everyone was clear of the cabins for now, or she'd never have started this chore. Mercy started to back away, but she couldn't resist the temptation to listen.

Jack Billington was talking to his younger brother, who was throwing up. "Francis, where did you get those extra biscuits?"

"Stole them from that sailor, Bart, the one that keeps mocking us."

"The one who attacked Mercy Clifton and busted my lip?"

"That's the one."

Hearing someone coming, Mercy jumped into the sheep pen to hide. It would be too embarrassing to be caught eavesdropping.

Peering through the slats of the pen, Mercy saw the sailor the boys were discussing. What was he doing down here again? She clung close to the bulkhead in the deepest shadows she could find.

Opening curtain after curtain, he seemed to be doing exactly what her father had asked her to do—emptying chamber pots! Or was he using that as a cover for stealing anything of value that he might come across? There was nowhere to run. She stayed still as a corpse under the straw, as the sheep nibbled around her.

She could hear him open the curtain that concealed the Billingtons.

"What in the . . ." Then his voice changed to a taunt. "Why aren't you two topside with them other psalm-singers?"

"We're not with them!" young Francis retorted.

"Maybe you should be; you're the worst little puke-stockings of the lot! Look at you! I can hardly wait to feed your carcasses to the fishes!"

"And I'd like to feed yours to the whales!" Francis snapped back.

"Why, I oughta . . ." But before the brute could catch him, Francis dashed away through the maze of cabins with Jack quickly following. Both of them flew up the ladder and out of sight.

After Bart left, Mercy carried up on deck the pots she'd put down. Careful to take them to the leeward side, she emptied them into the ocean.

The next afternoon Dr. Fuller asked the girls to help him. It wasn't John Howland who needed nursing; it was the sailor, Bart. He lay deathly ill with a fever.

Dr. Fuller shook his head. "He seems to have every infection I've been battling in all these sick folk put together. It's taken him so fast, there's nothing I can do. He'll be gone by sundown. But I can't figure how. I just don't understand."

Mercy thought she did. Looking down at the suffering sailor, she felt sorry for him, but could not help feeling that he was so filled with hatred toward the Saints that he had it coming.

A hand gently rested on her shoulder. Mercy looked up; it was her father.

"Forgive him, child. He's dying. If you don't, a part of your soul will go captive to the grave with him." He paused. "When we forgive, it is we ourselves who are freed."

Mercy sighed. She knew he was right; she knew he was waiting for her to quote the verse she'd memorized. Her mouth could say the words, but her heart was dragging behind.

Finally she took a deep breath. "Love your enemies, bless them that curse you, do good to them that hate you, and pray for them which despitefully use you, and persecute you."

She looked down at Bart. "All right," she whispered, "I forgive you."

Shaken with convulsions, the sailor didn't hear her. But she felt at peace.

Elder Brewster joined them. He asked all to pray who were witnessing the sailor die in such a desperate manner. While he read portions from his Bible, heads around him were bowed. "If thine enemy hunger, feed him; if he thirst, give him drink."

He closed the Bible and said solemnly, "It has pleased the Lord to put a just hand upon him. But let us plead for God to have mercy on his soul."

No sooner had they responded, "Amen," than the sailor, his eyes rolling back in his head, gave a final gasp and was gone.

The Elders had a proper funeral for the wretched man, sliding his body into the sea from a plank. He who had threatened to throw them all to the fishes was now himself food for the deep. Even as Mercy thought this, John Alden, surrounded by children, pointed out the spout of a whale.

10

LAND HO!

At last the cruel sea seemed satisfied; it ceased to punish the small vessel. Waves that had once towered halfway up the mast had disappeared. Now the surface was completely calm, as smooth as glass.

Leaning over the port rail, Mercy was able to see her reflection in the water. Behind her the sails hung limply from the yardarms. She frowned. No wind was just as bad as too much wind. They were drifting, no more in control of where they were going now, than when the storm blew them off course.

Gazing out to where the horizon vanished, as the milky blue sea blended seamlessly with the sky, she thought it was like a placid tub—until the Almighty whipped it like a cook beating eggs into froth. And once He withdrew His hand, awe of Him settled over everyone. Seeing God's hand in the sailor's death, after the funeral the crew didn't mock the Saints anymore, nor did the Strangers murmur against them. All was peaceful.

Yet Mercy felt uneasy within herself. Did God really strike down Bart? She wanted to talk with someone about it, but who?

She thought of Elder Brewster, the most spiritual person she knew, and found him sitting on a barrel in the bow, quietly looking over the ocean.

At her approach he turned and smiled. "Your face betrays you, young lady. You need answers, don't you?"

She nodded.

"We all do," he assured her. "And that, no doubt, is the plan of the Master of this sea. While there was nothing but disharmony aboard this vessel, it practically had to founder before our hearts would become of one accord. Now all of us ponder both the troubles and wonders that the wind of His breath brings."

"I like that," said Mercy, sitting down on a pile of coiled rope.

Elder Brewster looked at her, his brows knitting. "What's really troubling you, lass?"

"Bart's death. Could God have taken him because of what he did to me and Francis, and his hatred of us all?"

Elder Brewster tilted his hat back and smiled at Mercy. "We have continually prayed that God would watch over us, this ship, and its crew. And I believe He does. We were saved from sinking when the beam cracked.

"God's ways are mysterious, Mercy. Perhaps He allowed Bart to die to protect us from even greater harm that his evil heart would have inflicted on us later. We will never know for sure, but we do know that God cares for those He loves."

As Mercy pondered his wise words, Elders Carver, Bradford, and Winslow walked up at a quick pace. Brewster rose to greet them.

"With Master Jones' permission," declared their governor, "I've called a meeting for the entire ship's company. While the Almighty has everyone's attention, we must seek a lasting unity; for we are all pilgrims together, Saints and Strangers alike. We must not allow this opportunity to pass."

Half an hour later the deck was packed with people. Everyone waited for Governor Carver to speak. He stood resolutely, legs apart, arms folded across his chest over a purple doublet of fine serge, with a long row of neatly fastened buttons. Mercy had not seen him wear this before; obviously this was a special occasion. He was the picture of leadership, she thought, badly needed in a crisis like this.

She surveyed his audience—just over a hundred weary passengers—sailors still sobered by the loss of their shipmate, Strangers still mindful of the miraculous rescue of their own John Howland, Separatists encouraged by the amazing repair of the split crossbeam yet preoccupied by the worsening condition of the ill among them.

The only sound was the red pennant beginning to flap gently at the peak of the mainmast—curious because as yet no wind disturbed the glassy calm. Looking up at it, she smiled, wondering if anyone else had noticed.

With the Elders standing behind him, Governor Carver solemnly addressed the assembly. "In order to help pay for the cost of this voyage, Mr. Weston, representing our backers in the London Virginia Company, recruited extra passengers, you who once were Strangers to us." He smiled, his gaze seeking out the Hopkinses, the Billingtons, John Howland, and John Alden.

"We knew you not when this journey began, and we all understand that our reasons for coming are different. But we've been through so much together that in times of crisis we have begun to act as one. Who among us would not agree that Mr. Howland's rescue was a miracle? And were we not united in prayer and hope when the cracked crossbeam nearly doomed us?"

Mercy noted sympathetic nods everywhere—many among the Strangers, who actually outnumbered them.

The response seemed to encourage Governor Carver, who went on, "Let us agree, then, friends, that we face a situation where we need to be united. The recent storms have blown us far north of our intended course. A Divine destiny now lies before us, one that our navigator never charted. We must now continue west with all due speed to make landfall as soon as possible, before the dead of winter sets in, as it is already the ninth of November." He paused thoughtfully, "But we are in God's hands."

At that moment, as if to confirm what he was saying, the mainsail began to luff. The red pennant was now streaming in a gentle breeze that quickly became a wind filling the sails!

No one knew whence the wind had come, but all rejoiced at its coming. The *Mayflower* was underway!

A cheer went up from Saints, Strangers, and crew, uniting them in hope.

Several hours later a cry rang out from the lookout atop the sail in the ship's bow—the two hopeful words that all had been longing to hear for weeks: "Land ho!"

11

A CHANGE IN PLANS

All eyes eagerly scanned the silvery western horizon. There, shimmering in the morning haze, was a thin sliver of land, the first they'd seen in more than two months!

"At last!" cried Mercy. Two skirts swirled past—Priscilla and Elizabeth, cavorting like lambs. Each taking her by the hand, they formed a circle, dancing this way and that, shouting, "We're saved! Land!"

Tears of joy sprang to Mercy's eyes at the sight of everyone celebrating. Even the dogs began barking.

And now the sails filled, as if God Himself were blowing into them. The ship began rocking as their speed increased, but all were too happy to care.

It took Master Jones striding out of his cabin with a rolled-up chart in his hand to sober them again. "Captain John Smith of Virginia once explored this coast," he announced to Governor Carver and the others. "According to his chart, that land is a peninsula he labeled Cape Cod. But this wind, so strong from the south, may hinder us from rounding its elbow, further delaying our arrival at the Hudson River."

Hearing that, Stephen Hopkins said, "Captain, the Virginia Colony boundary extends only as far north as the Hudson. If we *don't* reach it, we won't be under the King's Charter." Thoughtfully, he turned to the others. "We won't be under any charter."

"Don't give up too quickly," Master Jones reassured them. "I'll do my best to get around the southern tip of this cape." The ship began to roll under the increasing wind. "But as it's getting a bit rough up here again, I'm afraid I must ask you all to return below."

For two days the *Mayflower* battled merciless headwinds, made more treacherous by the sudden appearance of barely submerged shoals off the elbow of the cape. Mercy couldn't bear the thought of coming all this way, within sight of land, only to run aground! If they were shipwrecked now, with only the ship's little boat to take them to safety, they would choose to save lives rather than what remained of their dwindling provisions. And even then some might not make it. It was a nightmare too horrible to think about!

At dawn on the third day, she brought a pot of hot tea and some biscuits to the captain's cabin, where Master Jones was meeting with their Elders. She put them down on the table next to Charlemagne, who was curled up in a catnap, oblivious to the discussion. Then she excused herself and left—but not before hearing what they were discussing.

"Gentlemen," Master Jones declared, "today is the eleventh of November. We cannot afford to lose yet another day in attempting to beat around this cape. We must go north. If the Smith chart is accurate, there's a curl at the end where we can find protection from this wind. We'll anchor there and send a shore party for fresh water while you decide what you want to do."

There was a brief discussion, and then Governor Carver's baritone voice proclaimed, "It seems clear that for whatever reason, God wants us here. Go north, Captain."

Master Jones nodded. "A wise decision. I'll reverse course at once, while the shoreline is still visible." He paused. "From the look of the sky, we'll be seeing our first snow within the hour."

By the time Mercy had finished her next chore, filling the braziers with embers from the cook's furnace, snow was indeed falling. Pulling her shawl close to protect her face, she paused to watch the delicate flakes blowing across the deck.

Every year before this one, she could hardly wait for winter. Cozy by a warm hearth, she and her mother would spend many happy hours knitting, watching the blizzards through the diamond-shaped panes of the leaded glass windows in their snug stone cottage. She'd loved the snow's soft white blanket over Holland's countryside, bringing life to a magical standstill.

But there would be nothing cozy about this winter, she thought. Below, in the 'tween decks, she found Governor Carver announcing their decision to give up any further attempt to reach the Virginia Colony. Now they would shelter in the lee curl of this peninsula and see where God would plant them.

Mercy looked around. Faces were drawn with anxiety. She noticed Mr. Hopkins and Mr. Billington whispering and felt a chill as she realized what they were thinking: If they were not going to the Virginia colony, they would not be under its charter.

Mercy's brow furrowed as she thought about the problem. As long as they were at sea, Master Jones was their final authority. But once they were ashore, who would be in charge then?

That was the problem—no one!

They would have no government at all.

She glanced at Governor Carver and realized that he had noticed Hopkins and Billington, too. He cleared his throat and continued speaking: "It seems to us that God would have us stay in these parts. As we have no existing form of government, we must covenant together to form our own.

"We propose to base it on the Bible, something men have not done since the time of the ancient Hebrews. We ask every one of you to join with us."

Handing the governor a tattered letter, Elder Brewster explained its contents: "Before we left Holland," he told everyone, "Pastor Robinson gave us wise guidelines for governing of ourselves. They will be a worthy model for the future."

Mercy noted that most were nodding, but not all. A few Strangers were looking to Hopkins and Billington.

"For the creation of this new government," Governor Carver concluded, "we need your prayers and a unified spirit, that we might find God's Great Design."

There were some heartfelt "Amens," but again, not from everyone.

Now William Bradford spoke up. "I was a lad of thirteen when I joined the Separatists, but in a way my journey is just now beginning. Whatever lies ahead, I must keep a good conscience and walk with God." He searched the faces staring at him. "If we all seek to do this, then wherever God plants us, He will bless us."

Elder Brewster put a hand on Bradford's shoulder and declared, "In matters of conviction we must stand firm before the Almighty." He smiled at the Strangers and chuckled. "But, as you get to know us better, you'll understand that we think no better of ourselves than we do of any of you."

Mercy watched the faces of many of the Strangers relax.

Now William Bradford shared their vision for the future. "We have a great hope of advancing the Kingdom of Christ in these remote parts of the earth."

Carver searched their faces for commitment. "That's why we've embarked on this adventure to the New World. Will you join with us?"

There was not a peep from the Strangers until John Howland weakly raised his hand. "I did not come on this trip for your purposes," he declared, "but I know God delivered me from death. I now choose to number myself among you."

"And I, as well," echoed Miles Standish, as his pretty young wife, Rose, nodded in agreement.

"And I," declared John Alden, raising his hand with a broad grin. Others were quick to join.

Mercy clapped her hands. But where was Jack's hand? She scanned the crowd but couldn't see him anywhere.

What was this? There was his father, Mr. Billington, shaking his head. "Not I," he said defiantly. Her heart skipped a beat. He was glowering over at Stephen Hopkins, demanding agreement from him.

But Hopkins shook his head at him! "Nay, I stand with them. I'm going to need their prayers and help—this very night, in fact! My wife has just gone into labor!"

Mercy rushed to Mistress Hopkins' cabin. If the poor lady was going to survive and deliver a healthy baby, it would take all of the women acting as one—unity, indeed!

12

OCEANUS HOPKINS

The tiny newborn that Mercy cradled in her arms reminded her of just how fragile life was. Oceanus Hopkins had just arrived in his own new world. His birth had been a difficult one, leaving his mother so weak that she had yet to hold her new son—the first baby born on a voyage to America.

Dr. Fuller recorded the birth in his medical log. The midwives who'd assisted him through the night had departed for rest, so Mercy stayed by Mistress Hopkins' side.

"She needs water," Dr. Fuller sighed, "lots of it." But Mercy knew that after two months at sea, what little was left in the bottom of the water barrels was foul. If they didn't get fresh water soon. . . .

Wrapping a blanket around the baby, Mercy nestled the wriggling bundle into his mother's arms. The privacy curtains parted, and an awed Mr. Hopkins looked in.

Gathering up his things, Dr. Fuller laid a reassuring hand on the new father's arm. "He may be small, but he's hardy."

Oceanus wailed, showing off his strong lungs. "And sings as good a tune as those brawny sailors!" the doctor added with a laugh.

Mr. Hopkins smiled. "I'll need a strong lad to help me trap for furs in this wilderness."

Mercy was about to follow Dr. Fuller when Mr. Hopkins whispered, "No, lass, please stay. I'm not much good at carrying babies."

Mercy took the child back, as Mr. Hopkins looked adoringly down at his wife. "How did you manage it, especially during the battering winds of these past few days?"

Mistress Hopkins smiled weakly and closed her eyes. Squeezing his hand, she murmured, "Mercy prayed for me."

"Then she'd best pray for us all," he muttered, his voice hardening. "We've yet to find this safe harbor that Master Jones promised. We'd have been to the Hudson River by now if the captain knew how to sail his ship!"

Mistress Hopkins opened her eyes, a look of alarm on her face. "Oh, no, Stephen," she moaned. "Not another mutiny!"

Another *what?* wondered Mercy.

Stephen Hopkins bent close to his wife's ear. "Billington says that since we'll not be under the Virginia Colony's charter, we needn't take orders from these Separatists." He looked at her. "And since there is no official government, it will not be mutiny."

Mercy saw tears well up in Mistress Hopkins' eyes. "*Please,* Stephen," she begged, keeping her voice low, "don't cause trouble here, as you did after that shipwreck on Bermuda. They almost hanged you!"

So *this* was the mysterious side of Mr. Hopkins that had made the Elders wary of him!

Mr. Hopkins dropped his wife's hand. "I stayed alive, didn't I? Had I not helped them build those two ships that took us castaways off that god-forsaken island of Bermuda, we'd have all died there!"

Mistress Hopkins clutched the corner of his jacket. "The winds of fortune blew you to Jamestown then, but where shall you hide in this vast wilderness? Billington's never been here, but you know better."

Mr. Hopkins fell silent.

"The Jamestown colonists rescued you and your first wife. Yet she perished anyway, and it broke your heart. Don't break mine, Stephen. I've come with you, to give your dream one last chance. But if you leave these people, you'll be at the mercy of the savages. We need them! If you strike out on your own, I'm going back to England and taking Oceanus with me."

Mercy marveled at the strength of her resolve. Mr. Hopkins looked at the helpless baby again, its innocence silently begging for a father's protection. He hesitated, then squeezed his wife's hand and left.

Mistress Hopkins turned to Mercy. "Promise me, Mercy Clifton, you won't say one word of this to anyone. Please!"

Oceanus, suddenly hungry, let everyone know, and his cries drew some of the older women back. Grateful to avoid making the promise, Mercy gathered up the swaddling cloths and took them topside to wash them.

The deck was glazed with ice, and as Mercy reached for the safety rope, the first mate came up to her. "Afraid ye can't be moving about freely today, miss. Too slippery."

"I've got to wash out these cloths for the newborn down there."

The first mate smiled. "Heard about that, we did. Never happened before on this ship!" He smiled.

"Um, I'll let you stay a while, if you promise a favor in return."

Should she trust him? Not every sailor was like Bart, but still, what did this one want?

"Draw me another one of those sketches you make."

Mercy laughed in relief. She had never realized how much the sailors enjoyed watching her. "I would. But Bart threw my chalks overboard. And I guess my dream of being an artist went down with them."

"The first mate has a few chalks for charting our course. I'll see what he says about that." The sailor grinned. "But a promise is a promise, miss."

Mercy was amused. "Yes! Of course. A chalk for a picture."

He reached out his hand. She shook it.

"Well then, follow the ropes to the bow, but mind the ice. Behind the cook's fire you'll see a bucket with a rope. Haul up seawater in the bucket, and after you've washed the clothes in it, you can rinse the salt out with the rain water in the barrel. Just take care not to slip."

Mercy thanked him, edging her way carefully around the deck. "Oh, sir?" she called after him. "Would it be all right if I take a bucket of water to the mother and baby?"

He nodded his permission.

Mercy didn't see another soul on deck until she approached the cook's quarters. Up ahead in the bow there stood a lone figure, leaning into the rail.

It was Dorothy Bradford, with no cloak in the freezing damp air. She was watching the weather-beaten landscape drift slowly past—wind-blown pines on cliffs silhouetted against the heavy overcast, beaches strewn with gray boulders shrouded in snow.

Mercy moved quietly toward the cook's fire and the rain barrel without speaking to the solitary figure.

But the woman heard her and, turning to look at the bleak eastern horizon, she said in a strange, disconnected voice, "I can't see my home anymore. You know, I left my son back there."

Mercy didn't know what to say. "I know, Mistress Bradford. But, uh, maybe it would cheer you up to visit Mistress Hopkins and her new baby."

Mistress Bradford didn't respond.

Mercy studied the ghostly forlorn image, dressed all in gray. Her coif was missing, allowing wisps of hair to blow across her face.

The woman leaned over the railing, looking down at the black water below. "He's crying for me," she murmured, more to herself than the girl. "He wants me to swim back to him. But he knows I can't swim." She leaned over farther.

Oh, don't! You might fall in! Mercy worried. But she couldn't rebuke an adult. "Mistress Bradford? It's cold out here; you're shivering, ma'am. We need to get you below now."

Mistress Bradford let the girl put her arm around her shoulders and lead her gently away from the railing. Then she asked, "How is Goodwife Hopkins doing?"

"Mistress Bradford, since you miss your child, I shouldn't have brought it up, except the whole ship is celebrating the birth and. . . ."

The faraway look left Dorothy Bradford, and her expression lightened. As they made their way below, Mercy wondered what had brought her back into reality.

Now Mistress Bradford looked in her eyes, and in an assured tone befitting an Elder's wife, she said, "This business of Saints and Strangers is weighing heavily on you, isn't it, child?"

Mercy nodded, at a loss for a reply.

"Are the Hopkinses upset about our loss of the Virginia charter's authority?"

The girl choked. It was the subject she'd gone topside to avoid! She longed to unburden herself of it, but Mistress Bradford seemed too ill.

The older woman smiled and tapped her hand. "Say no more; I shall speak to Mr. Bradford about it, for it troubles him, too."

But what will she say, wondered Mercy. And what will happen to Mr. Hopkins?

13

DROPPING ANCHOR

It was not long before William Bradford sought out Mercy. "Mistress Bradford tells me that I ought to have a word with you." When the girl did not reply, he added gently, "We share your concern, Mercy. I want you to come with me to the captain's cabin. Governor Carver and the Brewsters are there."

Mercy shrank back.

"Don't worry, child; you're not in trouble. We just need to hear what you know."

Reluctantly she followed him.

In the cabin Mistress Brewster summoned Mercy to her side and patted her hand, but it did little to ease her anxiety.

"Mercy, what can you tell us?" Elder Brewster asked simply.

"I was asked not to tell," she replied in a small voice.

"As it affects the fate of the entire expedition," said the most senior of their senior men with a grave but gentle smile, "I absolve you of that request."

Still she hesitated. Then with a sigh she told them what she knew, concluding, "I don't know for sure, sir, but I think Mr. Billington is unhappy about joining your plan for the colony and is trying to get Mr. Hopkins to agree with him."

Governor Carver pursed his lips. "We must gather the Elders at once. We'll draft a covenant and form a government before anyone goes ashore, or else we will have a full-scale rebellion to deal with."

Mercy was dismissed, and the Elders were sent for, with Miles Standish standing guard at the captain's door.

As she walked toward the aft ladder, Mr. Hopkins was ascending it. "There you are! Mistress Hopkins needs you! Where have you been?" Before she could reply, he noted Captain Standish standing in front of the door to the captain's cabin. "What's going on in there?" he asked the captain.

"A meeting."

"About me, I'll wager."

Captain Standish looked him in the eye. "I have no idea." His eyes narrowed. "But suppose it is? Do you intend to stand with our company or with Billington's group?

Hopkins took a long moment before answering, and then the wind seemed to go out of his sails. He said quietly, "Because my wife pleads with me this day and because she is in great need, I shall do her bidding. I stand with you."

Mercy breathed a sigh of relief and started below. As Hopkins turned and followed her down the ladder, he assured her, "You did no wrong in telling them, lass."

"I did not purpose to reveal you, sir."

"I know. It's all right, Mercy; I forgive you."

At Mistress Hopkins' side they were startled when Billington poked his head through the privacy curtain.

"How dare you, sir!" exploded Stephen Hopkins. "Leave at once, or I'll thrash you!"

Billington glared at him. "Traitor!" he spat out in disgust, then departed.

Mr. Hopkins now addressed his two servants, Doty and Leister, who were standing nearby, watching Billington leave. "He's spoken to you, hasn't he?"

Neither man replied.

"Understand this: You are *my* indentured servants, not his. You contracted with me to serve seven years in exchange for your passage. Until you fulfill the terms of that contract, I will decide where we will stand." He paused for emphasis. "And we're standing with the Separatists. Understood?"

Chastened, they lowered their gaze.

Now Billington returned, a folded piece of paper in his hand. To Mr. Hopkins he said, "Thomas Weston and The Virginia Company Adventurers in London recruited us Strangers as *paying* passengers." He held up his copy of that agreement. "They intended us to be planters together, but not here. Like you, I signed on for planting further south, in the Virginia Company grant. How do we know if we can even grow anything in this cold wilderness?"

He glanced around and, seeing no one within earshot, continued. "The Leiden Saints seem to have taken charge, but Squire Weston and his investors are going to hear about this. Then the courts of England will decide who's in charge of our destiny!"

Stephen Hopkins was not cowed. "You're not the only one who can write letters. And I promise you, I will not allow you to ruin us."

"We'll see," retorted Billington, stalking off.

It was late afternoon when they glided into the sheltered lee of the peninsula's tip. Master Jones ordered the great iron anchor lowered. To make way for the crew to get to the capstan in the bow, Mercy and others had to move a menagerie of sheep, goats, chickens, and pigs. She was lifting a chicken cage when it slipped out of her hands. The door flew open, and a hen escaped—gleefully squawking and flapping its wings, it ran through the maze of cabins.

Furious, Mercy unwound her tangled skirts and pursued the feathered fugitive. So did Loyal, yipping with delight at the new game, until she passed Mercy and nearly caught the chicken. Seeing the chase and feeling left out, Cromwell began lunging at the stout rope tying him to Mr. Goodman's cabin, his booming bark echoing through the 'tween decks.

Pursuing the chicken and Loyal, Mercy suddenly saw a hand whisk out and grab the hen by one leg! Holding it upside down, out of Loyal's reach, there stood Jack, laughing. "She'd better lay an egg every day, or she'll wind up in your stew pot!"

Breathless, Mercy brushed back her hair and thanked him. She took the chicken and stomped off, which brought forth gales of laughter behind her.

As soon as the area around the capstan was clear, two men inserted long wooden poles into the wooden spool around which the anchor rope was wrapped. Carefully they unwound it, and Mercy watched the heavy rope slipping out through the drafty hole they called a "cathead." She heard the great splash as the anchor entered the water.

After the rest of the passengers had hurried topside to catch their first close-up glimpse of their new home, Mercy helped her father up the forward ladder while he leaned heavily on his cane. The view of land from the starboard side of the ship was bathed in the golden light of the most glorious sunset she'd ever seen.

"I want to remember this day forever, Mercy, but I'm afraid I'll soon be bedridden like your mother."

"No, Papa!" she responded cheerfully. "You'll get your strength back as soon as we get ashore!" But her heart was full of dread; she could hear him wheezing.

Tucking herself under his arm, she tried to enjoy the crimson afterglow of the sunset. Along the shore, against the dry underbrush, were the last wild beach plums.

"Ah, if only I could go into town and buy you more chalks. Wouldn't it make a lovely scene?" Her father knew her longing all too well.

"Indeed it would, Papa," Mercy said, keeping her tone cheerful. "Someday we'll build a fine village, and ships will come to visit us and bring chalks." But even as she spoke, she wondered if either of her parents would see the beach plums blossom, when spring came to this new land of promise.

That sad thought was banished by the crew singing a sea chantey, as they hung over the yardarms or crossbeams on the two masts, from which hung the sails. They were "furling" the sails, gathering them in and tying them tight so the wind could not tear at them. Meanwhile on the main deck other seamen were uncovering the ship's boat that would take the first small party ashore.

They had arrived in the New World!

14

A BODY POLITIC

Mercy, Elizabeth, and Priscilla hardly slept that night, so excited were they about the next morning. Whispering into the small hours, they imagined what the natives might look like, and designed their future houses.

Shortly after dawn, Elders Brewster, Carver, and Bradford climbed down a rope ladder into the ship's boat, manned by two seamen. As everyone watched them being rowed to shore, Brewster's prayer could be clearly heard over the still water: "Blessed be the God of Heaven, who has brought us over the vast and furious ocean and delivered us from all the perils of two months of agony and miseries."

The Elders climbed out onto white sand, their arrival announced by noisy seagulls. As they knelt on the beach to dedicate this new land to their Creator, those watching from the *Mayflower* bowed their heads and prayed with them.

Mercy felt someone come up next to her. Head still bowed, she looked sideways. It was Jack. What did he want at a sacred moment like this? The joy on everyone else's face was missing from his. Why wasn't he with his family? His mother was there, but where was his father?

Looking around the ship, she finally saw Billington hovering close to the ladder. Was he waiting to help the Elders back onto the ship?

"What's your father doing?" she whispered.

"I know you pray," murmured Jack. "Now would be a good time to do so."

Mercy noticed tiny beads of sweat on his brow. Suddenly she was filled with dread. Her eyes darted about, looking for Mr. Hopkins. He was missing too!

The Elders were coming back to the ship. When the boat arrived, Billington steadied the ladder for them. But no sooner had the last one climbed aboard than he loudly announced, "Our turn now! Time to do some exploring!"

As had obviously been prearranged, three other Strangers emerged from the crowd and clambered down the ladder to join him. "Come on, lads!" they now shouted to Dody and Leister. "We're going adventuring! You don't want to miss out on the fun!"

The two servants quickly joined them.

At least their master was not among them, thought Mercy.

Captain Standish, musket in hand, stepped to the ladder and commanded, "Come back up here! No one goes ashore without proper permission!"

Governor Carver joined him, calling down to the man who had clearly organized the rebellion. "Mr. Billington! No one leaves this ship until we have *all* signed the covenant we have written. We will *not* have every man for himself."

"You already have it, Governor!" snarled Billington. Turning to the others, he ordered, "Man the oars!"

Captain Standish put his matchlock musket to his shoulder, took careful aim at Billington's chest, and announced, "I am ready to give fire, sir."

None of the Strangers moved a muscle.

"Dody? Leister? What in blazes are you doing down there?" It was Stephen Hopkins, having come up from looking after his wife. "You get back up here! Right now!"

Sheepishly the two servants hastily climbed the ladder. The three other Strangers followed them. Though his rebellion had failed, Billington refused to leave the boat.

"Please, Mr. Billington," cried his wife Eleanor, holding firmly onto Francis, "don't do this! Don't leave me a widow in this awful place!"

Jack didn't move from Mercy's side, though she could sense him doing his best to disassociate himself from his father. Her heart went out to him.

Now Governor Carver addressed the man in the boat, not unkindly. "Mr. Billington, your family needs you. We need you. Come back aboard and join us, and we will put all this behind us."

A minute passed. Then, teeth gritted, he climbed up the ladder. Without a word he stalked past them, going to his cabin.

Governor Carver pulled a document from his shoulder bag and announced, "Here is our compact. You need to hear this and sign it before we do any more exploring today."

He handed it to William Bradford to read aloud.

"In the name of God, Amen," it began and then declared that they covenanted together and combined themselves into a civil Body Politic, which would have the power to make laws and ordinances and to elect officers, to whom, for the good of the Colony, they promised all submission and obedience. In witness thereof they would subscribe their names below.

When Bradford finished reading, a cheer went up, and men began calling out, "Let's sign it now!"

Master Jones opened his cabin for the solemn ceremony, and they spread the document out on his chart table, so that each could read it before adding his signature to it.

As the men lined up, Mercy asked Jack, "Will your father sign?"

"I hope so. But no one's ever going to forget what he did today. How could he make such fools of us?"

Mercy smiled. "You're forgetting forgiveness. We don't think like you do. Remember how we forgave John Howland for rushing up on deck? It's a new day for all of us."

Jack brightened up.

"Besides, your father didn't break any laws, because they haven't agreed on any yet. That's what this is all about."

Jack gave her a hug. "I won't soon forget this." And he went forward to the bow alone.

Mercy might have followed him, but her ailing father needed her help in taking his place in line.

"Papa, you shouldn't be standing up here any longer. Come below," she pleaded. "They can get this done without you."

He shook his head. "I did not come this far to not do my part. It will take all of us to make this happen."

Upon seeing the resolve of their oldest passenger, the Elders beckoned to Mercy to bring her father inside the cabin to the front of the line. As he dipped the quill into the inkwell, James Clifton said, "Daughter, never forget what you've witnessed this day. Not since Moses in the Sinai desert have men covenanted together in a wilderness to form their own civil government founded on God's Word. Had the English ruled themselves this way, with the Almighty in charge, we would never have had to leave. I pray America will always be a place of free worship for all."

Suddenly he was struck by a dizzy spell, and seeing it, Elder Brewster motioned for Mercy to help him into the captain's chair. There they watched, as one by one, the men of their company, Separatists and Strangers, signed. When there were no more, Elder Brewster asked, "Have they all signed?"

William Bradford checked the signatures and shook his head. "Billington's not here."

Governor Carver turned to Captain Standish. "Take John Alden with you and bring him here."

In a moment Billington, accompanied by Captain Standish and John Alden, arrived.

Governor Carver said graciously and a little sadly, "Mr. Billington, we asked you to sign our compact."

"And I declined your invitation."

"Then we shall have to insist."

"And if I refuse?"

Captain Standish stepped between the two men and looked Billington coldly in the eye. "Then you will be put in irons while we send word to the backers in London and await their instructions." The two men glared at each other. "I'll wager it'll be about a year before we hear back from them," said the captain with a wry smile. "Or longer."

For a long moment neither man moved. Then with a scowl Billington yanked the quill from its inkwell and signed.

After he stormed out of the cabin, Mercy and Captain Standish got her father to his feet. As they did, Edward Winslow picked up the document with all their signatures and locked it safely away in a metal box. "Since this was signed aboard this ship, perhaps some day people will call it 'The Mayflower Compact,'" he mused. "In any event, now we are one."

"Hear, hear," murmured the Elders—all save Governor Carver, who thoughtfully rubbed his chin. "We'll see."

15

THE STORYTELLER'S CIRCLE

Later that afternoon Mercy found Jack by the rail, no better off than before. Unable to look her in the eye, he moaned, "My father's shamed of our whole family."

She touched his arm. "You are not your father, Jack! In this New World, you have a new life." She pointed to the land stretching away before them. "It's a goodly land, wooded to the brink of the sea. Why, the possibilities are endless! You can be your own man."

Gazing at it with her, he took a deep breath and exhaled slowly. "If you believe in me, I can be."

Mercy blushed. She had to answer something, without committing more to him than her heart would allow. "It's not if I believe; it's what you believe about yourself."

She waited. Was he listening? She looked up. He was staring at her.

Just then Captain Standish approached him. "Did you not hear the call, young man? I've chosen you for my exploration party. You're strong and able enough to man an oar."

Jack was speechless.

"We leave in an hour. Ask the first mate what to bring."

"Aye, Sir!" was all he could say, as the captain sought the next man on his list.

"You see?" exclaimed Mercy. "They're *not* against you!"

He beamed. "You're the wind in my sails, Mercy girl! I've no idea what adventures await, but I'll tell you all about it when we return!" And with that he planted a kiss on her cheek and strode off to join the expedition.

Mercy put her hand to her cheek, still tingling with his kiss, as she watched the sixteen bold adventurers depart, swords and muskets by their sides. Once again he was the dashing hero she'd admired before discovering his family's rebelliousness.

After that expedition and each one thereafter, Jack would entertain Mercy and her two friends with fascinating tales of his exploits, while Loyal snoozed at Mercy's feet. The children they were looking after would gather in a circle around him, hanging on every word. Desire Minter paid close attention, too. Interrupting him frequently for more details, she began to annoy Mercy, though Jack seemed not to mind.

Well, at least Desire could not read or write, thought Mercy, as she carefully recorded Jack's exploits on large white strips of birch bark he'd peeled for her, using twigs he'd blackened in the campfire.

He told of their gathering of juniper, the fragrant scent of which filled the whole ship; of the encounter with six savages and a dog and how the Indians had run from them, whistling for the dog to follow; how they had uncovered a rush basket filled with Indian corn, buried beneath the frost level. They also had found that the roots of a sassafras tree boiled in water made a tea that soothed their stomachs, after they had gotten sick eating raw shellfish. But the most wonderful news was the discovery of freshwater springs, which they so desperately needed!

As each expedition brought more supplies of partridge, deer, firewood, and water, those who had not been ashore grew restless to disembark. No matter how crude, a settlement ashore would be far better for the new mothers than this disease-ridden ship. Mary Allerton was overdue and deathly ill, and Susana White had endured a life-threatening delivery that had gone on all night. Dorothy Bradford, standing by Susana's bed, had tried in vain to calm her screams as they rattled through the ship. Then Dorothy herself had become hysterical and had begun hallucinating until Goodwife Winslow led her away. In her own cabin Dorothy continued to mutter about Indians coming in canoes to sneak aboard and steal the womenfolk while their men were away.

Mercy had her hands full, keeping Mistress White's new baby boy warm. She watched Dr. Fuller record his name: Peregrine, Latin for "Pilgrim." But when his quill inscribed the birth date, November 20, she realized that winter was almost at hand, and there was still no decision about where they would settle.

She wrapped their last clean blanket around Peregrine and handed him to Elizabeth. "I'm going topside to wash out these cloths."

Walking through the 'tween decks area, Mercy saw the children she normally cared for tucked into blankets around the feet of Desire Minter. And in their center perched "Prince" Jack, carried away with the admiration of his young audience, as he spun yarn after yarn.

So much for being the only wind in his sails! With a twinge of jealousy, Mercy turned away and bumped into William Brewster, who was listening to the story of the discovery of an iron kettle, buried by earlier European explorers. It was still full of seed corn—ten bushels of it—for the natives' spring planting.

Mercy was about to ask Elder Brewster's forgiveness, when he put a finger to his lips. He did not want her to interrupt the next tale of finding a bent-over sapling above kernels of corn strewn in pine needles, to bait deer into its snare. Suddenly the sapling sprang upright, and dangling from it, upside-down, was none other than William Bradford!

The children gasped, then shouted with glee! And Elder Brewster laughed so hard his stomach shook.

When their mirth subsided, he stepped into the storyteller's circle. "Now, children, who knows that it's wrong to take something that is not yours?"

All hands went up.

The wise Elder knelt among them to be closer to their eye level. "What Jack did not tell you about the seed corn is that while we need it to make a crop next spring, we've marked the place where we found it and mean to repay its owners, as soon as we discover who they are."

Looking around the circle, he gravely added, "Explorers came here before us and were mean to the Indians. They captured some and sold them into slavery. So we must treat them well. Do you understand?"

Every head in the circle nodded, including Jack's.

But behind Elder Brewster's back, as he got up to leave, Mercy noticed one of the older children scowling. It was Jack's younger brother, Francis.

The next day Jack was again delighting the children, and the more they laughed, the more he dramatized his tales. While describing how they had shot at a wildcat, he showed them one of the muskets. Then, from his rucksack he produced a squib, a small tube of gunpowder, used to prime the musket before firing.

Of course, every little boy in the circle immediately wanted to feel it.

Alarmed, Jack quickly put the gun away and the squib back in his sack. Shaking his head, he warned them, "You'll have to grow up to be big like me before you can fire this!"

An hour later there was a sudden explosion from the hold below! Everyone rushed to the hatch where thick, black smoke was rolling out. From it appeared Francis Billington, covered with soot.

Two seamen hurried below while Dr. Fuller carried the lad to fresh air.

"We're afire!" came a cry from the hold. "There's fire and open gunpowder down here!"

People started scrambling to the main deck, carrying the sick as best they could. Mercy wept when she was unable to get either of her parents up.

Master Jones descended into the hold and took charge, calling for buckets of water to be sent down and directing his men where to douse the fire.

When calm was restored, he and Governor Carver sat a badly frightened Francis down to find out what had happened.

Francis had taken his brother's musket and squib down to hide below and done his best to shoot it off. Seeking to load the gun with a real powder charge, he had opened a cask of gunpowder but had managed to spill most of it on the deck. When he finally got the musket to go off, it produced quite a flash, igniting the loose gunpowder. He did not know why the open cask of gunpowder had not exploded.

When he finished, the ship's captain and the governor stared at each other. Then Carver murmured, "It is a miracle we are still sitting here!"

"Aye to that, sir," exhaled a shaken Master Jones. "Aye to that!"

16

SECRET TREASURE

Finally, under John Alden's careful supervision, their sailing longboat called the shallop was assembled and caulked—all thirty feet of it! Its first assignment? To take thirty-four of their most able-bodied men around the inner perimeter of the peninsula to see where God would plant their colony.

The day before they were to leave, Mercy, Priscilla, and Elizabeth got their first chance to go ashore, to wash the ship's foul laundry in freshwater, and to get the weevils out of the last of the cook's hard biscuits. Mercy could hardly wait! It had been so long since she had set foot on dry land! And the thought of clean drinking water was like a dream.

Jack Billington and John Alden had volunteered to help the girls load the ship's boat, row them ashore, and stand guard while they did their chores. The girls passed down two baskets of bread and four baskets of heavy and smelly laundry to John, who stood on the rope ladder. He in turn handed them to Jack, who stowed them in the boat.

As the girls made ready to climb down into the boat, Elizabeth called out, "I'm afraid of falling!"

"I'll go first," offered Priscilla, hiking up her full skirt and starting down the ladder.

John Alden reached up quickly to help. "Here, take my hand," he said, helping Priscilla into the boat. Then he helped Elizabeth.

Mercy climbed down quickly without his assistance.

Jack and John rowed them ashore as the sun's warm reflection sparkled on the green water.

Mercy trailed her fingers in the cold water while they glided along. She couldn't get over how wonderful the fresh air smelled. Free at last from being cooped up in the gloomy darkness of the 'tween decks!

When the boat grounded on the beach, Jack and John helped the girls step out on the sand. They immediately slipped off their shoes.

"Oh, it feels *so good!*" Mercy exclaimed, as she took her first few steps. The sand was firm and secure beneath her feet. Giggling with delight, the three girls linked arms and began to dance in a circle. A southerly breeze brought the welcome scent of beach grass and pine trees.

After a few moments of gaiety, Priscilla said, "Well, I guess we'd better get on with our chores."

"We'll show you where the freshwater is," Jack offered, and after the girls had put their shoes back on, he and John started off through the dunes away from the beach.

Looking down into the clear water of the spring, Mercy raised a handful of it to her lips and tasted it.

"*Ahh!* I had forgotten how sweet water could taste!"

After everyone had drunk their fill, Jack and John brought the baskets of dirty laundry and bread up from the boat, and the girls got to work. Thoroughly washing each garment and spreading it on a nearby bush to dry took them nearly two hours.

While the men kindled a fire, the women soaked the biscuits in buckets of spring water until weevils crawled out and floated up! Scooping them off the water's surface, they toasted the bread over the fire and packed it up again, good as new—almost.

Once the clothes were drying on the bushes and the bread was toasting, Mercy found herself with time for a brief walk with Jack. She realized that she had mixed feelings about the shallop's departure the next day because he would be going with them. "How long will you be gone?" she asked, as they wandered over the dunes. "All of us will miss you and your stories."

He looked at her, a half smile playing on his lips. "Look what happened the last time I told a story!"

"And look how God saved our ship—again," she wryly pointed out. "You are not your little brother, any more than you are your father."

She drew back and stared at him. "You are your own man, Jack Billington! You must make your own way."

He took a deep breath. "You make me want to be better than I am, when you talk that way."

"You're better than you think you are," she quickly replied. "Our key men are taking you with them. That's how highly they think of you. Now model yourself after them, and when you return, you will be a better man!"

He laughed. "You've just done it again, Mercy girl! You've lifted my heart."

She just smiled. Then she said, "If you want to be useful, you can help us load our baskets back into the boat and row us back to the *Mayflower*."

When the expedition left at dawn the following morning, Jack did something he'd never done before. He waved to her until they were out of sight.

After this, every time she was on deck giving Loyal and Cromwell some exercise, Mercy's eyes strayed to the horizon, hoping for a glimpse of the shallop's sail that would signal their return. Master Jones had warned them that a proper exploration around the bay could take two weeks or more, but she couldn't help searching the horizon, again and again.

One day an unusually gorgeous sunset brought many passengers up on deck to see the spectacular layers of red-orange and scarlet. Mercy was flanked at the railing by Elizabeth and Priscilla.

"I wish God would give us a sign that they were all right," Mercy fretted. "I pray for Him to hold them in the hollow of His hand, but how do I know He is doing it?"

"With a sky like that," observed Priscilla, "it's hard to believe He isn't."

They were silent for a while, as scarlet shaded into crimson and finally purple.

"Maybe the natives have killed them," mused Elizabeth. "Or maybe they've swamped the shallop and all drowned so no one's left to tell us."

"Oh, thanks, Elizabeth! That's helpful!" exclaimed Mercy, fighting back tears.

Shivering, Priscilla blew on her hands. "It's so cold, maybe they simply froze to death. You know, that can happen while you're sleeping, without you even knowing it—like frost creeping up a windowpane. Dr. Fuller says it's the kindest way to die."

"No!" cried Mercy. "God didn't save us when the crossbeam broke and Francis almost blew us all up, just to let it all end here. I won't believe that!"

"Then neither will I," Priscilla promised.

"Nor I," added Elizabeth.

Suddenly Cromwell's deep throaty bark echoed across the still waters of the bay. They whipped around to see Charlemagne, the captain's calico cat, clinging to the mainmast, about ten feet up, gazing down at the big brute who had treed him. This time it was Loyal who was frantically struggling to get free and join the hunt. Tied to the railing beside Mercy, she nonetheless yipped encouragement to her big mastiff friend.

But Charlemagne, seemingly trapped, had devised an escape plan. Hurling himself through the air, he jumped down on the upturned ship's boat.

Cromwell reacted quickly, even while Charlemagne was airborne. He turned and threw himself after the cat in hot pursuit, with great lumbering strides and frantic barking. Charlemagne didn't wait for developments. He took two large bounds forward; and then, in a remarkably agile in-flight maneuver and with a hair-raising screech, he launched himself down the forward hatch.

Cromwell, bounding eagerly after the cat, suddenly found himself on a patch of ice. With all paws scrambling, he desperately sought to regain a semblance of balance. No use. His momentum carried him crashing into the raised sill around the hatch, and down he toppled to the 'tween decks below, his great baying voice suddenly altered to a pathetic croak.

After a moment Charlemagne, who had gone through the 'tween decks and come up the aft ladder, came sauntering out on deck as if nothing had happened.

Then Mercy heard something else, which she had not heard in sixty-six days at sea or ten days at anchor. *Laughter!* Gales of it! Looking aloft, she spied sailors everywhere, howling with laughter. And the passengers were laughing just as hard, holding their sides.

She began to smile, and soon her laughter joined all the rest.

A few evenings later, as she was tending to the chamber pots, someone whispered her name. Mystified, she looked around but could see no one. She shrugged and was about to resume her chore when she heard it again. This time she saw a crooked index finger beckoning to her from the Bradfords' cabin. Since Mr. Bradford was away with the shallop, it had to be Mistress Bradford. Hesitantly, she went over.

Dorothy Bradford opened the curtain and bade her come in. "You know that Billington fellow is planning a mutiny," she whispered. "He means to take over this ship and sail her to France."

Mercy very much doubted that, fearing that the poor woman had lost even more of her fragile grip on reality. But she said nothing.

"Well," prodded Mistress Bradford, "do you not think he means evil?"

"Mr. Billington signed the covenant," replied Mercy, keeping her voice calm and reassuring. "He's been forgiven, and I think he deserves a fresh start."

This was not the response Dorothy Bradford was hoping for. "You're so innocent! He has never stopped plotting."

Sighing, Mercy gathered her skirts to leave, but Mistress Bradford put a hand on her arm. "You know, I caught him in here, snooping in Mr. Bradford's journal."

"What?" Mercy took a deep breath. "Mistress Bradford, Mr. Billington is away with the men on the shallop, along with your husband."

"He is? It must have been before, then."

Mercy tried to leave. "I really must go."

No," said Dorothy Bradford firmly. "You really must stay."

She reached under the mattress. "I want you to read what Mr. Bradford has written about Mr. Billington. That is what that rogue was trying to see."

"But why me?" Mercy whispered, striving to keep her voice down.

"I want a witness who can read, and whom I can trust."

Before Mercy could object, Mrs. Bradford pulled out a green velvet bag with a leather-bound journal in it. She started thumbing through the journal to find the passages in question.

But Mercy was more intrigued by something else that had come out from under the mattress along with the velvet bag. It was an old red leather pouch that had partially opened to reveal its contents, an ornate silver cross set with five dark red stones.

Seeing that it had accidentally emerged, Dorothy Bradford hastily tucked the pouch and cross well out of sight. "Now, here," she said, indicating a passage in Mr. Bradford's diary, "this is the first time he mentions Billington, and there are three others." She obviously hoped Mercy had not noticed the other items, but she *had* noticed, and as she read what William Bradford had written in his flawless penmanship, she could not get her mind off the silver cross. What was an incredible treasure like that doing aboard the *Mayflower*?

17

MISSING

Four nights later Mercy was awakened by the voice of Mary Brewster calling for someone. "Halloo, Dorothy Bradford! Where are you? Come, my dear, don't hide. We need to find you, to know that you are all right."

Oh, no, thought Mercy, *she's missing!*

She and Elizabeth and Priscilla tugged on their cloaks and went to Mary Brewster. "What can we do to help, Mistress Brewster?"

"You can help us look for her. She's nowhere to be found, but perhaps you will think of a hiding place that we haven't."

When the three girls separated, Mercy went up on deck, drawn to the bow where she had once before found Dorothy Bradford. There was a heavy fog, and the deck was slick with ice, so she was careful to keep a hand on the lifeline.

But there was nothing, no sign of anyone having been there. She turned back to see that the sailors had joined the search.

"Dorothy Bradford," they cried repeatedly, their calls echoing in the fog. The candle lanterns they held on high made eerie golden glows in the fog. Two men had gone down into the hold and looked everywhere. One had even climbed up the mainmast to see if by the remotest chance . . .

"Dorothy Bradford . . ."

Three men were in the ship's boat, rowing slowly around the *Mayflower* in the fog. Two manned the oars while a third held up a lantern, searching the black water and calling her name.

Finally, the wind picked up, blowing out the candles. A freezing rain began to coat everything with a glaze of ice, and Master Jones called off the search. "It's no use. She's vanished without a trace."

But Mercy could not let it go at that. She tugged on Master Jones' sleeve. "Please, sir. Could someone not take the boat out again? Maybe she tried to swim ashore!"

Master Jones looked at her with compassion. "Even if she could swim, she might last fifteen minutes in these frigid waters. She could never make it to shore; no one could."

Mercy remembered the afternoon the two of them were in the bow, and Dorothy Bradford had told her she couldn't swim. She went to find Mary Brewster, to tell her.

She was relieved to find her with her husband, because they were the only two people on board to whom she felt she could unburden herself. Barely able to speak, she related the incident that had occurred in the bow of the ship, and what Dorothy Bradford had said about not being able to swim.

She shook her head as tears welled up in her eyes. "I can't help thinking I could have done something to prevent this—told you sooner, been more of a friend to her."

"Don't torture yourself, child," said Elder Brewster. "Her condition was getting worse, and we all knew it. It had nothing to do with you."

Mistress Brewster put her arm around Mercy. "Don't even think about it, Mercy. She was ill and probably simply slipped. In any event, she is at peace now."

She paused. "Pray for Mr. Bradford. This is going to crush him, when the men return."

Mercy slept fitfully that night.

"Sail ho!" came the cry from the bow.

"Where away?"

"On the starboard quarter. She's hull down on the horizon, but she can only be the shallop!"

Everyone gathered on deck to greet the returning explorers. As thrilled as Mercy was to see Jack, she dreaded seeing Mr. Bradford, and chose to stand close by Elder Brewster and his wife.

Well before the shallop was within hearing distance, the shouting and cheering began and did not let up until the shallop tied up alongside. One by one, as the men climbed up the rope ladder, their loved ones greeted them with hugs.

William Bradford was one of the first, and so brimming with good news was he that he practically ran to Elder Brewster. "Wait till you see the plantation the Lord has provided! It is on a gentle hillside, perfect for drainage.

There is a natural harbor, well protected on three sides, and so deep that the *Mayflower* will practically be able to tie up at the shore! Best of all we found not one spring but *four!* With the sweetest water you have ever tasted! Oh, the Lord is good!"

Then he noticed the look of deep concern in the Brewsters' faces.

His smile faded. "Dorothy."

Elder Brewster nodded. Without saying anything he put his arm around his old friend. That and the tears in his eyes said it all.

His shoulders shaking, Bradford put his hands over his face and let his old friend comfort him, and lead him into the privacy of the captain's cabin.

Everyone gathered outside, mourning with him and waiting to give words of sympathy.

By and by the door opened, and Elder Brewster beckoned Mercy inside.

"Child, will you tell Mr. Bradford what transpired in the bow?"

She did, reporting Dorothy Bradford's certainty that Billington had been into his diary. "If only I had been with her more," Mercy lamented, while Charlemagne rubbed against her legs in sympathy.

William Bradford comforted her. "I don't know how I'll get on without her, but I'll not have you blaming yourself, Mercy. She was slipping away before I left, and now she has gone to a far better place."

Mercy finished the thought for him out loud:

> *Yea though they should lose their lives in this action, yet might they have comfort in the same, and their endeavors would be honorable.*

William Bradford raised an eyebrow. "What did you say?"

"Your wife read me a page from your journal. She loved it. My father taught me to write, and I'm also keeping a journal of stories."

"You are?" He was impressed. "It's rare for a young woman to posses such a skill. I trust you will continue." He gazed out the window. "As for me, I cannot bear to put quill to paper today."

He sighed. "Following God's will sometimes costs us more than we expect. It has cost me dearly, and yet, blessed be the name of the Lord." He thought for a moment then added:

> *Precious in the sight of the Lord is the death of His saints.*

A weight seemed to lift from Mercy's heart. Somehow, once again, God's meaning and purpose had brought good out of sadness.

"You know, Mercy," William Bradford said thoughtfully, "the biggest help you could give me today, would be to get together with Jack Billington and record his account of all that happened on our voyage to and from the place we named Plimoth, after the town we sailed from months ago."

18

"IF YE BE MEN . . ."

As William Bradford had requested, Mercy rejoined Jack's storytelling circle with birch bark and charcoal twigs, ready to record his tales of adventure. Seated cross-legged on the capstan, Jack smiled at the children's intense expressions, as they eagerly awaited the stories.

Several days after they had left the *Mayflower*, Jack began, they'd spied Indians on a stretch of beach that John Smith's charts called Eastham.

"We drew the boat close to shore to see what the savages were doing. There were ten or twelve of them, wearing deer skins and wolf furs and kneeling on the shore around a great black fish. It was smaller than a whale but larger than any fish I ever saw."

To their utter delight and surprise, he suddenly flopped down on his belly in their midst as if he were a great fish, and said, "Master Jones told us it was a Grampus!" They giggled at the silly name.

When the Indians saw us coming, they ran off. We built a barricade out of brush to protect us and camped there on the shore, frying some pieces of Mr. Grampus for supper."

The children got up and pranced around the circle, chanting "Grampus! Grampus! Grampus!"

As they settled back down, with a look at Mercy, Jack added, "We also found some Indian graves there, but we were careful to leave them alone."

Mercy knew he did that because of her strong reaction to one of his earlier tales. They'd gone ashore in the ship's boat to explore and had found some Indian graves. Jack had immediately started digging into them, looking for arrowheads—and his father had let him. Mercy had scolded him for disturbing the graves. How would he like it if some Indians had dug up his parents' graves, looking for something to steal?

She smiled at him now, which was obviously what he'd hoped she'd do, but the memory of it troubled her because she remembered something else he'd said, in a moment of private honesty. He'd told her he was not the hero she thought he was. He just happened to be where trouble was. The night John Howland went up on deck? Jack was at the hatch because he was about to do the same thing!

Mercy was beginning to regard him with negative feelings. To be sure, he was handsome and dashing, and he was having the time of his life entertaining the children. But there was something unsettling about him, something she couldn't put her finger on. You'd better put a guard on your heart, Mercy Clifton, she told herself.

Jack started whooping like an Indian and pretending to shoot arrows from a bow. "One day some natives shot their arrows at us!"

"Oh," cried the children in unison. "What happened?" they pleaded, eyes wide with excitement. "Tell us! Tell us!"

"It was while we were at breakfast," Jack began. "We heard shouts, then one of our guards came running in crying, 'Savages! Savages!' Soon arrows flew among us, but no one was hit."

"The mercy of God, to be sure," breathed Mercy, as she wrote down his words in charcoal. Jack glanced at her and resumed the story.

"Captain Standish and others of us fired their muskets at them, but the savages kept shooting, all the while yelling dreadfully. It sounded like this." Jack cupped his hands to his mouth and shouted, *Woach woach ha ha hach woach.*"

The children covered their ears while some of the passengers came over to the circle to see what the noise was about.

"One of their leaders shot three arrows at us, which we avoided," the storyteller continued, "and finally one of our musket shots struck a tree near him, and off he ran, with the rest after him. We took up some of their arrows. Here are two!"

Jack reached behind his back and produced two Indian arrows, one tipped with hammered copper, the other with an eagle claw. The little ones passed them around the circle with oohs and aahs.

After a lunch of peas porridge soup, dried beef, and cheese, the children insisted that Jack tell more adventures. By now the circle had grown to include a number of adults standing around the outside.

"A rough time we had of it, the day we found the harbor," Jack said quietly, looking around the circle at the children. Then he raised his voice. "Wind blowing a gale, it was; snow and rain hard in our faces, and the waves getting higher by the hour. Suddenly, the sea broke our rudder! We could only steer by the oars now. We were in great danger!"

The eyes of all listeners were fixed intently on Jack.

"The night was coming on fast; we feared we would miss the place we sought. Anon, our first mate, Master Coppin, bade us be of good cheer; he said he saw the place. But now came the worst of it, for having hoisted much sail to get in, the gale was so stiff that our mast was broken in three places!"

The children squealed with anxiety, and the adults groaned.

"We were almost wrecked, but we had the tide with us, and great waves pushed us into the harbor. Yet we were not safe! When we tried to run the shallop ashore, we came near to giant breakers and would have been cast to pieces on the rocks, had not seaman Clark shouted, 'If ye be men, about with her, or we are all cast away!'"

"We rowed with fury and snatched her from the waves! As darkness fell, we found a small island in the lee of which we spent the night, every man exhausted."

The listeners exhaled in relief.

Just then, William Bradford parted the curtains of his cabin and nodded approvingly at Mercy, who was writing down Jack's story. He held up his journal for Mercy to see.

Seeing him, Jack pleaded, "Sir, you were there. Come, tell us yourself what happened next."

People were shocked that Jack would presume to disturb Bradford's grief over his wife's death, but to their surprise he walked over to join them, journal in hand!

"I shall indeed, young man, for I cannot leave my heart with my dear wife at the bottom of the sea. It is time to be with the living."

At that moment Mercy came to deeply admire this man who laid aside his sorrows to take his place of leadership among them.

Bradford told them how they had spent the next day and the Sabbath on the island in the harbor, which they named for seaman Clark. "On Monday, December 11, we went ashore and found a pleasant land and four running brooks of good water that drain into a deep-water harbor. And to our amazement, there are many harvested cornfields."

Who farmed the fields, the children wanted to know. Were there English there already?

Elder Bradford shook his head. It seemed to have been Indians that had done it, but the cornstalks were old. No one had tilled the fields for several years. "And we found many skeletons of people scattered about that place," Bradford added.

"*Ewww,*" the children cried, wrinkling up their noses.

"Who might they be?" asked several of the adults. "How did they die?"

"We could not tell," replied Bradford. "Perhaps the natives who lived there were killed in a battle, though none of their skulls were crushed, which would have been the case had they died fighting. Perhaps they died of a plague. It is a mystery. But no one lives there now. It seems to belong to no man."

He looked around the circle. "We believe it has pleased the Lord to have protected that place for us, and we shall make good use of it after we bury those who used it last."

"How soon can we land there?" Mrs. Clifton weakly called from her berth. "I'd like to see this New World at least once before I . . ."

Die? Mercy grimaced. After Mrs. Bradford's death, all her mother would talk about was her own. For weeks she had not had enough strength to leave their cabin and had wasted away to a mere shadow of the plump woman she'd once been.

"How soon?" Mercy looked at William Bradford.

"Sooner than you might think," Governor Carver announced, coming down the forward ladder.

"Master Jones plans to sail tomorrow. He says the waters here ice over in January, which would trap his ship. He wishes to drop us off and head back to England as soon as we've built a common house to shelter ourselves."

Hearing this, the women started happily pulling down the privacy curtains and packing up the storage chests they yanked from under their mattresses! They would soon have proper homes at last!

"Not so fast, dear ladies." Mr. Bradford cautioned. "We'll need this ship for protection. The slave traders who preceded us left the savages in a fury. Divine Providence may have blown us here, but Divine Grace must help us change their hearts, before it will be safe for you ladies to live ashore."

19

"YOUR MAJESTY!"

The next morning, as crewmen came down to wind up the anchor rope, Mercy begged her father to come topside to watch them sail across the bay.

Weakly he declined. "I just cannot, dear girl," he told her through dry parched lips. He had not drunk any water in days and now was only able to take in moisture by sucking on a wet rag. His eyes had become cloudy and his bones showed through his transparent yellow skin. Mercy had been reading his Geneva Bible to him because his eyes could not focus on the print anymore. All he wanted to hear from it now were the passages about heaven.

"You need fresh air, Papa," she pleaded. "Let me help you go topside."

"Dear Mercy." He patted her hand. "I've lived to deliver you here. That was my dream."

"No, Papa!" cried Mercy, struggling to hold back her tears. "No! We're going to build a house and live in it together, just like we dreamed."

"You go and watch for me. Draw for me what you see as we go there. I'll enjoy it that way." He smiled. "Go."

Reluctantly Mercy pulled on her cloak and tightened a wool scarf around her neck, picked up a piece of birch bark and some charcoal twigs. She climbed up the ladder and stepped out into a bone-chilling wind that made her grateful for every ounce of clothing.

Picking a corner of the deck where she would not be in the way, she watched the sailors untie the heavy sails from the yardarms and scurry back down to the deck to secure them. The canvas fluttered until the lines were tightened, and then with a *whumph* the canvas filled out, and the ship, her anchor raised, began to move.

She wished her father could see it all; but she would be his eyes, this time, and draw it for him. Mercy poised her charcoals over a white piece of birch. It had curled up a bit in the dampness of her cabin since Francis had pressed it under a rock. But she could still manage. What to draw?

A shout from the starboard railing drew everyone's attention. John Alden was pointing to a herd of seals jumping in the water. There were dozens! One would poke his whiskers above water, coming up for air, until a playmate would knock him off balance and beckon to be followed to the depths. She watched, transfixed, marveling that the seals could be so frisky in these icy waters. She started sketching the seals, quickly drawing one after another with her homemade charcoals.

Just then the first mate called to her from the poop deck. "I see you're making one of your drawings again. Here," he said, tossing a chalk down to her. "A sailor begged me to give you one a few days ago. We like your pictures. Not much else on this ship to amuse a body, is there?"

At last, after fighting adverse winds for two days, the *Mayflower* reached Plimoth Harbor on December 16. Mercy, sitting beside her sleeping parents, listened to the cries of the First Mate as he called out the water's depth by means of a weighted fathom rope.

Suddenly Jack came up to her. "You've got to come up and see this, Mercy; we're making history!"

She didn't move.

"Your father wouldn't want you to miss this moment."

Looking at him, she knew Jack was right. If he were awake, he'd be saying the same thing.

As Mercy emerged out on deck just behind Jack, the splash of the ship's anchor signaled that they had arrived.

The ship's rail was lined with passengers eager to catch a glimpse of their new home, but Master Jones had anchored the ship so far out in the bay that it was hard to make out details on shore. They could see a cleared area of land sloping upward to a hill several hundred yards from the water. And on either side were plenty of trees, to supply the timber for houses.

Excitement mounted among both passengers and crew throughout the next day and the Sabbath, as a landing party was selected from the passengers and crew to go ashore in the shallop Monday morning. Once again Jack was chosen.

That evening, when they returned, Jack bounded down the forward ladder to find Mercy keeping vigil by her parents' bed as they slept. He was eager to tell her everything. "We marched along the coast in the woods for seven or eight miles. We didn't see any Indians, but we did see where they had planted their corn.

"The best news is that the Elders were right; there are four brooks of sweet, fresh water that all run into the bay. The land is good. We saw many trees—oak and walnut, beech, ash, birch, and others. Vines are everywhere, and cherry and plum trees, and others we don't know. It is a fine place, Mercy!

"Tomorrow we will take some of you back with us." Mercy couldn't help but smile at his enthusiasm, though her heart was heavy with worry about her parents.

"Listen to the boy," Mercy's mother whispered. She wasn't asleep, after all. "We'll still be here when you get back."

The next morning dawned gray and overcast. When Mercy climbed into the shallop, she found Mistresses Brewster and Carver, as well as Priscilla, Elizabeth, and Desire Minter.

"How's your father?" Mercy asked Elizabeth.

"Poorly. I don't want to think about it."

"I know; mine is too." They hugged each other.

As the oars dipped, Mercy was grateful to put the *Mayflower* out of her mind for a while.

John Alden pointed to a large rock at the shore. "Glaciers brought it here," he informed them.

"Aha!" exclaimed Mercy. "God put it here for our stepping stone! He knew we were coming!"

Standing up in the boat, and nearly losing her balance in the process, she struck a pose as a grand lady in Shakespeare's theater. "It shall be His footstool," she theatrically declared, "and we," with a grand sweeping gesture she included them all, "His kings and queens, to rule forever in this noble land."

Laughing, they all applauded her.

As the boat bumped against the rock, John Alden hopped out first and then stretched a hand towards Priscilla who, unsure of her footing, pulled back, giggling shyly.

Hiking up her skirts, Mercy boldly walked the boat's length. "I'm not afraid!" she cried, clasping John Alden's outstretched hand and stepping out onto the rock.

"Since I'm the first woman to step on Plimoth's rock," she cried laughing, "you may call me the Queen of Plimoth."

John Alden bowed and handed her an oar, held upright like a scepter. "Your majesty! May your dominion be great and your descendants many."

Jack scowled at him. Fishing for something in his pocket, he pulled out an arrowhead and held it up to her. "My gift, your majesty," he said without smiling. "You'd better hope no queen of savages challenges your crown."

When all were ashore, the women stepped quickly past the skeletons lying about the shore and headed for the hill they had seen from the ship. They found it covered with a dried bed of wild strawberries, a useful winter herb. Further exploring the area, they noted that the moist, dark earth looked promising for the gardens each woman would plant in the spring.

Mercy had to stop and rest several times. It had been over two months since she'd walked much, and her "land legs" tired quickly.

Meanwhile the men came upon some half-buried Indian pots near the cleared cornfields. In them was a great store of leeks and onion bulbs, the best foundation for a hearty winter soup.

Growing near the marshes of the creek was wild flax, excellent hemp for making rope, which would be needed to pull logs from the nearby woods. Miles Standish said they'd be twisting strong rope together to pull their two cannon up the hill. The high ground was defensible with the cannon.

Mercy was deeply pleased. Everything they could possibly have asked for was here.

That afternoon, back aboard the *Mayflower*, young Francis Billington whispered to his brother Jack. "Did you see all those dead Indian bones lying around?"

Jack glanced in Mercy's direction, as she sat by her sleeping parents, and deciding that she couldn't hear them, he nodded. "A bad omen?"

But she did hear them—and was disgusted that the Billingtons were always preoccupied with death and Indians.

20

THE LONGEST, COLDEST NIGHT

Before long everyone was preoccupied with death. In spite of the abundance of pure water and fresh provisions gathered from the harbor, men weakened by the rigor of the voyage were at last succumbing to the dreaded scurvy. The limes they had brought with them had run out several weeks before.

Mercy had convinced Elizabeth to surrender the hidden cache of the limes she had refused to eat. She'd squeezed them for her father. But nothing could reverse James Clifton's symptoms now; his breathing was labored as he slept.

And it was getting progressively colder. One night the temperature dropped lower than it ever had before, driven well below freezing by a fierce wind that prohibited a fire, lest sparks ignite the ship.

Before dawn James Clifton breathed his last tortured breath.

Though her father had tried to prepare Mercy for his death by talking of heaven, nothing could prepare her for the sense of loss she felt. She sobbed on Priscilla's shoulder; and a little while later, so did Elizabeth, who had lost her father and her youngest brother, who were caught away by the death angel while they slept.

The comforting care of her beloved friend did little to sooth her agony. Jack tried too, but his words couldn't lessen her pain; neither could her mother, herself so close to death.

Now Elder Brewster came and put a comforting arm around Mercy. With him she could unburden herself. "I didn't even get to say good-bye," she sobbed. "He couldn't hear me."

The kindly white-bearded man gently raised her chin and looked into her eyes. "You don't know this, but a few days ago he told me how proud he was of you, being the first woman to set foot on our new land."

Mercy sniffled. "He did?"

"Your father's parting request was that I promise him I'd see to it that you would know coming here was not in vain. He wanted you to help plant the Gospel of Christ in this savage wilderness. You were the only surviving child of their lifelong dream, and he prayed that God would bless you with many children in this New World."

Within hours five other families requested a burial party to entomb bodies on land. But Master Jones objected. If the savages discovered their numbers were being weakened by death, they might well attack. He advised burial in the bay.

The grieving families were upset. How could they dump their loved ones over the side of the ship in bags weighted with cannonballs?

At last Governor Carver prevailed over Master Jones's objections. He assigned Miles Standish to take an armed party and bury the dead ashore— at night, under cover of darkness.

Jack was to go with them. As Mercy watched Mrs. Brewster wrap her father's body in strips of bedding, Jack said softly, "Mercy, I'll mark the spot on the hill where we'll bury him; and I'll take you there later, I promise."

She made no reply; she could find no words for anything.

Gently Mrs. Carver gathered the forlorn girl to her bosom, as silent wrenching sobs wracked her.

There was a brief ceremony on the ship in pitch-black darkness as Governor Carver committed the souls of the deceased to God. Then the shallop's sad cargo was rowed ashore.

Each day the great sickness grew worse, and Mercy couldn't seem to find any prayers to pray against it. A number of the children she'd cared for had passed away, and that was the hardest of all. Instead of living to see the land of the stories they'd come to love, they went to an unmarked grave.

The shallop now left regularly to the shore, for some felt it healthier to be in the fresh air, cold as it was, than to be among the sick and dying. Mercy could not stand it in the 'tween decks, with the constant coughing and the smells of feverish and unwashed bodies.

She tended her mother in the morning, as the sun came up, and fed her in the evening if she was awake. But during the day she and Priscilla were often among those going ashore to wash linens and clothing. This was a great help to all on board, who were grateful to be able to change their garments after long weeks at sea. But Elizabeth was now too sick herself to accompany them, and Mercy and Priscilla worried constantly about their dear friend.

On December 25, as Mercy and Priscilla unloaded their laundry on shore and prepared a fire, Jack surprised them with an unusual gift.

"Don't get too busy on your chores yet!" he called and scaled a tall tree near the hill, on which were growing green vines with berries. Grabbing some, he scrambled back down the trunk and brought them proudly to Mercy, holding them above her head.

"Ah! The winter solstice!" sighed Stephen Hopkins, who was passing by with a musket in one hand and his axe in the other. "I miss the mistletoe and the lighted tree." He winked. "How could we forget to have a bit of Christmas today?"

And with that he planted a kiss on one of Mercy's cheeks, as Jack did on the other.

Picking up on the idea, John Alden held a clump of berries and greens aloft and kissed Priscilla's forehead.

Then the young men went merrily on their way to cut logs, leaving the two girls staring blankly at each other.

"Winter solstice?" asked Mercy.

"Lighted tree?" responded Priscilla.

"The old Heathen Feasting Day," explained John Howland, who had ventured ashore for the first time after his long recovery. He recited a poem from England's festivals:

> *When winter is the bleakest,*
> *And its icy grip like death,*
> *That's when Winter Solstice comes.*
> *Its celebration brings new breath.*

And then he added, "When the sun has finally reached its greatest distance below the equator, we celebrate because we can look forward to spring instead of winter."

Spring. Mercy liked the sound of it, but these Strangers certainly had different customs than Saints. "We don't celebrate birthdays, not even the Christ Child's. That would be worshipping ourselves," she said firmly. "The day you were born is not as important as the evidence of God's hand in your life. That is what should be honored."

"We're not going to have any foolishness of Winter Fests here today."

They turned to see Governor Carver, with Elders Brewster and Bradford beside him and Edward Winslow not far behind, pulling a sled for towing wood up the bank.

"We have too much to do," the Governor went on, "trees to fell, and a common house to build up there on the hill. There'll be no drunkenness or reveling, such as happens in the streets of London this day. We've been purified from that."

"But surely there will be a Christmastide goose," pleaded Mrs. Billington, who was among the Strangers who had gathered. She held up a wild turkey that her husband had shot the day before. "I'll build the fire myself, and we'll all partake of it together for the midday meal!"

Governor Carver sensed a dispute brewing. The Strangers obviously wanted to celebrate a holiday from a culture the Separatists didn't tolerate. Of course, everyone wanted to eat the scrumptious turkey, but there was no time for a day off with so much work to do and so few able-bodied hands to do it.

Elder Brewster came to the rescue. "The Old Testament prophet Jeremiah condemns the heathen practice of cutting a tree from the forest to 'deck it with silver and gold.' That is one of the beliefs we live by, and it is clearly not yours," he said to Mrs. Billington. "However, since we've had our own share of religious persecution, the last thing we want to do is to inflict hardships on anyone else in the name of religion. So we'll spend the day cutting trees for a house and not for a Christmas Yule log. But this evening we'll all enjoy the turkey together, grateful that this long winter shall pass because God has appointed the change of seasons."

That bit of diplomacy impressed Mercy as having been heaven-sent.

Everyone smiled but Mr. Billington. He nodded his head soberly, picked up his saw, and marched to the forest to catch up with Mr. Hopkins.

Work continued on the Common House. Rain, snow, or shine, the men labored on, sometimes working up a sweat, which soon turned to chills in the freezing temperatures. More fell ill.

And Master Jones's crew was also getting sick and dying. Mercy had heard him hotly discussing with the Elders his extended stay in the harbor, which had already gone long past the agreed-upon time. He'd quartered the sailors as far as possible from the sick passengers, but it did no good.

Climbing the hill one day, Mercy could see far across the bay. With their houses built on the hill, they would all enjoy this view. Governor Carver had shown them the plan for their little village—a long central street with houses on both sides and a cross street bisecting it in the middle. She would not have a house of her own; she was resigned to that. Her father was gone, and she knew her mother would soon follow him. The Elders would assign her to another family. She hoped it would be the Winslows; but, she told herself, she should be able to be happy wherever they put her. At least, she would have a garden plot of her own.

That is, *if* she stayed. Without a family this was a hard place to live. And Jack was too much of a question mark to figure into any serious plans. She'd begun thinking about returning to England with the *Mayflower*. She could get to Holland from there—back to her cousin and Pastor Robinson and a real bed and hearth fire. Never had the comforts of home seemed so appealing.

21

A MOUND IN THE SWAMP

January 3, we go exploring, wrote Mercy in small, neat script on a piece of flattened birch bark. She was seated in the shallop, being rowed ashore with other young people, the younger children, and the two dogs. Next to her was Elizabeth Tilley, who had recovered, thank God, and was looking after the two Brewster boys, Love and Wrestling. After so many getting sicker and sicker, to have one person getting healthier brought hope!

Jack had been put in charge of this expedition to collect reeds for the thatched roof of the common house, and clay to caulk the rough-hewn boards of its sides. It was breathtakingly cold, but Dr. Fuller had prescribed this outing.

"I don't know how you do that, lass," murmured a kindly voice just behind her. "Writing while we are moving. In fact, it is rare to see a young lady writing at all."

She turned to see the smiling face of Edward Winslow. "My father taught me back home, sir."

"Do you miss home, Mercy?"

"Yes, sir," she admitted.

"One day you will call this home."

She nodded, but wondered if that day would ever come.

Captain Standish greeted them and helped them off the boat. He had been camping in a lean-to of saplings to guard the common house under construction. Now, as he stood shivering before them, Mercy could see the poor man was frozen to the bone, his campfire offering precious little warmth in the wind.

They all listened as he instructed Jack to stay close to the creek that ran near the hill. "The Towne Creek, nigh the common house, is a safe place to venture. The swamp, however, is *not* a safe place. Do *not,* under any circumstances, go in there." He paused. "Is that understood?"

Having discovered that the cattail rushes from the banks of the frozen creek would make good thatch, the Pilgrims began harvesting them.

Wrestling Brewster suggested, "Let's weave those rushes into baskets for the clay!" When Jack agreed, his brother Love and some of the others wove the baskets and filled them with clay from the creek bank.

As the sun rose toward noon, they continued walking farther away from the hill, along the creek. No one noticed how dark the woods had become.

When they'd pulled enough reeds for thatch, Jack announced it was time to turn back. Taking a head count, he found that all were present except one, his younger brother. "Has anyone seen Francis?"

Scowling, Jack studied the creek bed, and sure enough, there were his footprints leading away. Following them into the swamp, they found Francis on his hands and knees, busily digging something up.

Jack grabbed him by the collar. "Francis! We were calling you! And you've led us into the swamp. Didn't you hear Captain Standish?"

"I'm not afraid of any ol' swamp," Francis bragged. "It's the best place to find Indian arrowheads," he exclaimed triumphantly, holding up a muddy piece of chipped flint.

Mercy shivered in the gloomy shadows. She didn't like the feeling of the swamp, and it was obvious that the others felt the same.

"I feel like a million eyes are watching me!" whispered Desire, as an owl hooted.

"Aw, it's just birds!" Francis snapped. "Girls! Sissy scaredy-cats!"

Ignoring him, the girls started to leave.

And then one of the boys pointed to a strange mound under a dense covering of scrub oak and cedar.

"Hey!" yelped Francis with delight, "It's just like the graves you told us about at the First Encounter Beach, Jack!" And before anyone could stop him, he'd pulled away from his brother's grip and bounded toward it. The younger boys ran after him, nearly knocking Mercy over.

"Someone who worries about curses coming on grave robbers ought to know better than that!" Mercy shouted after Francis, who climbed the mound and then scrambled up a tree to get away from his brother.

All at once Francis shielded his eyes, gazing into the distance. "Hey! There are Indian huts over there!" He pointed. "And someone's there, 'cause there's a fire going. Let's go have a look-see!"

"Francis!" commanded Jack. "Come down from there! If there are savages this close and we're on their burial ground, we need to be getting out of here!"

"*You're* afraid?" Francis mocked.

But just then the limb he was balanced on gave way, and he fell out of the tree in a heap.

"We've got to be getting back. Now!" Priscilla insisted. "Besides, they need our clay and thatch."

"There's another reason to get out of here!" Love Brewster pointed at the swampy trail leading up to the mound. There were strange footprints and a second set of impressions belonging to a creature with four pads on its paws.

"What made those?" Mercy asked.

Jack had Francis by the collar again. "The big ones are made by moccasins. And the others . . ." Before he could say it, the howl of a wolf pierced the dark swamp. And it sounded close.

Hackles rose on every neck as a spooked owl flapped out of its perch above them.

Mercy snatched up Loyal and grabbed Cromwell's collar before the spaniel and the mastiff could investigate the sound.

"*Yeech!*" cried Francis, rolling his eyes, "And they've set wolves to guard their buried treasure! But I'm not afraid of any ol' wolf! I'm gonna come back here and dig it up and. . . . "

"No, you're not!" declared Mercy, handing Loyal and Cromwell to Priscilla. In a flash she grabbed his arm and dragged him back down the trail as fast as she could. "Whatever the Indians buried there," she announced to the other boys, "it's going to stay there!"

Though Francis tried to hit her, she refused to let go of his arm until they were back at the campsite.

"You're not my mother!" the lad screeched, as several wolves bayed in the background.

"And thank heavens, you're not *my* brother. But I'm not about to let you cause trouble with the Indians this close to our plantation."

Francis didn't say a word and calmed down just in time to enter the camp looking like a perfect angel.

22

LOST IN THE WOODS

January 9 was unseasonably warm, like spring! Mercy felt so grateful for the glorious morning that she was teaching the children prayers of thanksgiving to their Creator.

Suddenly one of them, Francis, pointed overhead. "Look at the big bird flying over the woods!"

Mercy was awestruck. "An eagle!" she breathed, as they all watched it gracefully soaring upward. "It's like it's going to touch Heaven!"

"Ow!" cried Francis, behind her. Mercy turned to see Mr. Billington pull him away, boxing his ears and scolding him about not fetching some fish he'd strung on a line for breakfast.

In that instant Mercy saw why the boy was so rebellious. Who ever let him enjoy anything?

She sighed, and picked up her father's hoe. Taking advantage of the January thaw, she and others were preparing the soil for their own plots, before the ground froze over again.

Though she was happy to go to work, Mr. Billington wasn't. After he'd finished his fish, he began grumbling about having to work on the common house again. Elder Bradford came looking for him.

"Mr. Billington, it's high time you did your share of the work if you expect to be housed with the rest."

"Why should I?" Billington snarled. "We came to build our own houses, and could have had them nearly finished by now!"

Elder Bradford did not raise his voice. "Some are not as robust as you, nor as healthy. But your turn may come to be sick, and if it does, you'll be glad someone else is working for you."

Mr. Billington slowly got to his feet. His embarrassed wife took her pots to the creek to wash them, grateful for an excuse to depart.

Governor Carver appeared, and William Bradford took him aside for a private word. He did not want Billington to hear, but apparently he did not mind Mercy hearing. "John, this pooling of labor does not seem to be working as we'd hoped; it's breeding much confusion and discontent, and slowing the speed of our efforts."

Mercy sensed he was concerned about Billington, who was showing greater resistance to being governed day by day.

"What do you propose?"

William Bradford thought a moment. "I suggest that as soon as the roof is completed, we turn every man to his own plot and the building of his own house. Perhaps that will help them work faster."

Governor Carver nodded and informed Billington of their decision.

"About time!" muttered the latter, as he shuffled off to get his tools.

Mercy watched him get as far as the common house, but then he sank down for a little snooze behind it.

They could have used his help. That afternoon the balmy weather turned frigid again. As the temperature dropped, the sweat the men had worked up in the warm sun began freezing, and they developed coughs and chills they couldn't shake.

William Bradford worked harder than any of the older men. Mercy sensed he was hammering pegs into the wooden posts of the roof with a force that drove away the grief he was suffering from losing his wife. As Mercy watched him, he looked feverish to her, but he would not come down to rest.

Noting that the roof would be finished in another few hours, she joined the other women, who were already moving in bedding and provisions. The fireplace was drawing well, with a fire crackling in it, so perhaps the men could get some peaceful sleep there that night and not have to sleep with the sick onboard the *Mayflower*.

But that evening at sundown, the promise of a peaceful night was smashed by terrible news.

Two of their men were missing!

At noon a party of four, accompanied by both dogs, had gone to gather enough thatching material to finish the roof of the common house. Only two of the men had returned. The other two had searched for them, calling and hollering, but neither Peter Brown nor John Goodman nor either of the dogs was anywhere to be found.

What to do? The Elders and Captain Standish decided against sending out a search party at night with torches. If the Indians had indeed taken the men captive, as many feared, they might be waiting to ambush anyone who came looking for them.

At dawn, the captain would lead a dozen armed men on a scouting expedition to search the swamp and, if necessary, go to the Indian village.

And in case the Indians were holding Mr. Brown and Mr. Goodman hostage, they would take items to barter for their lives—two axes, a mirror, a necklace, and Stephen Hopkins' luxurious beaver fur coat, which he had donated.

"What are we supposed to do in the meantime," blurted out Edward Winslow. "Just sit here, doing nothing?"

"We must go back to the ship and tell the others," responded Elder Brewster. "But there is something else we can do: we can pray—all of us."

As soon as they were in the shallop, rowing back to the *Mayflower*, Brewster led them in prayer for the missing men. The rest of the ride was spent in anxious silence.

On board the ship, when Mercy prayed along with Elizabeth and Priscilla, she found that she was not only worried about the missing men but also about Loyal. With her father gone and her mother soon to follow, the little, sad-eyed spaniel was the only thing she had left on this side of the ocean.

At dawn twelve of their able-bodied men, the only ones not sick, assembled on the top deck of the *Mayflower* with their muskets. Captain Standish organized them in pairs and told them (and those who had come on deck to see them off) that if they had not found the men by sundown, they were to break off their search and meet at the big rock on which they had come ashore.

Mercy and Priscilla and Elizabeth passed among them, distributing bundles containing a day's rations. She saved the last for Jack, so that she might have a word with him.

"You once saved Loyal for me," she murmured. "I shall pray that you do so again."

Jack smiled at her mischievously. "Aren't you worried about *me,* that *I* might not return?"

Mercy shrugged, trying to show indifference. "No, should I be?"

"Well, you heard the wolves. And what if we run into savages again like we did at First Encounter Beach, and they start shooting arrows at us?"

"Oh, I'm sure you'll be able to scare them off." She kept her smile, as the men got into the shallop and headed for shore, but he had definitely given her something to worry about.

At sundown, the vague worry became harsh reality. When the shallop reached the *Mayflower*, Captain Standish was the first up the ladder. He went straight to Governor Carver, whose fever had prevented him from going, and Mercy, standing nearby, heard their exchange. Now Jack was missing!

"The Billington boy was with Stephen Hopkins, who was wearing his fur coat. It slowed him down, and the lad grew increasingly impatient until finally he told Mr. Hopkins that he had an idea where they might be, and he would see him back at the rock. Mr. Hopkins reminded him of their instructions not to get separated, but Jack just left."

Governor Carver spat over the railing in disgust. "You told the men to stick together. You could not have made it more clear."

"Yes, sir, and I repeated it ashore before we started. Jack may be smart, but he has no idea of what it means to follow orders."

"So now we have *three* men missing."

Just then Jack's father came storming up. "What's the meaning of this? Why have you come back to the ship?" he demanded of Captain Standish. "Why aren't you searching for my son?"

"For the same reason we did not go searching last night," responded Miles Standish. "We do not yet know the minds of these savages. If they mean us harm, they could deal us a crippling blow in the dark, as we stumble about in an area which they know well. If they have no ill will toward us, then the worst thing that will happen is that Jack will have a cold night of it."

Muttering under his breath, Billington turned and stalked off.

Mercy slept fitfully that night. Several times she was awakened by the baying of wolves only to realize that she had been hearing them in her dreams.

In the morning the search party went out again, this time with Billington taking the place of his son. There were no smiles at their departure, only the grim assurance that those staying behind would be praying.

To occupy the minds of the little ones, the girls took them ashore to gather kindling for the common house. Mercy kept Francis close to her side that morning as they scoured the hillside for kindling. She was seeing a side of the boy she'd not seen before, an endearing side.

"They should have taken me!" he told her emphatically. "I could've told them what tree to climb. I saw those Indian fires. I saw their huts!"

As he looked up at her, the hurt and anger went out of his eyes. "I'm scared for Jack, Mercy," the boy suddenly blurted out, for the first time honestly speaking about his fear.

Without speaking, she put her arms around him and realized that she, too, was scared.

As the sun began to settle on the horizon, the search parties straggled back to the rock. All were bone tired and grateful for the flagons of hot water from a kettle on the common house's hearth fire that Mercy handed to them. Wearily they made their reports to Governor Carver. They had seen nothing, found nothing.

Captain Standish and John Howland were the last pair to return. The Captain quietly informed Governor Carver that they had better prepare themselves for the worst. Even if the three missing men had not been taken captive, it was unlikely they could survive three nights in the wild with no warmth and no food.

Mercy heard this and wished she hadn't. Now, in addition to her father and probably her mother, she was going to lose Loyal and Jack. In her head she had denied that he meant anything to her. But she could not deny the terrible dread in her heart.

Twilight was turning to night, as Governor Carver called all ashore to get in the shallop, and return to the ship. Mercy was about to step on the rock, sadly remembering with what joy she had first put her foot on it, when she paused. Was her mind playing tricks on her again, as it had when she was awakened by the wolves?

Or did she actually hear the distant sound of a dog barking?

23

HERO OR REBEL?

Far down the shore a black-and-white bundle of fur propelled herself over the sand and rocks, as fast as her little legs could carry her! As she drew closer, she caught sight of Mercy and redoubled her efforts, finally leaping up into her outstretched arms!

The others, now visible behind her, were not doing so well. Peter Brown and Jack were supporting John Goodman between them; and Cromwell, the Bull Mastiff, was limping along behind.

A cheer went up from the searchers as they ran down the beach to escort home their stricken friends. When they arrived back at the common house, the two older men collapsed from weakness and hunger.

That was soon remedied as women ladled steaming stew into bowls for each of them. Mr. Goodman dropped his, and Mercy realized that his fingers must be numb with frostbite. Dr. Fuller confirmed her fears as he carefully examined Goodman's hands. But his feet, soaked in swamp water and then frozen, were in worse shape. Once the doctor had removed his boots, the flickering light of the hearth fire revealed that several of his toes were blackened.

Dr. Fuller shook his head. "We'll do our best to save them, John," he whispered, "but if the color does not return, they may have to go."

Mr. Goodman closed his eyes and nodded.

Governor Carver gave each man a small amount of warm brandy. "This will help," he said, and it did. It also inspired Jack to resume his familiar role as storyteller, with himself as the hero of each story. The two older men, shy to speak in public, let him carry on, adding gestures of agreement now and then.

"Those two had found a lake, following after the dogs that had gone chasing a deer. I heard them barking and followed. When I found them, we'd gone so far that we couldn't find our way back before nightfall. We'd all gotten our feet soaked in the swamp and then frozen when it started to snow. I told them about the savages' huts that Francis had seen the other day, thinking if we found them, we could get warm."

"But we had to give up; they were too far from us to reach before nightfall. When night came, we were forced to make our bed in the dirt."

Mercy looked around the dimly-lit common house. Everyone was listening.

"And that's when we heard two lions roaring and climbed a tree!"

Everyone gasped at that. Lions? No one had ever seen a lion in Holland, or in England either, for that matter. A wild place, this New World!

Jack, delighted at being the center of attention, spun his story out. "We couldn't stay up in that tree very long because of the wind. And when the lions drew near, we could barely hold the dogs back. But they must have scared them off because we never saw them again."

The faces around the common house relaxed, as Jack continued the saga. "I tore off some fir boughs and covered us, but those other two sat up all night, watching for wild beasts. At daylight we tried to find our way back, but somehow we turned in the wrong direction."

Looks of concern again came to the faces of his listeners. "In the woods we discovered many lakes and brooks. We should have marked the trail, but we were exhausted."

His audience nodded in sympathy.

"Then while those two took a rest, I kept exploring with Loyal. We drew near a swampy area I thought I recognized, but suddenly wolves leaped at us from a bluff. I had no musket. And Loyal had no sense; she chased the wolves.

"But when the wolves turned on her, she ran back between my legs. All I had to protect us was a rotten log lying on the ground. I picked it up and threw it at the lead wolf. Luckily, it hit him square in the head. He ran off yipping, and the others went after him."

Seeing his listeners hanging on every word, Jack continued. "But now me and Loyal were lost!" he paused. "in the swamp, where no one wants to go.

All nodded in agreement. "Luck struck again! I found the burial mounds that Francis had discovered."

His brother stirred up at that.

"That's when I recognized the Towne Creek flowing nearby. I went back and got the other two, and here we are!"

Applause and smiles greeted this happy ending.

But Mercy noted that John Goodman had raised an eyebrow for some reason, though he'd said nothing. She had a funny feeling about Jack's story, and deep down inside she wondered what had *really* happened.

The next day she returned to the common house with Dr. Fuller, to look after their patients. Everyone else was outside, sawing and trimming trees, to be cut into planks for the building of their houses.

After a warm night of sleep by the fire, John Goodman was better able to talk. "Would you like to hear what really happened?" he asked Dr. Fuller in a low voice. Mercy went about her business at the hearth. Then Goodman said to her, "You, um, may not want to hear, lass. Everyone knows you're kinda sweet on him."

Mercy blushed.

At that moment Mistress Carver walked in with a bucket to scoop ashes from the hearth. When she left, Mr. Goodman resumed. "But right's right, and wrong's wrong."

Mercy looked squarely at him. "I am just his friend, Mr. Goodman, not his defender. What has he done?"

The latter scowled. "He got us lost, that's what! Nearly caused our chilling to death, he did. I didn't want to say anything last night, in front of his mother. She must have been worried sick about him."

Mercy agreed; the poor woman had experienced all she could bear.

"But he's no hero. We told him to go right back to the other men, with the message that we would be following the creek downstream. Instead, he went off messing around in that swamp!"

Mercy felt her anger rising. "Near that Indian burial mound?"

"I don't know, miss. Whatever he was up to, they never got our message, and we wound up spending another night in the wild. And now I might lose my toes."

Now Peter Browne spoke up from his cot. "And then he slept the night away and wouldn't take his share of the watch. We nearly froze while he stayed warm as a bear in hibernation under those fir boughs."

They painted a far different picture than Jack had the evening before, and Mercy believed them. But what had Jack been doing in that swamp again?

24

THE EAGLE IS DEAD

Mercy dropped the ladle and rubbed the blister on her thumb. It seemed like she'd been spooning out soup from the iron cauldron in the common house kitchen all morning. The men, both the mildly sick and the well, were putting up houses as quickly as they could, and Governor Carver had instructed them to stop by for a bowl of soup to keep their strength up.

Someone reached down and retrieved the ladle for her, and Mercy looked up to see Jack. "Oh, it's you."

"Nothing heroic this time, Mercy. I'd just like another bowl."

"Another?" she snapped. "No one else has dared to ask that but you!"

"It's not for me."

"An act of charity for one of the sick ones?"

"No."

She drew back the ladle and put it under her apron. "Kitchen's closed."

"My father sent me."

"Too lazy to fetch it himself?" retorted Mercy. "What's he been doing all day? Or you, for that matter? I haven't seen either one of you working."

"We've been fishing. Somebody's got to catch the food we eat around here."

"Well, I saw the men putting nets into the harbor and setting up traps for lobsters. What part did your father play?"

"He watched."

"Like the other morning when he watched them finishing the roof?"

"Why are you so harsh with me today?" asked Jack. "Didn't I save your dog yesterday?"

Mercy's anger rose. "That isn't the whole truth, and you know it! You made me believe all your fancy stories. Whatever you were doing in that Indian graveyard may have cost Mr. Goodman his toes and maybe his life! Have you heard his cough today?"

The veins in Jack's forehead stood out as he glared at her. "I found something there I was going to show you. A secret. Something buried."

Mercy had heard enough. "Good men had to give up work time to go looking for you in the woods. My father died, my mother is dying, and many of our men are, too. But you Billingtons never seem to get sick. Is it because you just aren't working as hard as everyone else?"

Jack picked up a shovel. "At night, while you and the good saints sleep, some of us dig graves in this frozen ground so the savages won't see us. There are already twenty buried up there on the hill, and from the looks of things, there'll soon be plenty more! I'm exhausted after a night like that, and so is my father! It's none of your business if we sleep in the day while the others do their share. We bury. They split logs."

Mercy said nothing, but she was fairly certain some of their men were working all day and burying all night. Jack seemed to be an expert at twisting things his way.

Three mornings later Mercy was helping Mistress Brewster pluck five geese that the men had shot. One of the great blessings of the New World was the abundance of wild game, she thought. God had indeed prepared a table for them in the wilderness. There were codfish, smoked and salted, and now drying in the sun. And the carcass of a deer, freshly shot and slaughtered, would soon be roasting over an open fire. If only the sick would recover.

When the geese were ready, she turned her attention to preparing the buns they were about to bake in the clay oven they had recently built. The dough had been rising for two days. She was just cutting a cross mark in the top of each bun she'd placed on the baking paddle when Jack showed up again.

Beaming, and obviously proud of himself, he dropped a huge bird at her feet. "Your Highness, here is a creature big enough to feed all of your sick."

But her response was the opposite of what he'd hoped. Looking down at it, her eyes began to fill with tears. He'd shot the eagle.

"Oh, Jack, how could you?"

His smile fell. "What's wrong? I thought you'd be proud of me! You said I had to be my own man. I did this for you."

But all she could think of was the day they had watched that noble bird soar into the heavens, lifting all their hearts with him. The eagle had made her feel connected to her father, and now this beautiful creature was dead.

Jack interrupted her grief. "It's only a bird, Mercy. We'll eat it. I can't seem to do anything to please you."

Her nose tingled. Something was burning! Oh, no! The bread!

Frantically pulling it out, Mercy moaned. "I've even wasted that! A day's work gone. Can't anything turn out right?"

Behind her, someone shouted. It was Mr. Billington carrying Governor Carver over his shoulder. He'd passed out, his face red with fever!

Mercy stood by helplessly as they passed. That's when she heard Mr. Billington's snide comment to Jack. "Looks like our noble leaders are dying. When we bury them, we'll bury their covenant with them."

25

LORD, WE NEED A MIRACLE!

The next day, January 13, Mercy rode ashore in the back of the shallop, away from any further conversation with the Billingtons. She'd decided the only right thing to do was to tell William Bradford what she'd heard. If their leaders were going to die, they should know about any mutinous threats and be sure to put capable leaders in their place before . . .

She glanced up at the sky. Please, Lord! No graves with Bradford or Carver on their headstones!

At the common house she sought out Carver and Bradford, but neither had any strength to eat breakfast, much less concentrate on what she needed to tell them. When they weren't mercifully dozing, they were caught in the throes of uncontrollable coughing spells. Sadly, they both struck Mercy as being not long for this world.

She walked back to the fireplace, sat down, and surveyed the common house. The men had moved in a few days before, to spend all their available time ashore erecting houses. Today the sickness was worse than ever. Cloaks and hats were strewn everywhere because so many of the men were unable to get out of bed.

She had fixed a breakfast for them of oatmeal, spiced with cinnamon and dried prunes. But as the sun rose higher, only a few stirred. She finally realized that the only people not sick were her, the Billingtons, the Brewsters, Captain Standish, and a few other men! As she went from bed to bed, she found many delirious with high fevers.

As she neared one bed, Elder Brewster stopped her. "No, Mercy. That's not a fitting sight for your eyes." He drew a cover over the dead man's contorted face.

Mercy ran from the building, her stomach churning. She climbed the hill up to her favorite perch on the rocks, and sat down to watch. From this vantage point she could see them bringing out ten wrapped bodies, one after another. There they would lie until nightfall, when they would be buried. With Elizabeth and Priscilla caring for the sick back on the ship, the whole common house was under the care of Mistress Brewster, Eleanor Billington, and herself.

She gazed across the bay, past the *Mayflower*, and imagined what Dorothy Bradford must have seen—a home in Holland, calling her back across the sea. She would give anything to hear the gentle beat of the windmill paddles or see the fields of red and yellow tulips! And towns full of living people! Not like this disease-ridden death camp!

Sinking her head in her hands, she felt despair wash over her. "Lord," she murmured, "you helped the Israelites in their wilderness. Please help us! We need a miracle here in ours."

The air was still, but she heard something in her heart—two Bible verses she had memorized that she had not thought of in a long time: "For I know the thoughts, that I have toward you,' saith the Lord, 'even the thoughts of peace, and not of trouble, to give you an end and your hope. Then shall you cry unto me, and ye shall go and pray unto me, and I will hear you.'"

Her father had rewarded her with a kite for learning those verses from the prophet Jeremiah. She was just six years old.

Mercy's soul soared at the memory. God *does* give us hope! He *does* promise to hear our prayers! But how to pray for the plantation?

"Lord," she cried aloud, "we just can't take any more dying. At this rate we'll all be dead soon. Yet I believe that we did hear You say to come to America."

She looked up at the sky. Did the overcast seem to be lightening a little? Or was it her imagination?

"I'm just a girl, Lord, not an Elder. We took the Lord Jesus into our hearts and wanted to worship Him according to the simplicity of Your Word, instead of by all the rules and regulations of the King's Church. And they persecuted us for that.

"So you brought us here to live according to Your Word, in freedom."

The cloud cover was definitely lighter than it had been, she thought.

She paused and then summed up their case: "If you let us all die, then the King's Church people will say that they were right and that none of us Separatists understand You or follow what You put in our hearts."

She sensed there was something else. "Oh, and Lord? It would be like Pharoah, remember? He mocked Moses and said You couldn't deliver the children of Israel from his hand. King James doesn't think so, either."

As she got to her feet, the sun broke through the clouds! Coincidence? Or a sign that God had heard her prayer?

26

FIRE!

When Mercy returned to the common house, Elder Bradford was awake and for the moment not being tormented by his cough. Propped up on one elbow, he motioned for her to come near. Carefully skirting the powder kegs, she settled down beside him.

"Child," he said with a smile, "I trust you're keeping your journal. There's only mine back on the *Mayflower* and Edward Winslow's and yours. If anything happens to me, you must be sure to keep a good record of everything that happens."

Pulling her pocket pouch off her waist string, she opened it and pulled out the pieces of birch bark she'd been writing and drawing on.

Just then Mrs. Billington called for her to help with the fresh loaves of bread that were ready to wrap up and put away.

"May I look at these?" he asked.

Mercy hesitated, then smiled. "Of course. I read yours, didn't I?" Giving them to him, she went to help.

While they were wrapping the loaves, Mercy heard something on the roof. A squirrel? A rat? Then it stopped.

A few minutes later, Jack came running through the door. "The roof's on fire!"

Looking up, they could all see the licks of flame, inside now, running along the rafters.

"Get those powder kegs out of here or we're all dead!" commanded Governor Carver, staggering up from his sickbed. Clutching his stomach, he pulled on his boots and cloak and stumbled out with one of the kegs. Standish and Brewster came running to carry out the other kegs, while Mr. Billington called his boys to drag away the muskets and balls.

Mercy, Eleanor Billington, and Mary Brewster frantically helped men up from their beds, throwing blankets around them as they pushed them through the door. Mary and Mercy ran back in for Elder Bradford.

The place was now so full of smoke she could hardly see, and flaming pieces of thatch were already falling from the roof.

Hopping over one, she ran for his bed. As she came near it, her eyes widened. The bed had caught on fire! Suddenly, a searing hot wind blew up her petticoats. She looked down. She was on fire!

"Roll!" cried Miles Standish, throwing her to the ground. Then Eleanor Billington pushed a water barrel over on her. That put the skirt fire out, all right, but half drowned her!

Sputtering, she got to her feet, only to hear the captain yell, "Get out of here, girl!" Stomping on the burning bedding, he took Bradford by the shoulders, while Jack took his legs, and they stumbled toward the door.

Then Mercy remembered. Her journal and her sketches! Running back to retrieve them, she stopped in her tracks. There they were, on the other side of Bradford's bed, just where she left them. But she'd noticed something else: on the near side of Brewster's bed was the Geneva Bible she'd loaned him!

Outside she could hear people calling her name. "Where's Mercy? Did she get out?"

Suddenly there was a great cracking sound above her and a shower of sparks. Pieces of burning thatch were falling everywhere. She looked up. The blazing roof was falling in! There was no time to rescue both the birch bark pieces and the Bible!

With a deep moan she grabbed up the Bible and ran through the smoke toward the door. As she jumped through the burning door frame, the roof came down behind her with a fiery crash.

Mercy sucked in a deep breath of clean air and staggered into Mary Brewster's arms. "Child! We were afraid you'd burned up!"

"I had to get my Bible." Her voice broke. "My drawings and journal are gone!" she sobbed.

Then she fainted from exhaustion.

When Mercy came to, the fire had burned itself out.

Days of writing and sketching gone to ashes, she thought bitterly. And no matter how hard they all had worked on the common house—no matter how the men had sweated and gotten chilled in their wet clothes, and taken sick and died—all their labor had gone up in smoke.

They weren't getting *anywhere!*

Loyal ran up and licked her face. She hugged the little spaniel tight, looking over the harbor. People on the *Mayflower* were calling to them, to see if they were still alive. Mercy stood up, and someone handed her a burning torch. She waved it high to let them know they were alive, while sparks crackled and flittered around her.

Sparks? She frowned. A spark had lit the thatch on the common house. But where had it come from? The chimney was tall enough to cool them and carry them away.

And what was that noise up on the roof, just before it happened?

She sat down and, looking at her scorched hem, retraced the day—the rocks, Jack, the clay oven bread, Francis left to play alone, and everyone too sick to pay attention.

She remembered watching the walls of the common house as they fell into the fire. How could he have gotten up on the roof? Then she recalled the moment the chimney had tottered over. Had she seen, just for an instant, the silhouette of a ladder?

A shadow fell across her shoulder. She looked up. Edward Winslow handed her the burned remains of her birch-bark journal and sketches.

Mercy's eyes filled with tears.

Edward Winslow said, "I saw them inside and pulled them out. I understand your loss. I know how I'd feel if I'd lost mine. "

Nodding, she smoothed out the curled-up birch pieces. Her words and sketches were nothing but smudges now.

Seeing Jack standing behind him, she said, "Jack, all your stories are lost."

He smiled. "Not up here, they aren't," he chuckled, tapping his forehead. "You just let me know when you want to hear them all again."

She smiled back at him through the tears.

Of the hundred and two passengers who had originally signed on, only sixty-seven were left alive. They had no choice now but to bring all the sick who had been in the common house back to the *Mayflower*. There was nowhere else to keep them, thought Mercy.

Would they be carrying their diseases back to the ship? Or would those in worse condition on the ship weaken these even more? And how much longer would it be before the Indians finally realized how many they were burying and attack them?

Mercy's head was swirling with questions when she returned to the ship with Edward Winslow and William Brewster.

Master Jones was waiting for them, a fist on each hip. "Ye cannot bring them back here! This ship is full of death already! I want you all off as soon as possible, before I lose what's left of my crew."

Miles Standish struggled to remain patient. "What would you have us do? You saw the common house burn. It's too blasted cold out there for even healthy men to survive without shelter."

Christopher Jones took a long look at the charred remains of the common house and then at the shivering men huddled in blankets in the shallop. "All right," he said with a sigh, "bring them aboard. But take any able-bodied ones with you and go build that house back."

He patted the railing of his ship. "If I don't take this old girl home soon, I won't be able to take her at all. There'll be no crew to set her sails or haul her anchor. My first mate, who sailed with me for years, went to a watery grave this morning. Soon she'll be a ghost ship, rotting in this harbor with all aboard dead, waiting for the savages and French pirates to pick her bones!"

Mercy shivered.

Edward Winslow and William Brewster stepped up. "Master Jones, we're at your mercy. If you leave now, we'll have to go with you, because no one can survive here without shelter. And most of us will join your first mate. We'll be tilting that plank all the way back across the ocean."

Mercy tried not to think of an endless succession of funerals at sea.

Then the white-haired Elder pleaded, "It will take us a month to build back the common house. Give us at least that long."

For a long time Christopher Jones remained motionless. Then slowly he nodded. "I will."

27

TO THE TUNE OF A DRUM

Everyone, it seemed, was dying. Elizabeth Tilley's two sisters and her mother went. And then Rose Standish slipped away. Dr. Fuller had said that the pneumonia could take Margaret Clifton any time, but Mercy knew it would be soon. Without her husband, Mercy's mother had no desire to face the New World alone.

As she drew her final breaths, Margaret made her dying wish known to Mercy, who leaned close to hear what she was trying to say. "I beg you not to stay in this awful wilderness." A violent convulsion seized her. Her lips went blue, and her eyes closed.

Mercy bit her lip to keep from weeping.

A few seconds later her mother spoke her last words. "Marry that young man. Go back to England." Her eyes fluttered open a brief moment more. "Your father's waiting for me." As if she could see him, she reached out and expired.

At that moment Loyal climbed onto Mercy's lap. Hugging her, Mercy let out all her pent-up grief in one long, tragic wail.

"Now," she sobbed, "I have no one!"

As if to remind her that was not entirely true, Loyal licked away her tears.

Mercy hugged her. "If I do go back with the *Mayflower*," she whispered, looking in the sad brown eyes of the little spaniel, "you're going with me."

Soon, as if in answer to their prayers, several days of sustained warm weather arrived. Though it was the end of January, it felt more like April, Mercy thought. And best of all, some of the men were beginning to recover!

They were responding to a new cure that Dr. Fuller had found—rose-hip tea, made from the dried pods of wild roses. Amazingly, it seemed to have the same curative power as limes! With more men able to work and a few warmer days, the rebuilding of the common house progressed so fast that it was finished on January 21, three weeks ahead of schedule! And since it was the Sabbath, Elder Brewster and Edward Winslow took every well person and the dogs over on the shallop for a dedication service.

For this happy occasion they pulled their best clothes out of the trunks they'd been waiting to open. They fetched their call-to-worship drum from the hold; and to its beat all the Pilgrims—Saints and Strangers alike—marched three abreast up the hill from the beach, led by Governor Carver, Elder Brewster, and Miles Standish shouldering his musket.

When Mercy arrived at the new common house, everything was neat and in order for the service. For pews, planks had been laid on powder kegs and barrels in two rows, running the length of each side of the long narrow building. The men were ushered into one side and the women and children into the other.

Keeping the young children from becoming unruly was no longer a problem. There were no more than a handful left. Mercy sadly recalled their wide-eyed wonder as they'd watched the *Mayflower*'s sails go up for the first time, at the beginning of their voyage.

She closed her eyes and shook her head, trying to shake the memory from it, as she sat down beside Mary Brewster. Mercy now regarded Mistress Brewster as her substitute mother. The feeling was mutual; the Brewsters had taken the newly-orphaned Mercy to their hearts as if she were their own daughter.

Everyone was there but the Billingtons. Intent on avoiding the service, Mr. Billington had been quick to volunteer for guard duty, and had taken his two sons with him.

Elder Brewster asked everyone to bow their heads as they prayed the Lord's Prayer. When they came to "deliver us from evil," Mercy glanced at the loaded and charged muskets lining the walls. Miles Standish had warned them stoutly to keep their weapons ready at all times, even when they were at worship.

Then Elder Brewster opened her father's Geneva Bible—which she had loaned to him—to Psalm 37. He sang one verse at a time, with his congregation repeating it after him.

The steps of a good man are ordered by the LORD:
and he delighteth in his way.

Though he fall, he shall not be utterly cast down:
   for the LORD upholdeth him with his hand."

When the service was over, Mercy and the girls stepped outside. Cold cheate bread with cold rabbit meat was their midday fare, for there could be no cooking on the Sabbath. A line formed, with the children serving the adults first.

Walking to the front to help, Mercy passed Jack and Francis.

"Psalm-singer!" Francis sneered under his breath.

Fed up with him, Mercy stooped down and put her face close to his. "See here, little man, I didn't spend two months on that ship and lose both my parents to be mocked by a little snot like you!"

Francis stamped on her toe and was about to dash off when Jack yanked his collar nearly off. "Say you're sorry, Francis!"

Francis buttoned his lip tight.

Jack stuck a finger in his face, "They didn't punish you for nearly blowing up the ship, now did they?"

Francis teared up a little. Then a worried look crossed his face.

"And they didn't punish you for climbing up on the—"

"So it *was* you on the roof," snapped Mercy. "*You* started that fire!"

"Sorry!" Francis blurted out, in the fastest apology she had ever seen. "Tell God, I'm sorry!"

Even Jack was surprised by his sudden repentance and let him wriggle away.

Their lunch might be cold, but the unseasonable warmth of that sunny day more than made up for it. Mercy was refilling their flagons with rosehip tea when she heard Governor Carver muse to Elder Bradford, "Despite our losses, William, we have much to thank God for, beginning with this merciful warmth. Had the bay frozen solid, as John Smith reported was often the case, the Indians could have crossed it at night and surprised us in our beds."

Mercy gasped. Just what Dorothy Bradford had imagined! But in God's mercy, it had never happened.

After the lunch remains had been cleaned up, Mercy was still reflecting on Governor Carver's words when she heard Cromwell barking furiously at something.

"What in the world?" John Goodman exclaimed, jumping to his feet and running out to see what his dog was up to. As Mercy followed him, she heard Loyal chiming in with her lighter barks.

When she and John Goodman rounded the corner to the back of the common house, the sight they beheld stopped them cold in their tracks.

"Oh, my!" Mercy cried, her hands flying to her mouth.

Next to a reed basket containing scraps of rabbit meat was a large skunk, facing Cromwell, who was crouched down about a foot away. His deep booming sounds were echoing off the nearby trees.

Loyal, prudently hiding behind her big friend, was barking as well.

Unable to get a response from this strange black-with-a-white-stripe Charlemagne, the big dog stopped barking for a second.

"Cromwell, come here!" commanded John Goodman.

Too late. The skunk calmly turned around and employed her ultimate weapon—a terrible, stinging spray—right in Cromwell's face!

Yowling with dismay, the poor dog sneezed violently and rubbed his nose and eyes with his paws. Now the stench was overpowering. He tried desperately to get the spray off him.

As the other occupants of the common house began arriving, the skunk beat a hasty retreat. Seeing Cromwell lurching from side to side, whining, and rolling on the ground, the latecomers soon understood what had happened. Priscilla, Elizabeth, and Mercy began laughing while trying to hold their noses at the same time because now the entire area reeked with the skunk's acrid spray

"What are we going to do with him?" asked Priscilla through her nose. "He stinks too much to have him around!"

"Your best hope is to wash him in the bay," Mistress Brewster observed.

John Goodman spoke up. "Well then, ladies, if you will help me, I'll see what I can do."

Soon a comical procession was making its way down to the shore of the bay. In the front, John Goodman led a still sneezing and reluctant Cromwell on a rope. He was followed by Mercy, Priscilla, and Elizabeth, waddling along in bunched-up skirts. Each of the girls was holding an old rag, a scrubbing brush cut from a bush, and a wad of cooking fat to use as soap. Loyal brought up the rear, trotting along at a safe distance.

John led his dog into the shallow water of the bay, then turned to the girls. "Mercy, if you hold his rope firmly, and Elizabeth, if you'll stand behind him so he can't back up, then Priscilla and I will do our best to clean him."

Loyal sat and watched while her friend endured a scrubbing, shivering with the shame and indignity of it all, his head hung low.

When his owner pushed Cromwell's massive head under the water, the dog tried to back away.

"Oh, no, you don't!" cried Mercy, gripping the rope. "Push on his rear, Tilley!" she called out to Elizabeth, and together the two girls kept him from escaping.

They scrubbed and rescrubbed until the soap was used up. Then the cleaning party led the large dog up out of the water.

"I'm afraid he still smells pretty bad," Mercy grimaced. "It seems like it will just have to wear off."

As if in response, the mastiff gave a vigorous shake of his huge body, thoroughly covering them all with cold salt water.

"Oh, you beast!" cried Priscilla. "Haven't you caused enough trouble for one day?"

With that, the girls fell on the dog with their rags, drying him off as best they could.

That night in her bed, Mercy chuckled as she relived the episode.

28

FOOTPRINTS!

Looking out the door of the rebuilt common house two weeks later, Mercy watched the cold rain beating down, turning the path into a muddy mess. At least it was rain and not snow, she thought. If it got much colder, and stayed cold, the bay would freeze over. Mercy kept imagining the Indians silently approaching the *Mayflower* over the ice, intent on murdering all of them.

With a shudder she commanded herself to stop thinking about it. As Elder Brewster had reminded them, with no knowledge of what the Indians were thinking, they must hope for the best but prepare for the worst.

Eventually the rain stopped, the sun came out, and the wind died down. It had become the long-awaited perfect day to transport the cannon from the ship to the common house. With these two pieces in place, they could feel reasonably secure.

Watching the men carefully loading the smaller cannon, known as a "minion," onto the shallop, Elizabeth leaned over to Mercy and whispered. "See! My patient has recovered."

Mercy looked at the muscular John Howland and giggled under her breath. "Ah! I do see! And tell me, dear Tilley," she asked mischievously, "does he know that he is thy patient?"

"Um, of course," mused Elizabeth. "And if he doesn't, he soon will."

Mercy pinched her for being so sure, and Elizabeth retaliated by reaching over and tugging Mercy's coif down over her eyes.

They giggled again, and then sobered up instantly when the young man in question looked their way. Snuggled shoulder to shoulder, they looked back at him like innocent lambs.

Carefully the men rowed the cannon to shore and returned to fetch its big brother. There was much prayer, for the slightest shift in weight could plunge their precious cargo irretrievably to the depths of the bay.

When both were safely delivered to the shore, everyone breathed a joyful sigh of relief. With the protection of the cannon, they all felt more secure living ashore.

"You two, come with me," Mistress Brewster summoned Mercy and Elizabeth. "It's time you paid your respects to your parents' graves."

As the girls got up and went after her, followed by Loyal and Cromwell, Mercy had mixed feelings. When she'd asked the older woman to accompany her, she'd been told that they would go up together in due time. Due time was apparently now. She'd been up to the burial hill before, but primarily to be alone and enjoy the view. Now it would be to close a chapter in her life.

When they arrived at the common grave, Mercy had a lump in her throat. At the time of their burial, the ground had been so frozen that it was almost impossible to dig. The burial party had been forced to put the bodies in the same plot. And since there were no markers, there was no way of being certain who was where—Allerton, Standish, Tilley, Crackstone, White, Martin, More, Clifton. One day there would be proper headstones here.

Pondering the site, Mercy murmured, "Losing one parent is bad enough. But losing two. . . ." Her voice trailed off.

"How about losing all your brothers and sisters, too?" responded Elizabeth, eyes brimming.

Mercy put an arm around her friend. "It's a good thing our leaders aren't buried here. Because if they were, Mr. Billington said he'd bury their covenant with them."

"*What?*" demanded Mistress Brewster. "When did he say that?"

"When the Governor and Elder Bradford were sick in the common house."

"Did you tell anyone?"

"I was going to," Mercy replied, "but they were too sick to speak with, and then the common house burned down, and Mama died. And I saw Mr. Billington helping and hoped that meant he'd changed his mind."

Mistress Brewster pursed her lips. "Let's hope he has."

For a long time they stood without speaking, bidding their loved ones a silent farewell. Above them the sky was bright blue; and below them, to Mercy's surprise, there was also blue. The first blue buds of wild crocuses, encouraged by the unseasonable warmth, had pushed their way to the surface.

Noting them, Mistress Brewster smiled. "Since the flowers are up already, we should start planting grain here, to hide this spot from the Indians." She paused. "Rye and barley, I think."

As Mercy and Elizabeth bent to pick the delicate, bell-shaped buds, suddenly both dogs began to circle the spot, sniffing.

Wondering why they were so agitated, Mercy studied the ground. Then her mouth fell open. She pointed to a fresh set of round footprints encircling the new graves—different from the heeled shoe prints of the grave diggers, and on top of them. Whoever had made them had come after the burial party had left.

"Moccasins!" Mercy gasped. "I've seen footprints like this before, in the swamp."

She looked at her alarmed companions. "Indians have been here." She bent and felt the earth. "They're still soft," she murmured, straightening. They were here this morning, before we came!"

"Mercy!" exclaimed Mistress Brewster, and she was not using the girl's name.

Elizabeth was walking slowly about the site, staring at the ground. "There were at least ten of them," she announced quietly. "Maybe more."

Mistress Brewster looked at each of them. "If the savages have been this close to our common house, we need to leave immediately. They could be watching us right now."

Mercy suddenly felt that it was true.

Seeing her expression, the older woman forced herself to smile. "Don't panic," she whispered. "We don't want them to think we're afraid of them. Quick! Pick a bouquet of those flowers. If they are watching us, they won't realize we've noticed their footprints. They'll just think we're picking flowers."

Each snatching up a handful, they skipped fast down the hill. At the bottom Mercy glanced back and was relieved that no Indians were following them—at least, none that she could see.

As day followed day with no further Indian sightings or tracks, gradually the little colony began to relax. There were houses to be built, plots to be planted, wells to be dug.

The good news was that the dying had stopped, and with the promise of spring becoming more of a reality each day, hearts were lifting.

And then one afternoon Jack came running back to the common house with an expression Mercy had never seen on his face before: fear.

He had gone duck hunting, she heard him tell Governor Carver and Captain Standish, over by the creek. Waiting for the ducks, he had hunkered down, hiding in some tall cattail reeds. Suddenly he'd heard reeds breaking. He sank closer to the ground, crouching, ready to run. Was it a wolf? A mountain lion? Had it picked up his trail there, all alone? He waited.

And then he saw twelve pairs of feet walking by him. Indians stealthily approaching the colony, crouching down so their heads were not visible above the reeds. Focused on the plantation in the distance, they never saw him, right beneath their noses!

When he'd finished, Governor Carver looked at Miles Standish. "We must assemble the men immediately."

The captain agreed. He turned to Jack. "Go to John Howland and John Alden. Have them tell the rest. Every able-bodied man is to be here, as fast as his legs can carry him."

29

"WELCOME, ENGLISHMEN!"

As soon as the able-bodied men were assembled, Governor Carver addressed them. "Since an attack by the Indians is now a definite possibility, we must prepare to defend ourselves. We must form a military company at once and elect a captain."

"Aye, aye!" cried the men in chorus. Someone proposed they elect Miles Standish, and in their first democratic election in the New World, they unanimously agreed he was the man for the job. His first act as their military commander was to schedule a military drill for the next day.

Elder Brewster spoke up. "Perhaps the Indians are just as curious about us, as we are about them. It may be that they intend us no harm."

"Let us hope so," declared their captain. "We shall hold drills and be prepared to fight if they attack us, but it would be far better to befriend them."

The Indians were certainly becoming more bold. The following morning, as Mercy did laundry with the other women, Elizabeth Winslow looked up and gasped.

Looking to where she was pointing, Mercy saw two Indians on a hill, a quarter of a mile away. One raised his hand toward them.

Mercy snatched up her laundry to flee with the others toward the plantation, but it was sopping wet, too heavy to carry and run. She dropped it in the mud and kept running.

All she could think of was what Edward Winslow had asked Elder Brewster the night before. "What if all the different tribes around the bay got together and attacked us at the same time?"

Reaching the plantation, Mercy found Miles Standish already asking for a volunteer. "Who'll go with me to that hill?"

Stephen Hopkins' hand was up first. "I may know the language roots of these people. If I can converse with them, as I learned to do at Jamestown, then perhaps we'll find out what they want."

They watched as Captain Standish and Stephen Hopkins made their way through the wooded valley to the far hill. Sometimes they would see the men bobbing through the trees; other times they would disappear entirely.

Elder Brewster led the anxious watchers in singing Psalm 23:

> *Yea, though I walk through*
> *the valley of the shadow of death,*
> *the Lord is with me.*
> *His rod and His staff, they comfort me.*
> *He spreads a table before me,*
> *in the presence of my enemies.*

At long last they saw Miles Standish and Stephen Hopkins emerge and approach the hill. They stopped, and both laid their guns on the ground as a sign they'd come in peace.

Mercy held her breath as the two men beckoned for the Indians to approach.

The natives refused. Why?

Taking no chances, Governor Carver positioned their cannon to fire on the hill. But if it came to that, how could they avoid hitting their own men?

The Indians simply walked away.

When Miles Standish and Stephen Hopkins returned, the captain set the butt of his musket in the ground and leaned on the end of its barrel, crossing both elbows. "They'll be back, and we'll be ready."

"We don't want to end up in a war, like Jamestown did," Stephen Hopkins warned.

"If that happens," Mr. Billington blurted out, "we'll kill us a bunch!"

"Sure! And make them as mad at us as a swarm of bees!" muttered Jack behind his father's back. To Mercy's surprise, his father paid no attention.

"Pastor Robinson called on us to bring Christian love to these Indians," Edward Winslow reminded them, "not to kill them."

Mercy wanted that, too. But how?

Three days later, planting peas in her new herb garden, Mercy pondered their fragile existence in this harsh land. Would English peas even grow here? When summer arrived, would their vines be climbing the crude trellis she'd made?

With a sigh she tugged up her worn-out woolen socks, which were sagging around her ankles. She'd snagged them repeatedly on cockleburs as she hiked up the hill, and her mother wasn't there anymore to mend them. That had been Mama's delight, mending winter things, while she and Father planted their garden together.

Just then Francis Billington came running toward her. "Mercy!" he called. "Look! I'm a savage!"

He had deer antlers strapped to his back, and Mercy asked, "Where did you get those?"

"Found 'em in the woods."

She looked at him, her eyes narrowing. "You weren't digging things up again in that swamp, were you?"

The boy didn't answer. Instead, he pulled out a hawk's leg from the collection of claws and bones he now carried in a bag around his waist. Waving it in front of her, he bragged, "I'm just as brave as any ole Indian, snooping around that swamp. They don't scare me!" And making sounds of war whoops he'd heard Jack tell about, he hopped away.

But no sooner had he left, then he was back!

"They're down there!" he stammered.

"Who is?" asked Mercy, not looking up from planting peas in the holes she'd prepared. She had no more time for such foolishness.

"They're really there!"

Wiping her brow with the back of her wrist, she said firmly, "Listen, Francis, I can't be bothered. Now run along."

"*No!*" he insisted, tugging on her skirt. "*Look!*"

Irritated, Mercy glanced up and was stunned. There, standing in a clearing of brush at the base of the hill, was a dark-skinned native man, starring at them. She studied him as Francis trembled beside her.

"He doesn't have a weapon," she whispered to Francis.

The boy was too scared to speak.

And then the Indian, realizing he'd been seen, ran away.

A moment later Priscilla walked by with Elizabeth Tilley. "Imagine what they must think of us," mused Mercy. "Planting vegetables, building houses. . . ."

"Who?" asked Elizabeth.

Mercy pointed to the woods along the shore. "Oh, Indians."

"Savages?" asked Priscilla.

"*Indians.* You don't know if they're savage until you meet them."

Elizabeth frowned at her. "Take your head out of the clouds, Pilgrim girl!" she exclaimed, tapping her head. "They can't even speak our language! And every time they get close to us, they either shoot arrows at us or run away!"

Priscilla leaned into Mercy's face, too. "Just because Pastor Robinson had some romantic notion about evangelizing them doesn't mean that can happen."

Shocked at her criticism of their pastor, Mercy decided not to tell them about seeing the Indian she'd just seen and strode off down the hill.

"Where are you going?" asked Elizabeth.

"To get some water to water these peas. Maybe I'll meet an Indian or two along the way! That would be much more lovely than listening to you two sour ole biddies!"

"Old?" Priscilla smoothed her stray hair back into her coif.

"Biddies?" Tilley scowled.

"Likely to wind up old maids!" Mercy called over her shoulder. "Frowns turn into wrinkles and worries into gray hairs!"

A harmless shower of pebbles flecked her back.

A week later on a fair warm day, Mercy was watching the men drilling under Captain Standish, when suddenly a half-naked man came striding down the path between their new houses!

She jumped to her feet to run, but he walked straight past her toward the men. Other women were screaming, grabbing their children and dashing indoors; but Mercy was too curious to go inside. What could this Indian possibly want?

The men were as startled as the women. But when they saw that he didn't raise the bow he carried or take one of the arrows from the quiver on his back, they stood calmly to greet him.

Mercy wrinkled her nose at the smell of bear grease smeared all over his dark skin. *Maybe that's what keeps him warm,* she thought. All he wore was a deerskin cloth over his loins. His hair was in a long braid down his back, and the sides of his head were shaved.

Just as it occurred to her that she should cover her eyes because of his nakedness, Captain Standish threw a cloak over him. The Indian accepted the gesture as a gift, running his hands slowly over the fine material with delight.

"Welcome, Englishmen!" he declared.

30

NEIGHBORS

Once over his astonishment, Governor Carver led their Indian visitor to Stephen Hopkins' new home, the most complete of their private dwellings. There, while Mercy, Priscilla and Elizabeth served him a hearty meal of buttered fresh bread, lentil soup, and roasted venison, he and Mr. Hopkins did their best to decipher the tall, dark-skinned brave's broken English.

His name was Samoset. He was from a tribe five days' journey north of here, and had met and traded with many of the explorers and ship captains who had visited these shores. As the Indian talked, the Pilgrims learned the answer to the great riddle that had puzzled them since they arrived. Four years ago this place, called Patuxet by the natives, was struck by a mysterious plague that killed all the people who had lived here. Other tribes, fearing the land was cursed, would not even come near it.

Mercy put a hand to her mouth. So that was how all those skeletons came to be on the beach! The Pilgrim men had given them decent burials, but until this moment it had been a mystery as to how they'd died.

"To God be the Glory!" murmured William Brewster. When Governor Carver and Elder Bradford turned to him, puzzled, he explained. "Don't you see? Remember all our distress at not being able to make our destination in the Virginia Colony? At being blown so far off course? The Almighty knew that on the entire coast of the New World, north and south, this might be the only stretch of land that was not inhabited by one tribe or another."

Slowly people nodded in agreement, and then began to smile at their extraordinary good fortune. Even Samoset seemed pleased, announcing that he would spend the night with them. And after enjoying another round of Mercy's cooking at sundown, he snuggled down on a goose-feather mattress bag for a good night's sleep.

No one else in the common house slept well, least of all Mercy, who could not help imagining other braves sneaking in and murdering them all in their beds. And she was sure that hers were not the only ears listening for the slightest sound.

But as the first sparrows chirped in morning's pink light, Mercy realized that her fears were unfounded. Yawning, she pulled herself out from under a coverlet and stirred up the embers in the common house hearth.

As dawn broke, Samoset got up and waited for the girls to serve him breakfast. Seeing them appear in the doorway, he simply motioned to the water barrel nearby and waited for them to bring him some.

"He must think we're Indian squaws!" observed Elizabeth, tapping her foot indignantly.

"Shh!" Priscilla scolded under her breath.

As Samoset sipped his water, he told the Elders all about their neighbors, the Wampanoag. They were a strong people, united with many tribes in the area. But the mysterious plague had weakened the alliance and made them vulnerable in the sight of their more fierce neighbors to the southeast, the Nausets.

Listening to his terrible description of the Nausets, Elizabeth was a bundle of nerves, fumbling and dropping utensils. A much larger tribe than the Wampanoag, the Nausets had been provoked to great anger a few years earlier by a sea captain named Thomas Hunt. After luring twenty young Patuxet braves onto his ship to trade furs for trinkets, he'd kidnapped them! Then he'd sailed across the bay to the Nausets and taken seven of their braves the same way.

"So that's why they attacked us on First Encounter Beach!" William Brewster exclaimed.

With great agitation Samoset picked up a knife that had been used for cutting bread and drove it into the dirt before them, talking vigorously. Hopkins interpreted. "He says that no one ever saw them again. They'd been taken in by the promise of trading for English knives. Now the Nausets have vowed to kill their captors."

"And that's who they think we are!" Elizabeth whispered. "Ooh," she moaned, wringing her hands, "I wish I were back in Holland right now!"

"Shh!" Mercy scolded, pushing her out the door. "Go wash out these pots, Tilley, and pull yourself together!"

Elizabeth rushed out the door.

"As it happens, I know something about this, gentlemen." Edward Winslow stood up. "I met one of those red men, bought at a slave auction in Spain. Indeed, one of the merchants who arranged this voyage had him working at his estate when I visited. It troubled me that they'd been purchased for a mere twenty pounds apiece! A human life, worth as little as that!"

"We wish to live in peace with all tribes," Governor Carver assured Samoset.

To this Samoset grunted his agreement. Then in broken English, he acted out a vicious drama that had occurred a scant few months before the Pilgrims arrived—the slaying of eight French trappers and the narrow escape of three more!

Mercy felt chills racing down her own spine and was ready to join Elizabeth outside, when Master Jones arrived.

Miles Standish had sent for him to demonstrate to their new acquaintance that not all sea captains were like Hunt. With a smile Captain Jones removed the gold ring from his ear and gave it to Samoset, greeting him in a native tongue. The Indian received the gift with deep gratitude, and as he bade his farewells, Mercy liked to think that at least some of the damage between the Old World and the New had been repaired.

A few days later Samoset returned. This time he brought five native men with him, arriving during Sunday church!

Elder Brewster stopped in the middle of the Psalm he was leading, while Captain Standish and several other men grabbed up the loaded muskets that were leaning against the wall of the meeting house.

Seeing this, Samoset carefully laid down his bow, as did the braves with him. All wore tanned deer or wildcat skins about their shoulders and deerskin leggings with fringes. Their long black hair was bound by feathers, with foxtails hanging at the end. "Look at their faces," whispered Priscilla to Mercy and Elizabeth. Their cheeks were entirely covered with black artistic paintings.

The congregation sat staring at them.

Mr. Billington, who was supposed to have been guarding the door but who had fallen asleep at his post, now tried to make up for his neglect. Lighting the slow-burning match on his musket, he raised the gun and cocked it, taking aim at Samoset's chest.

"Oh no!" Mercy blurted out. "Somebody stop him!"

"Hold your fire!" commanded Mr. Allerton, the deacon by the door.

Billington did not pull the trigger that would lower the match into the powder charge, but neither did he remove his finger from it.

Then Jack, who defied his father on Sundays by listening outside the door to Elder Brewster's sermons, walked toward him. Contemptuously his father made a dismissive gesture, as if to brush him away. He raised the barrel slightly, pointing it now directly at Samoset's face.

Governor Carver stood up. "Put down your weapon, sir."

Captain Standish now raised his own musket and centered it on Billington.

Samoset, eyes narrowing, extended his arm, ready to take up his bow in an instant. The brave behind him reached for an arrow in his quiver.

One quick move by anybody, thought Mercy, and people are going to die.

Suddenly Jack stepped in between Samoset and his father, looking first at one and then the other. Mercy noticed the barrel of the musket in Mr. Billington's grip begin to tremble. Then slowly he lowered it and put it down.

Mercy remembered to breathe. She swallowed the lump in her throat.

"Welcome," said Governor Carver, repeating the first word Samoset had spoken to them. And then he added, "In peace."

Slowly, solemnly, Samoset replied, "Peace."

31

SQUANTO

Samoset's unannounced visits became a regular occurrence in the early spring. One clear day at the end of March, he brought with him a shorter, younger brave wearing an Englishman's top hat.

As they approached, Edward Winslow stared at the man with Samoset, and dropped the roasted squirrel he had been enjoying. "Tickle my whiskers!" he exclaimed. "That's the Indian I saw in John Slanie's service in England! But how on earth did he get here?"

"Let's ask him," said Elizabeth Winslow, calling the girls to come with her.

Mercy gathered up her skirts and hurried after her, joining the throng that had gathered around the Indians. Stephen Hopkins was slowly repeating the Indian's name, *"Tis–squan–tum,"* so that the Pilgrims could pronounce it.

Tipping his hat in the manner of an English gentleman, the young brave pointed to himself and announced a short form of his name, "Squanto."

As Squanto told them his story, Mercy noted that his English was far better than Samoset's. Captured by a fishing captain and taken to England in his teens, he had come into the service of Sir Ferdinando Gorges, who was planning England's colonization of the New World. Quickly learning the English language, he adapted to English food and customs. Only several months after having been brought back across the sea by another fishing expedition, the unscrupulous Thomas Hunt had lured him and nineteen other Patuxet men on board his ship by showing them trinkets.

How awful, thought Mercy. Twice he's been taken away from his people by the English.

Squanto continued. Hunt had sailed to Malaga, Spain, and sold the Indians on the slave auction block. When it became Squanto's time to be auctioned off, a monk walking past from a nearby monastery took pity on this forlorn Indian and bought him. Squanto had lived with the monks for a time and there had learned about "the white man's God," as he put it.

"Our God saved you!" Mercy blurted out.

Squanto fastened his gaze on her and grunted in agreement.

But the Indian had never forgotten his village and his people, he said. Obtaining his freedom from the monks, he found his way back to England, where his mastery of English proved to be his ticket home. There he had lived in John Slanie's home, where Winslow had seen him. After several years, the English brought Squanto back to America to act as their interpreter for the fishing expeditions. But, tragically, when he finally reached the site of his village, he found all his family and friends dead from the plague.

"All dead!" he exclaimed; then sadly he pointed to his chest, his voice breaking. "I am the only one."

Mercy thought of her long-lost siblings back in England and how much she would like to see them again, if only to tell them of their parents' death. She knew how Squanto had felt, being gone all those years, with no one on either side of the ocean knowing if the others were alive or dead.

But as he continued, Mercy realized that Squanto seemed to be enjoying the privileged status that his command of English gave him among the Pilgrim Elders. And the Wampanoag seemed to regard his return as something miraculous, entitling him to great prestige. Moreover, there truly were no hard feelings on his part toward the Englishmen who'd come to settle on the land where his people had once lived.

Of course, Squanto was not exactly a saint. As the days passed, with the Indian spending as much of each day with them as possible, Mercy could see that he was far from the most humble person on the planet. Indeed, he seemed to be inflated by all the attention he was receiving.

But she also felt sorry for him. He had lost all his family, just as she had. Maybe that—and the fact that the Wampanoag, with whom he'd been living, were not his tribe—made him willing to adopt the Pilgrims. And adopt them he had, for he now preferred their company to that of the Indians.

Just when they began to think that nothing Squanto might do would surprise them, he managed to do just that. While speaking with Governor Carver, he mentioned that King Massasoit, chief of the Wampanoag and the

Great Sachem, or ruler of many tribes, was close by. "He wants to treat with you," he told the Governor.

He pointed to a nearby hill, and there stood Massasoit with sixty warriors, the most the Pilgrims had ever seen! Thanks largely to Squanto's influence, however, they were no longer afraid of their native neighbors.

"I'll go," Edward Winslow volunteered to Carver. "I can speak for you, and you are more needful to this plantation than I am."

All agreed he should go, and so he went, taking along a pair of knives and a bejeweled copper chain as a peace offering. Captain Standish insisted that Edward Winslow wear a breastplate, a helmet, and a sword to impress the Indians. As Winslow marched off with Squanto, everyone wished him good fortune and then prayed that he would receive it.

One hour went by, then two. When at long last Squanto returned, it was with King Massasoit and twenty warriors. Mercy was immediately struck by the bearing of the sachem. He really looked like a king, with high brown cheekbones and deep-set eyes. Physically powerful, he was handsome yet grave. Around his neck he wore a chain of white bones, and his face was decorated with a red mulberry stain.

Squanto addressed Governor Carver, explaining that King Massasoit had graciously accepted his greeting in the name of King James, and that he desired to make a peace treaty with the Pilgrims.

But where was Edward Winslow? Why had he not returned? Miles Standish voiced the question in all of their minds.

Squanto explained that Massasoit had wanted to buy Winslow's armor, and when Winslow had refused to sell it, the chief had told his brother Quadequina to hold him as a prisoner.

Elizabeth Winslow looked faint.

"Very well," replied the captain calmly to Squanto. "Would you and the king and his party kindly wait here, while we discuss this?"

As Squanto and the others waited, Governor Carver, Standish, and the Elders went into the common house. Going in to get their guests some tea, Mercy heard their earnest conversation.

"We should ask their king for seven warriors to hold hostage during negotiations," Captain Standish proposed. "That will show them how highly we value Edward Winslow."

"Agreed," said Governor Carver, and he proceeded to summarize the situation. From what Squanto had told them, the warlike Nausets to the south and east of them would like to take revenge on the Pilgrims for the braves that Hunt had kidnapped and sold into slavery. But they were afraid of the plague breath of the white men, which had blown over the Patuxets and killed them. They also feared their portable fire-sticks—the muskets—and the two big ones guarding the settlement, the cannon.

Yet Massasoit had an even greater problem than the Nausets. To the west were the Narragansetts—a very large tribe, exceedingly warlike. While the Patuxets were alive, they and the Wampanoag and the Massachusetts to the north were together strong enough to hold them off. But, now . . .

"Now they need us as much as we need them," Governor Carver concluded. He summoned Squanto. "You may inform his majesty that we will treat with him as soon as he sends seven men to us."

Squanto dutifully informed the king, who seemed pleased, and promptly provided seven of his men to stay in the common house as hostages until the peace treaty was concluded. Standish escorted Squanto, Massasoit, and a few of his warriors to one of the half-finished houses, motioning to Mercy, Priscilla, and Elizabeth to accompany them. Several of the Pilgrim women quickly spread a green rug and some cushions on the dirt floor.

As soon as the chief was seated, Governor Carver appeared, escorted by a drummer, a trumpeter, and a few Pilgrim men with muskets. The Governor, in an act of honor and respect which impressed Mercy, bowed down and kissed the king's hand. The king did the same in return.

Governor Carver called for the girls to bring some brandy water and fresh meat. After he and Massasoit had exchanged hearty toasts and the meat had been passed around to all, they got down to the business of the treaty. After some discussion they agreed to do each other no harm, leave their arms behind when visiting each other, promptly return stolen tools, and properly punish anyone who should violate the treaty. Most important of all, they pledged to come to each other's aid if they were attacked by a third party.

When the negotiations were finished, Master Allerton produced a trumpet and played a few heraldic notes on it. Both Pilgrims and Indians laughed gleefully, and several of the Indians begged to try it, producing pathetic little squeaks to the hilarity of all. Laughter rocked the common house as both Indians and Pilgrims rejoiced in their new unity.

Mercy noted that only one person was not entering into the gaiety, King Massasoit. He was trembling, as he had been throughout.

"Why does he shake like that?" she asked Elizabeth Hopkins, who had just arrived.

The older woman grew serious. "Massasoit is a chief, Mercy. He is at war with the Nausets, who have just cause to settle a score with the English.

When they find out, and they will, that he has made a covenant with white men, they will be angry with him and perhaps us!" She clutched Oceanus tightly. "He is also on a war footing with the Narragansetts. Against them his only hope is our muskets and our cannon."

"And he thinks that our weapons will be terrible to them and frighten them away?" Mercy promptly wished she hadn't asked her.

"Ooh! Don't say that! Please!" begged Elizabeth Tilley. "Surrounded on all sides!" she cried and grabbed Mercy's arm.

"Be brave!" Priscilla scolded.

"Don't know how," Elizabeth sniffed.

At long last, after the Indians had been fed another meal, both sides returned their hostages, and the king and his company of men departed— not back to their village, but into the surrounding woods where they encamped with their women. Through the trees, Mercy could make out their flickering campfires.

But she was too exhausted to be anxious. She slumped down in a heap with Elizabeth and Priscilla on their mattress in the Common House and laughed. "We thought they only wanted to scalp us! But now we can't get rid of them!"

"As long as the food holds out," chuckled Priscilla.

"And after that, what?" queried Elizabeth, ever the worrywart.

They looked at each other. Then Mercy burst out laughing. "That's when we find out what they can cook!"

They giggled and fell asleep, more soundly than they had since they'd first arrived.

32

OF EELS AND EAGLES

On the first warm Friday in April, Squanto announced that he and Samoset would teach the young people how to catch eels. Mercy wrinkled her nose; eels were ugly, slippery things, like swimming snakes. But as Mistress Brewster shooed all the girls down the hill for a day in the fresh air and sunshine, she was glad for the break in her daily routine of cooking, cooking, cooking.

Walking down the path, she looked across the harbor at the *Mayflower*. Sailors who had regained their health were up in her rigging, repairing sails, splicing lines, getting her ready for departure.

Directly below her, in the sandy bottom of Plimoth harbor, Mercy was fascinated by what Squanto was doing. He was working the eels out with his feet, as he slowly waded into the tidal water. Then suddenly he would shove his weight down with all his might and spring back up again with a long, black creature wriggling in his bare hands.

Taking each eel from him, Samoset added it to the pile in front of all the squeamish young people who were watching onshore. *"Askooke,"* he called the eels.

But Squanto wasn't satisfied with them remaining spectators; he wanted each of them to learn to do it, themselves.

"Nippe," he said, pointing to the surf breaking on the shore. *"Nippe!—water!"*

Gingerly Mercy waded into the freezing water. "Ooh!" she squealed, as she squished her toes into the low-tide muck. "Too cold!"

Turning back to hop to shore, she slipped on an eel slithering underfoot, lost her balance, and fell backwards, *kersploosh!*

"Aagh!" she hollered. The *nippe* was *really* cold! Soaking wet, she struggled to her feet, her chestnut hair hanging down in strings.

On the shore Squanto laughed. Soon Samoset was laughing with him, and then they were joined by Jack.

At first she was angry at Jack for joining the laughter at her expense. But then, when she realized how ridiculous she looked, she finally burst out laughing, too. When the hilarity finally subsided, she was grateful to Squanto, who had given them back the gift of fun.

That night Squanto showed them how to cook eels on sticks. *"Miidjin! Eat!"* he commanded, as he handed the first roasted eel to Mercy.

Her stomach rolled; its dead eyeballs were looking at her! With eyes squinted shut, she took a tiny bite—and to her surprise discovered that eel was sweet.

Their feast was a fitting end to a grand day. For while the youth were fishing and splashing gaily in the harbor, the plantation's Elders were busy re-electing Governor Carver for one more year. It was unanimous, as Mercy knew it would be.

The next day Squanto wandered over to where Mercy was minding the bread oven. Should a young woman talk to an Indian alone? She was about to make up an excuse to leave when she realized she was perfectly safe, with everyone within earshot.

Just then Francis came by. He stood a ways off, glaring at the Indian. The Indian glared back, studying the boy closely. Francis put his hands on his knees. The Indian did the same. Mercy wondered if Squanto was playing with Francis.

He threw the boy a smooth round purple thing.

Snatching it up, Francis examined it. It was marbled with white and polished.

"Wampum."

"What's that?"

"Like pounds."

Mercy and Francis looked at him blankly.

"Money," explained Squanto.

"Oh!" said Mercy with a smile. "Indian money is like English money?"

Squanto nodded. "From shells."

Mercy tilted her head and frowned. English money, gold and silver coins, had great value and was hard to come by. But shells on the shore were plentiful.

Francis didn't care. He started to scamper off, yelling to his older brother, "Jack! I'm rich! Indian treasure!"

Squanto called him back. "Brave, you come!"

Francis stopped in his tracks. "Me?"

Mercy saw his face light up. He'd pretended to be an Indian every day, and now Squanto was giving him that chance.

"Trade," said the Indian, pointing to Francis' neck.

Francis glanced down at the necklace he'd strung together of all his bird claws. Mercy had seen him staring hard at Massasoit's necklace which, she supposed, was a sign of his rank, as no other Indian wore one. Francis had made one of his own.

"My. . . eagle claw?" the boy gulped. Mercy knew it was his pride and joy. Squanto shrugged. "Give back *wampum*!"

Francis screwed up his face. "All right! You win!" He unfastened the claw, gave it to the Indian, and ran to find Jack, waving his *wampum*. "I'm rich!"

Squanto held the eagle claw in his hand ever so long. "*Wobsacuck*," he murmured.

Mercy guessed that was the Indian word for eagle. But was that a tear in his eye?

Reverently he held the claw to the sky and said some native words that she guessed were a prayer. Watching him, she remembered that back in Leiden Pastor Robinson had put a desire in her heart to show Christian love to the natives of the new land. Many had thought it impossible, but here was one who was praying!

"Excuse me," she said gently, "but are you crying?" She pointed to his brimming eyes.

"For many moons, eagle flew over Patuxet." In the sand he drew stick people, then the sun rising over a hill.

"Your people," Mercy said.

Squanto nodded.

"Sunrise?"

He shook his head, no.

"First light?"

Squanto agreed to that.

"People of First Light?"

He nodded emphatically.

Mercy put it all together: "Patuxet: 'People of First Light!'" she exclaimed.

"The eagle flew over People of First Light. Carried prayers to Great Spirit," Squanto added softly, pointing to the sky.

Mercy looked where he was pointing. "To heaven?"

Squanto nodded. "She made better my sad. . . ." He thumped his heart but didn't seem to know the word for it.

"Heart?"

"Heart," he repeated. "When I came, my people were dead."

The eagle was all that came to comfort him in his sorrow! Mercy felt his grief.

He held up the claw, and his voice wavered. "Now she gone, too."

Mercy didn't know what to say. As she pondered what comfort she might possibly bring him, Jack walked up, with Francis behind him.

"Mercy, you know anything about this?" he asked, holding out the *wampum*. Francis was grabbing for it, but he held it high out of reach.

Squanto looked at Jack. "You killed *wobsacuck*."

Jack blinked. "What's he saying?"

"You killed the eagle," she gasped. How did Squanto know?

Jack turned pale and lied. "Um, my hunting party shot it."

"No." Squanto extended the eagle claw in his face. "You."

Jack backed off.

"He's cursing you, Jack!" Francis shouted. "Run!"

The two boys fled quickly down the hill and out of sight.

Mercy looked at Squanto. He'd said nothing, cursed no one. He sat there silently.

Finally she pointed to her heart. "My prayers go to the Great Spirit, too."

Squanto looked at her. "You pray to the white man's God."

She wondered what she should say. Then she had an inspiration. "Squanto, did you see the big book, the Bible, in the house?" She pointed at the common house.

He nodded.

"The Book tells us that the Great Spirit loves all people, red and white, and sent His Son Jesus to earth many moons ago to die for our sins, so we can live forever with the Great Spirit."

He heard her, but she knew he didn't understand.

"We will read the Book to you," she explained. "We will help you understand."

He nodded, smiling but still mystified.

Never mind, she thought gratefully. It was a start.

33

AMIE

A few days later Squanto took all the youth with him to the creek below their little colony. When they reached the bottom of the hill, Mercy looked back at the houses, nestled among dogwood and redbud trees. The white dogwood blossoms and emerging redbuds added welcome color to the sun-drenched scene, augmented by tiny snow-white moths trying their new wings.

Two of the men were thatching Mr. Hopkins' roof while others were framing Elder Brewster's and Mr. Allerton's houses. Mercy decided that if this was to be her home, it was as pretty as any landscape in Holland.

Squanto led them single file down a well-trodden trail, past brown cattails turning green along the creek. Purple violets peeped through the underbrush beside the path, and robins twittered in the branches above them, making new nests. After the long, cold, deadly winter, spring was here at last!

Mercy inhaled the fragrant fresh air. What a difference from the fading memory of the stench in the dark belly of the ship!

All at once Squanto stopped and raised his hand. They froze. Sure enough, some large animals were stirring beyond the cattails in front of them. Mercy frowned. She could see flashes of bright color. What were they? They appeared to be headbands! Woven headbands, flashing through the trees along the bank. Indians!

Leathery hands parted the reeds, and Chief Massasoit stepped through, followed by a company of braves, women, and children. The Indian women were shy, but the young ones stared boldly back at the English youth. Mercy was delighted when one of the older girls, about her age, stepped grace-fully forward. She was dressed in beaded moccasins and a tanned buckskin blouse and skirt. Around her neck were numerous necklaces of different shapes and sizes. Long silky black braids, twisted with brightly painted clay beads, fell across a fox fur draped over her shoulders.

"Amie," called Massasoit, summoning her to his side.

"She is the king's daughter," Squanto explained.

"She has the longest lashes I've ever seen!" whispered Priscilla jealously.

Mercy thought she was beautiful, a real Indian princess!

Stepping up behind her, Jack whispered in her ear, "Well now, Mercy, Queen of Plimoth, how does it feel to meet *real* royalty?"

Mercy flushed, remembering how she'd pretended to be royal as she placed the first female foot on Plimoth Rock.

"Shh!" she whispered back. "Bow!" She yanked him down on one knee, as she clumsily curtsied, with Elizabeth and Priscilla following her lead.

Amie giggled softly, putting her hands to her mouth. But her father seemed pleased with the girls' ceremonial response. And now Mercy saw who was standing behind him: Edward Winslow.

"Oh, sir!" she gasped, assuming they must have been conducting business, "Forgive us for interrupting!"

"Quite all right, Mercy. This young lady," he nodded at Amie, "was most curious about all of you. She's been up there on the hill, watching you every day."

From her neck Amie took four necklaces and placed them over the necks of Mercy, Elizabeth, Priscilla, and Desire. As the girls ran their fingers cautiously over the smooth beads of intricate painted designs, she said boldly, "Amie. Friend."

"Amie," Edward Winslow elaborated, "is the French word for friend. She was probably named during an important agreement with French fur traders to the north."

Amie didn't understand what he'd just said, but she smiled intelligently.

Appreciating that, Mercy decided she would befriend her well enough to teach her English, and then show her new friend Christian love.

Now Stephen Hopkins came up beside Mr. Winslow. "When Amie heard Squanto bringing you all down this path, she begged to go fishing with you today. She has free run of the woods. It is her domain." He frowned. "But there's always the danger of kidnapping. She's her father's great treasure, so be careful," he warned, "not to go too far away."

As Massasoit sent her off down the path with them, the girls swarmed around Amie, buzzing with curiosity. She, in turn, pointed to their coifs and indicated she wanted to try one on. She did and, bending over the creek, laughed at her reflection. She pulled her braids tightly behind her head, like theirs, and laughed some more.

Their many petticoats were the next source of amusement to her. She delighted in jumping high, and climbing a small tree with her bow slung over her back, to show them how freely she could move about while they were so weighted down.

Finally Squanto called them to help him. He showed them how to weave a net out of the long vines tangled in the underbrush. Then he had them string it across the shallow creek. Immediately their net began to catch shimmering little silver fish swimming upstream against the current. These were herring on their annual spawning run.

They also caught minnows, and Squanto was quick to differentiate between them. The herring were *nammos*.

"*Miidjin nammos*," he instructed, turning to his star pupil. "What did I say?"

"Eat herring!" Mercy was quick to reply.

Squanto now pointed to the minnows that he was scooping onto the shore. "No *miidjin*!"

Why? Mercy raised her eyebrows in a silent query, but he just smiled. "Secret."

When the herring harvest was completed, the boys packed them into five woven baskets, and all followed Squanto back to the plantation, where he dumped them all out.

Finding the common house's salt barrel, he proceeded to salt down all the fish and then tied lids down tight on the baskets with some twine Mercy gave him. After hanging the baskets from a rafter with vines, he pointed at Cromwell and Loyal circling under the baskets, sniffing at the feast of fresh herring over their heads.

"*Aunum*" he declared, laughing, "*Aunum no nammos miidjin!*"

"*No nammos miidjin*," chanted the children at the dogs. The dogs barked back, until Mercy scooped up Loyal and sent the children in to supper.

When she returned, Squanto was smiling, and she felt that she knew why. He had finally found his long-lost purpose in life. She knew Pastor Robinson expected them to be missionaries to the natives, but who could have anticipated the blessing this native would be to them? It was as if the Almighty Himself had sent Squanto to them; and indeed, perhaps He had.

Certainly Squanto was no savage! It upset her that people blithely referred to them that way before even knowing them. How many wars had that attitude caused?

Shortly before sundown Squanto found Amie with the Pilgrim girls at the kitchen hearth of the common house. It was time for her to go home, but Amie was teaching them to cook the corn kernels her father had sent. In a dry iron skillet, she parched the large purple and black kernels till they burst apart. *"Nokehick"* she said, teaching them the name for the popped corn.

"Corn," they replied in unison, until Amie repeated it.

They watched her pick up a rock and begin pounding it on the kernels on the hearth.

"Use this," offered Elizabeth, handing her an iron mortar and pestle set. They showed her how to use it, quickly grinding the corn to a fine powder. Amie was amazed!

"She's never seen this before," Priscilla mused aloud.

To the powder Amie added some dried dark-red cranberries. Giving each girl one to taste, she laughed at their expressions.

"Yech!" groaned Elizabeth, spitting hers out. "Just like limes!"

Amie worked on quickly. Taking some oil from the herring skins, she rubbed the corn mixture into it, then added water to make cakes. These, the girls put in the oven, but at that point Squanto insisted that he must return Amie to her home at once, before darkness settled in.

As Amie was leaving, she turned back to Mercy and lifted the fox fur on her shoulder. *"Whauksis,"* she said.

Mercy learned the new word for fox. But why was Amie bringing it to her attention, just as she was leaving?

"She wants to trade," interpreted Squanto.

Mercy looked at him questioningly. She had nothing as valuable as the fur.

After speaking with Amie in her native tongue, Squanto picked up the mortar and pestle. "She wants this."

"Oh, no!" exclaimed Mistress Brewster, hearing the exchange. "We can't do without that! We have too many mouths to feed!"

No sooner had she said it than she winced, realizing how selfish it had sounded.

Mercy rushed to the rescue. "Tell Amie we will ask our chief about trading with you, for animal skins."

The princess smiled, and they left.

34

FINAL WARNING

It seemed that the death angel had returned to their plantation. Now Elizabeth Winslow had been stricken by a sudden fever. Mercy climbed up the hill to her prayer rock overlooking the bay. *Dear God,* she prayed, *must we now lose another of our wives and mothers? Please, spare her.*

She gazed at the landscape below. It had been transformed into a patchwork of neatly sown little fields, planted by Pilgrims and Indians working side by side, having agreed to share the harvest. Did it resemble an English countryside? That made her look at the sailors swarming over the *Mayflower.* It wouldn't be long now before she was seaworthy and ready to return to England.

At that moment Mercy felt a hand rest gently on her shoulder. "Would you mind if I share this spot with you?" asked Jack.

Smiling, Mercy moved over, making room for him.

"Squanto taught us to plant three fish with every kernel of corn. Mr. White said the rotting fish would make excellent fertilizer." He pointed to the nearest acre. "We did that today!" he said proudly.

"Impressive," said Mercy, meaning it. She knew it was what he wanted to hear, and she wanted to encourage his new taste for hard work. Perhaps he would model himself after the Elders after all, instead of his lazy father.

"We'll be helping you women plant small gardens near the homes, too. Ours will consist of peas and other small vegetables."

Ours? Did he mean his and hers?

"You know, I have my own plot, Jack; and I'll be getting land when I'm an adult, because my parents would have had their share." She did not want him getting any ideas, since she really hadn't made up her mind about him.

He kept talking as if he hadn't heard her. "Mr. White took sick while we were working. It's unusually warm today, even for May. He felt light-headed and went into the common house to lie down. Dr. Fuller said he was burning up, but I think it's probably because we're not getting enough to eat."

"*What?* I ought to run you off, for that!" exclaimed Mercy. "You know how hard we've been working to feed you all. We've got every hearth fired up, even the ones in the unfinished houses!"

Then she saw the corners of his mouth starting to rise. He was teasing her again!

"*Ooh!*" She slapped his knee with the kerchief she'd used to wipe the sweat from her brow at the fireplace all day.

He laughed with that devilishly handsome grin of his, his dark brows lifting in merriment.

Then he asked, "Why did you come here alone?"

Her smiled faded. "Because Mrs. Winslow is sick, too. And I just can't bear the thought of any more dying. I had so hoped it was all behind us now! So I came up here to let my prayers fly up to God, like Squanto says about the eagle." Too late, she realized what she'd just said.

Jack's face reddened. "Now prayers don't fly to heaven around here anymore because I killed the eagle!" He got up and glared at her. "I have to bury all these people, and now it's my fault they die, too." He started to say more, but turned and walked off.

"I'm sorry," she called after him.

Without looking back over his shoulder, he muttered, "That savage is all you ever talk about, anymore—Squanto, Squanto, Squanto!"

What had she done? She buried her head in her hands. Misery was not the company she'd come up here to find, but all the news was bad. Elizabeth Winslow was ill, and now Mr. White, too. And on top of that, she had hurt Jack. Was life here ever going to work out?

Her gaze was drawn to the *Mayflower*. Maybe Desire Minter was right. Maybe this wilderness was no place for a young woman.

Later that afternoon Mercy was back in the common house kitchen, helping with the cooking for all their field hands, Pilgrim and Indian, when she saw Francis Billington attempting to string one of the little dead fish onto the necklace of claws and bones he wore around his neck.

"Oh, no, you don't! Those things you've collected are a fright! We'll not have you smelling up the common house! Drop it, Francis, this minute!"

When he didn't, she made a grab for it, but he was quicker, jumping up and down with it over his head. "You take it away, and I'll just sneak down there like an Indian and dig up another in the cornfield!"

Mercy decided to ignore him.

But being ignored didn't suit Francis. "Well, I'll wear it in my own house," he yelled. "We're moving in tomorrow, into a real house! Not like some people we know."

That hurt. A real home, a family—it all seemed an eternity ago. Why should the Billingtons, who hardly seemed like a family at all, enjoy what she could never have again?

Seeing that he had gotten to her, Francis renewed his taunting.

How to get back at her little tormentor? Hmm, a taste of his own medicine?

"Very well, Francis. String that stinking fish on your necklace; it'll be a great wolf-catcher."

"Huh?"

"Why, yes, dear. While we're all safe in the common house, where you won't be anymore, all the wolves out there," she pointed to the surrounding forest, "will smell you!"

Francis gulped. Before he could say, "That doesn't scare me!" Elizabeth Tilley, sensing they were about to teach him a lesson, was quick to bait him more. "They'll climb on your roof and slither down your chimney and seek out your bed at night."

Francis rubbed his collar.

"Imagine, Francis," added Mercy, "wolf breath in your face, nibbling at that tasty thing around your neck."

Pop-eyed, the eleven-year-old dropped the little fish back in the pile. "I'm going to tell my mother on you, Mercy Clifton!" And he trotted off to find her.

"Good!" called Mercy after him. "I wish you would!"

But no sooner had he left, than a pang of guilt hit her.

Elizabeth, noting her friend's remorse, said, "Well, maybe we shouldn't have done that, but he's such a pest. I just get tired of it."

"We all do, Elizabeth. Maybe if his father would pay a little attention to him."

She was interrupted by a woman's scream from the direction of the Billington house.

They ran to see what the trouble was, and were shocked to find an Indian whom they'd not seen before, tall and straight, standing in the doorway of the Billington house, with Eleanor Billington screaming at him!

And here came John Billington with his musket, and Miles Standish and Stephen Hopkins running from the direction of the fields.

As he once had with Samoset, Billington raised his musket, this time determined to use it.

And once again Captain Standish commanded him to lower his weapon.

Billington didn't obey. "I told you that your letting these cutthroat scalpers roam freely through this plantation would come to no good!"

The entire plantation was now gathered on the path between the half-way constructed homes.

Miles Standish raised his own musket. "Mr. Billington, I'm warning you: put it down! Now! Let's see how this man explains his visit."

"He came into my house!" stammered Mrs. Billington. "Looking for something to eat!"

Stephen Hopkins, speaking in Wampanoag, asked the unarmed visitor his side of the story. "His name is Hobbamock," he informed them. "He says he's one of Massasoit's *panieses*, visionaries that see into the spirit world. He's one of the Great Sachem's council, helping him rule these villages." He smiled. "If he's telling the truth, he's not someone we want to offend."

Mercy studied the Indian's painted face, all red with black tattoos on each cheek. In his hand he clutched two arrows, one with a point and one without—the native sign for peace!

Hobbamock kept talking, and Hopkins kept interpreting. "He says Samoset told him that in my house the women were feeding the men who were helping us plant corn. He just got the houses mixed up."

Just then Jack arrived on the scene. "Oh, no!" he groaned. "Not again!" He turned to his father. "Why must you always embarrass us?"

Billington slapped him.

Jack clenched a fist, then turned to his mother, who buried her head into her son's chest, sobbing.

Governor Carver confronted Mr. Billington. "One more transgression, and you'll have your head bound to your ankles, backwards!"

Mr. Billington said nothing, but Mercy thought the rebellion in his scowling dark eyes said it all.

On her way back to the common house kitchen, she found Francis curled up behind the cannon. He was crying.

Gently she folded her arms around the boy's heaving shoulders. "I'm sorry, Francis," she said softly. "I really am."

He just cried harder, and she let him, realizing that he was crying about much more than just today.

35

PRAYER WORKS

A great sadness settled on the plantation's small population the next morning. Two of their stalwarts had died of fever during the night—Mr. White and Elizabeth Winslow. No one could comfort Susana White, who clutched her newborn, Peregrine, in a trancelike state of shock. And Edward Winslow went off to the woods to mourn alone for his wife.

Mercy helped the women wrap up the two bodies laid out in the common house. As they grieved, Mistress Brewster acknowledged the entrance of one who had slipped in among them. "You're welcome here, Eleanor Billington. We don't hold your husband's actions against you."

Meekly Eleanor nodded. "I thought you might need my help."

Mercy eyed the pitiful character. She was thin as a rail, and her shoulders seemed perpetually stooped in shame. How could Mercy's mother ever have thought of her marrying into the Billington family? What if Jack turned out like his father, and she ended up like this miserable creature?

She studied Eleanor's forlorn face and noticed a purple mark under her jaw. Staring harder at it, she saw that it ran under the strings of her coif, all the way around to her ear! Raising her head only to talk, Eleanor was doing her best to keep it from showing.

When Mercy drew Mistress Brewster's attention to it, the latter reached over and tenderly cupped Eleanor's chin in her hand. "Eleanor Billington, does your husband beat you?"

The woman slowly turned her head, to reveal a long line of bruises on her jaw. "Like his child," she admitted, in a barely audible voice.

Mistress Brewster indignantly removed the woman's bonnet, and they all saw the bruises she'd endured recently. "Under the King's law, a man may discipline his wife like his child," the Elder's wife acknowledged. "But if it be determined that he has beaten her too badly, he could be imprisoned."

"Oh, no!" Eleanor Billington pleaded. "He's already in enough trouble! Please!"

"Well, I'll speak to my husband about this. We are in the New World. Things are different here; and this, too, must change. The King doesn't live here; we do!"

As Eleanor Billington retied her coif, her thin lips turned up with the slightest glimmer of hope. And now Mercy saw how beautiful the woman must have once been, when she married the man whose face must have been as handsome as his son's now was.

"Those bruises are new. Why has he done this?" Mercy boldly asked.

"I came upon him writing another letter to Squire Weston."

"He was forbidden to do that!" declared Mistress Brewster.

Before the poor woman could reply, the burial detail, under the direction of Miles Standish, arrived with a cart to collect the bodies of the deceased. Stephen Hopkins, John Howland, John Alden, and Mr. Billington were all carrying shovels.

Eleanor flinched at the sight of her husband.

"You see, Mrs. Billington? It's like I told you," he sneered at her. "They need me! Can't get along without me!"

"I wouldn't be too sure of that," someone declared. Into their midst strode Governor Carver and Master Jones. Mercy was surprised to see them, assuming they would be aboard the *Mayflower*, making final arrangements for the ship's departure in the morning.

"The reason we're here is this" declared the Governor to Billington, holding out several letters, their red wax seals broken. "Why did you write these?" the Governor demanded.

Billington glared at the seasoned sea captain. "My letters were for the Squire's eyes only! You traitor!"

"Nay, I am no traitor," replied the captain calmly. "You have betrayed the covenant you signed in my cabin, and have caused me great trouble with these worthy men who have hired my services."

Billington was shaking with rage, and Mercy thought he was about to lunge at the captain! So, apparently, did Miles Standish, who drew his sword in warning.

"The papers," Eleanor Billington murmured hardly above a whisper.

But her husband's keen ears heard her. "Has my whole family turned against me?" he growled. "Not only do you strip me of my rights as an Englishman, but now you meddle with my family authority, too! You are the scum of the earth and the rot of hades!"

Mercy covered her ears, as the crazed man began to curse every authority figure in the room.

Finally Governor Carver had heard enough. "Captain Standish, remove this foul-mouthed evildoer from the presence of gentlefolk, and clap him in irons!"

Mercy looked at Jack, who had just arrived and was comforting his mother. It was obvious he was angry, but at whom?

Jack confronted Governor Carver. "Since you deem it right to govern, but my father feels a deeper allegiance to the King, I plead with you, sir: let this matter be decided in the courts of England, not here."

For a long time the Governor weighed what had just been said. "Very well, young man, it shall be as you've requested."

He turned to Master Jones. "Captain, you shall have four passengers on your return voyage. Billington shall stay in irons and his family under guard. And he is not to be released until my own letter to Squire Weston is delivered."

As she watched the men marching Billington away, Mercy's heart could not have sunk lower. Jack, who'd once come to her for comfort when his father first defied the Elders, had finally turned against their authority. She would have nothing further to do with him.

But she could not dismiss the deep pang of sympathy she felt toward the one who'd once rescued her, and who'd delighted her darkest days with his stories. Had she failed him as a friend?

She looked at the sad woman leaning on his shoulder, walking numbly to the dreadful task of packing up their belongings and leaving their new cottage for the long sad voyage to an uncertain fate. Such a struggle merely to survive here was now ending in senseless tragedy. Would the curse of one man ruin their family for generations to come?

The next morning was warm but overcast, as the entire plantation gathered on the shore to bid farewell to the faithful vessel that had carried them safely through so many storms, and sheltered them from the ravages of winter.

From each family Priscilla Mullins had gathered letters destined for loved ones back in Holland. Master Jones had promised he'd see to it that they got delivered. Among them was the letter Mercy had written to her cousin, telling her of the death of her parents.

Eyeing the handful of sailors remaining, she wondered if Master Jones would even make it home. More than half his crew, as well as half the passengers, now lay buried behind them or at the bottom of the bay.

At last the moment she'd been dreading came. Jack bravely walked toward the shallop beside his father, who was hobbled in leg manacles and chains.

Would Jack speak a parting word to her?

As they came by her, Jack leaned close to her. "Pray, Mercy girl! I need a miracle!"

Her heart soared. Maybe he could be salvaged, after all!

At that moment Elder Brewster called the company to prayer. Many knelt, and all bowed their heads. He asked a blessing on the crew, and for courage to fill the hearts of those saying good-bye to their last link with England.

Mercy whispered to Jack, "Tell your father to bow his head."

"He doesn't believe in it."

"Make him do it anyway, as a sign of repentance."

"He'll never do it," he sighed.

As soon as Elder Brewster said, "Amen," Jack stood up, put an arm around Mercy, and gave her a hug.

"Bye, Mercy girl," he said sadly. "I'll never forget you."

Nor will I forget you, she thought, as Jack helped his mother into the shallop.

But where was young Francis? Searching the crowd, her eyes widened. He was still down on his knees, praying his little heart out!

When his father saw him, he was stunned. "I never taught him to do that!"

"Well, maybe it's time you learned yourself," Mercy heard Jack reply. "We could all use a miracle to get out of the mess you've gotten us into, Father."

Mercy stared in unbelief, as slowly the senior Billington's head bowed till it hung limply on his chest. Defeat—the fight was gone out of him, at last!

Elder Brewster noticed. "John Billington, what pardon do you ask of the Lord?"

"That I be allowed to stay here, sir, and that my family be restored to your plantation, sir. I see that there is no higher law here than God's, and that you are in authority under Him. I was wrong. The King is too far away."

An uneasy silence lingered for what seemed like an eternity, as the Elders conferred.

"All right then," Governor Carver pronounced. "Release him!"

Pointing his finger directly at John Billington, he sternly added, "One more defiance of any ordinance at all, and you shall spend the rest of the year confined in the stocks, until such time as another ship comes."

The women all went to Eleanor and hugged her.

Francis ran to Mercy. "It works!" he exclaimed, overcome with joy. *"It really works!"*

"I told you," she agreed, laughing with him. "Prayers always work better than curses."

36

THE CRIMSON CROSS

From her prayer rock on the hill, Mercy watched the *Mayflower* sail away. She'd run up there as soon as they'd weighed anchor. At first the old ship seemed large, tacking out of the harbor under only her stay sail. She'd still seemed large when she unfurled all her sails to take advantage of the following southwest wind.

But as she headed for the open sea, she got smaller and smaller, and Mercy grew sadder and sadder. Finally her topmost pennant was no more than a speck on the horizon. Then it, too, disappeared.

Mercy got to her feet. Her old life was over. As for her new life, there seemed precious little to recommend it.

She sighed. At least the weather was warm, even hot. The sun had burned away the overcast and was now blazing down without benefit of any cooling breeze. The New World's climate wasn't subtle; it could be numbing cold or blazing hot. According to Squanto, autumn would be the best, but that remained to be seen.

Going down the hill to help prepare the evening meal, she could not help admiring all the work that had gone into the fields—six acres of barley, twenty acres of corn, with beans, pumpkins, and squash among the corn. When it all came in, hunger, like untimely death, would be a thing of the past.

It could not be too soon. Their rations were now so meager—a peck of meal per person, per day—that she often felt like her stomach was bumping against her backbone. They were so low on flour that they no longer baked bread, unless the Indians were kind enough to bring them cornmeal.

She smiled. They'd proven so much friendlier than anyone had imagined! With their help there would be ample provisions for the winter. And the cottages were going up faster now, as the men finished plastering the sides with clay.

Walking past her own garden, though, Mercy sighed again. Her peas, her beautiful English peas, were not coming up. Fretting over them, she even dug up a dried seed to see if it had begun to sprout. It hadn't.

"You need crow!"

"*What?* Oh, it's you." Squanto had silently snuck up behind her again and scared the wits out of her. "I wish you'd stop doing that!"

But seeing she was smiling, he just smiled, too. He put his hands together, one over top of the other, slowly circling the thumbs, imitating a bird in flight. "Crows brought seed to our fathers from the great god *Kantantowit*." He pointed south. "Maybe you need his blessing?"

"No," replied Mercy with a smile. "I pray to the one whose Spirit flew away to heaven from the Cross. Remember the story the monks told you from the Great Book?" Squanto's expression didn't change. "Like your eagle, the man from the Cross carries my prayers to heaven."

Squanto remained unconvinced. "*Kantantowit* blesses the fields, or no peas porridge." And without waiting for a reply, he left.

Mercy understood the challenge. The Lord had better bless her peas, or Squanto might not believe in her prayers at all.

Mistress Carver came by then and leaned over the little picket fence to keep the livestock out. "A watched pot never boils, my dear. Neither does a seed, dug up before it has a chance to grow. Leave it alone and fertilize it with a little prayer."

"Yes, Mistress." Mercy loved the dear old soul. She was plump and grandmotherly to everyone. Even a dried-up pea patch seemed lovely as she hovered over it. She was a perfect match for the Governor, who could be a bit stubborn at times. She was the sugar to sweeten his spice. Everyone appreciated the combination, grateful for the steady courage of these two.

While they were chatting, Squanto came running back up the path, yelling, "He is hurt! He is hurt!"

"Who?" called Mercy.

"Governor!" Squanto panted. "I get doctor," and he ran to fetch Dr. Fuller.

Mistress Carver shrieked and ran as fast as her old legs could carry her toward the field where her husband was working.

Mercy ran after her, only to see William Bradford and Samoset carrying the unconscious Governor.

She gasped. "Is he . . . ?" She couldn't bring herself to say it.

Dr. Fuller arrived and bent over the still form, looking for signs of life. "He's still with us," he announced. "Take him to the common house."

Then he took Mercy aside. "Stay close to Mistress Carver," he said gravely. "It's not good."

Governor Carver never revived. His wife wore herself out, hovering over his bed until he took his last breath three days later. Then the life seemed to go out of her as well. A week later they had a second funeral.

Mercy could hardly believe they'd lost them both. How could life be any darker, now that this torch that had guided them in the wilderness was gone? Would the darkness never leave them? Not even tears could express this new heartbreak. Silence, this time, suited them all better; for no one could bear even to discuss this latest and greatest disappointment. The *Mayflower* was gone; their Governor was dead. Who would lead them now?

No sooner was Mistress Carver in the ground than Elder Brewster gathered the men and again read the covenant to them. Then he nominated William Bradford to be their new Governor. Bradford was voted in unanimously that very night.

But this did not still the doubters. Desire Minter, having no home to serve now that her master and mistress were dead, was so overcome with grief that all she could speak of was going back to England on the first ship to arrive. She said it so often that Mercy's own heart now felt the tug more than ever. Finally Mistress Brewster, who had taken Desire in, forbade her to mention it again, lest every heart be infected with her despair.

Even Governor Bradford seemed to need encouragement. John Carver had been his dearest friend. Now he was left alone to chart their course through uncertain waters.

One bright day, Mistress Brewster sent Mercy to deliver the midday meal to him at the common house. Though his own house was finished, he chose not to live in it until all were housed. The common house was house enough for him, he said, and a draped-off area with a bed, a table, and a chair served as his living quarters. He was at the table now, studying the documents of their agreements with Squire Weston and the London merchants.

Mercy tiptoed around the table. She set down a trencher of cod stew, baked in clam sauce—a savory dish, spiced with a gift from the Indians, wild garlic and leeks. Governor Bradford thanked her and went back to his studies.

Lying on a carved chest behind him were other books with Hebrew and Greek letters on their tooled leather covers. A short candle with a charred wick showed that he must be poring over them at night.

The bed was nothing more than a straw mattress, but there in the middle of it lay the red pouch Dorothy Bradford had once tried to hide from her. Mercy had brought two clean towels for him and hovered over the bed, as if trying to find a convenient place to put them. Looking down at the pouch, she caught a tantalizing glimpse of ornate silver and rubies.

"Would you like to see it?" Governor Bradford had seen her looking at it, and without giving the startled girl a chance to respond, he withdrew the cross from the pouch and held it up in a shaft of sunlight. The silver filigree of the Cross was delicate, almost like lace. As he turned it slowly in the light, the five rubies seemed to catch fire!

"What do you think?"

Mercy could hardly speak. "I think it's the most beautiful thing I've ever seen!"

"It is called the Crimson Cross. We know that it came originally from the Holy Land. At least, that's what the man who gave it to me was told when it was given to him. We do know that it is ancient and has been to the New World before, when God sent others who sought to do His will, as I seek to do now."

He smiled and returned the cross to its pouch. "There is more to it, and perhaps I will tell you the rest one day."

That night it was hard for her to get to sleep. Her mind was too busy thinking about the Crimson Cross. How had it come to the New World? Who gave it to William Bradford? Had some English knight bought it in the Holy Land? Had it belonged to one of the ancient Apostles?

37

GRAVE ROBBERS

Whack! With her hoe Mercy dug into her pea patch, turning the soil around each tiny sprout. She'd done it often before; the soil was well turned. But these sprouts were taking forever! She'd tried fertilizing them with prayer as Mistress Carver had suggested, but the stubborn little plants seemed unresponsive. Now she whacked away at the ground around each one, as if by threatening it within an inch of its life, she might persuade it to grow faster.

"I'm glad I'm not a pea in your patch," said someone behind her. It was Jack—the cause, she suddenly realized, for much of her pent-up feelings. Mainly because she couldn't make up her mind how she felt about him.

She was thrilled when her prayers—and his, and his brother Francis', and even, finally, his father's—had been answered, and the Elders had relented and not shipped them back to England. Yet more than ever she sensed that at bottom he was shifting sand, hardly a firm foundation on which to build a house—or a future.

She looked up at him and smiled. "Good day, Jack," she said pleasantly. "Off to join the other men in the fields?"

Hurt by her formality and distance, he said, "I see that it might not suit you now to be seen as my friend in Plimoth, or my wife."

Wife? Mercy blushed. Why was he still considering that, after siding with his father . . .

"Well, I don't blame you," he went on. "But I want you to understand: I had to defend my father. He's family, and I could not let my mother be destroyed along with him."

"I do understand. But I can't . . ." She was suddenly, uncharacteristically, at a loss for words.

He waited; and when she said nothing more, he added, "I just want you to know: things aren't always what they seem."

His dark eyes searched the depths of her soul, a look that always stunned her senses into numbness. Even now.

The handsome brows lifted. "We may not be held in much esteem here, but I actually am not as bad off as my father. He inherits nothing more, but I am the principal heir of my uncle's entire fortune, and I didn't want my father to go back and mess it up. Had they kept him in the stocks, however, we'd have had no other choice. You can't live in such a degraded state for long."

She cut him off. "It was not the Elders' fault! Your father brought it upon himself!" She was angry now, as if he'd attacked her father along with those who had now become her fathers. Her eyes narrowed. "Why do you brag of fortunes you don't have? And why don't you Billingtons work as hard as everyone else?"

While she waited to see how he might respond, Loyal came trotting down the newly-named Leiden Street and joined her, growling at Jack.

He kicked at her, and Mercy gathered the dog up into her arms.

"Whoever heard of making a pet of such a foolish mongrel!" Jack exclaimed. "She can't return your affection like a husband could, and she's liable to go off somewhere and get eaten by wolves, anyway. Why do you care for her more than me?"

Sensing he had found a crack in her armor, he pressed the attack. "A dog that doesn't even belong to you, and a dried-up pea garden without a house! That's all you have, Mercy Clifton. Not a very strong position to snub me from, is it?" Jack smiled, holding her eyes with his, looking for the spark that had once drawn them together. "Why don't we Billingtons work? We are gentlemen, and gentlemen let their servants do the work for them."

He tried to wrest the hoe from her grip; but Mercy, her jaw set, refused to release it.

"You will all labor to fill every returning ship with goods, because you've signed your lives away to Thomas Weston and his merchants." He paused and looked at her. "But it's not what goes into the ship that counts; it's what comes out of it!"

What did he mean by that?

"My fortune is movable," he continued, teasing her curiosity more. "I don't have to be in Olde England to claim it. Marry me, O Queen of Plimoth, and you could be one of the richest ladies in New England!"

"I've never cared to be rich," she retorted, "only happy, with the simple things of life. It must be your great invisible Billington wealth then that causes your father to behave as the laziest man I ever—"

"He knows who he is!" he cut her off. "He could care less about all the useless wasted effort of you poor people here! Why should he cast his future with such a pathetic lot?"

"And why should his son cast his future with such a foolish mongrel as me?" Her hand flew to slap his face before she even knew what she'd done.

Jack stalked off, the red and stinging mark on his cheek a sharp "no!" to all he might have hoped to salvage that day.

Well, that, she thought, *is the end of that!* And grabbing up the hoe, she hit the ground with such force that she broke its handle.

At that moment Squanto came by, bringing a basket of fresh leeks and spring garlic, a present to her from Amie. He was shaking his head; obviously he'd witnessed her fight with Jack.

And to make matters worse, here came Francis, flipping a little bag in his hand that dangled from his belt. "You seen Jack, Mercy? I got something to show him!"

Mercy looked at his shoes, caked with mud. "Where have you been, young man? You were supposed to be playing a game of shuttlecock with the other boys."

When he didn't reply, she looked at him. "You've been in the swamp again, haven't you!"

No answer.

"You know that's a dangerous place to go!"

"Not anymore. We don't have to worry about the Indians, anymore." He pointed to Squanto. "They're friendly to us now."

Squanto's lips tightened. "Not all Indians are friendly." He pointed to the south. "They spy on us."

Francis ignored him. "Don't be mad, Mercy,' he pleaded. "I found buried treasure there! I'm going to be rich."

"You're always going to be 'rich, rich, rich,'" she scolded. "That's all you and your brother care about!"

Francis stuck out his tongue at her and would have walked off, but Squanto stepped in front of him like a stone pillar.

"The swamp is sacred ground," he declared. "Do not bring trouble with my people! You stay out!"

Then he looked down and saw another eagle claw hanging from a necklace around the boy's neck, this one decorated with fine beadwork. He snatched the necklace off of Francis' neck. *"Where did you get this?"*

Mercy had never seen Squanto so fierce before.

"My brother gave me the other claw from that ole eagle he shot."

Was he lying? Studying the boy's face, Mercy decided that he was.

"No!" Squanto corrected him. "These beads are old."

Mercy watched him rub them, and then he bit one. "Very old."

He held the necklace up to the sun and wiped dirt from the clasp where the claw hung. It shimmered in the sun.

"Gold," Squanto said. "There is no gold here. . . . High Sachem got it from Cheepi god."

Suddenly he grabbed Francis' shirt collar and lifted him off the ground. "You robbed the grave!" He let out a bloodcurdling screech. *"Ahh-yeee! Ahh-yeee! Ahh-yeee!"*

Francis pulled away and ran off, terrified.

Governor Bradford came out of the common house to see what all the commotion was about.

"Those two brothers are bad blood!" Sqaunto declared, spitting on the ground to finalize his decree. "Bad blood."

As he strode off, William Bradford and Mercy watched him disappear down a wooded trail. "I must talk with those boys," said the new Governor, frowning. "Squanto will tell Massasoit. It could affect our peace treaty." He paused. "It could affect everything."

38

THEE, I WED

On the last Sunday in April, Mercy was sitting near the window on the women's side of the common house, which was serving as their church. In his sermon Elder Brewster was giving thanks for the beauty of God's creation. It was indeed beautiful. From where Mercy sat, she could see bright orange tiger lilies blazing by the creek. And on a low-hanging branch above them, a pair of cardinals preached their own sermon to the glory of that morning.

The only thing troubling her was that no one had seen Squanto—or Samoset or Hobbamock, for that matter—since the incident with Francis' eagle claw. She tried not to think about what bad possibilities their prolonged absence might mean.

All such dark thoughts were abruptly swept out the door, when Edward Winslow stood up and announced that he and Susana White would marry the following Saturday. A delighted gasp escaped the congregation, followed by applause and cheers. For these two, so recently widowed, to be joined in marriage was a sure sign of God's blessing and encouragement!

Three days later Mercy and Priscilla and Elizabeth took all the young children on a wildflower-gathering expedition. Equipped with reed baskets, they went deep into the woods, looking for flowers for a wedding arch under which the married couple would walk. When all the little ones were assigned to the older girls, they began their hunt.

Mercy and her three little charges were looking specifically for violets. They were finding some, though they were hard to spot.

All at once she felt a pair of eyes on her. Scanning the undergrowth ahead, she saw the faintest outline of a person. To her surprise, she was not afraid, sensing no danger, only peace.

Directing the children under her care to a promising patch of moss, she turned to her unseen observer, who now stepped forward. It was Amie!

"Hello," she said in a whisper, so as not to disturb the children.

"You speak English?" Mercy whispered back, astonished.

"Squanto teach me—little."

In a barely audible voice, Mercy said slowly, "It's good to see you!" She gestured to her own eyes and to her heart, and then smiled and pointed to her friend.

Amie nodded vigorously and smiled back. "Why you—" Not knowing the words, she indicated what they were doing and raised her eyebrows.

"Wedding!" Mercy exclaimed, almost forgetting to whisper. When Amie looked puzzled, she made elaborate gestures, using one hand as a man, the other as a woman, showing the two hands gradually coming together, and becoming as one. Then she clasped them together.

"Ah!" whispered Amie, understanding. With a broad smile, she asked, "When?"

"Saturday." Blank response. "Three days," and she held up three fingers.

Amie nodded and smiled.

"Mercy?" called Damaris Hopkins. "Look what I found! A whole field of them!"

"I'm coming," she called. But when she turned back to say good-bye to her friend, Amie was gone.

When they returned to the plantation with their baskets full, the older girls told the younger ones what each flower meant.

"Apple blossoms mean better things to come," pronounced Priscilla.

Elizabeth explained that honeysuckles signified loveliness.

"What about a red chrysanthemum?" asked Damaris.

"I love you," cooed Mercy.

To which a male voice responded, "The words my foolish heart longs to hear!"

Everyone turned around. All the girls laughed except Mercy, who recoiled.

It was Jack!

Oh! She got up and carried their garlands to the place being decorated for the wedding as fast as she could, to get away from him.

On Saturday morning, as the simple wedding ceremony took place, Mercy held Susana's small son, Peregrine, in her arms, so the baby wouldn't cry. The infant was no trouble, but Jack was. Through the whole service he just stared at her, till she flushed, hoping no one else noticed his brazen affections.

After the wedding couple, dressed in their finest and most colorful Sunday best, pronounced their vows and walked beneath the arch woven with wildflowers, everyone rose to follow them, to cut the layered cinnamon nut cake and the decorative cookies with designs that Mercy had sculpted in the dough.

As Mercy was about to step through the arch, Eleanor Billington offered to relieve her of the bundle in her arms, so she could help serve the newlyweds. But no sooner had Mercy agreed and given her little Peregrine, than Jack came up, tucked his arm in the crook of her elbow, and swept her through the arch and to one side. In the merriment nobody seemed to notice.

She whispered, "Let go of me!"

"No!" replied, Jack, smiling. "Not until my fair lady agrees to speak the same vows with me."

"Never!" Mercy struggled to free her arm.

Crestfallen, Jack let her go. "Look, Mercy girl . . ."

"And stop calling me that!"

"You used to light up like the sun when I said it," he protested.

"That was before. . . ." She searched for the right words.

"Before my father spoiled everything," Jack conceded. "But you once reminded me that I could be my own man. Let me have the chance!"

She was silent.

"You'll see, the Billingtons will fit in to this tight little society by and by, and all our ways and customs will one day blend."

"I doubt it," she responded, struggling to keep her voice down. "We will never become so worldly!"

"Mercy," he was pleading now, "join me in my dreams. They're bigger than you can imagine! Someday a ship will come in, and we'll have everything we need." His face glowed, as it had when he used to spin tales of adventure in the storyteller's circle—as it had when he had once captivated her.

Their eyes met, but this time something deep down inside her wouldn't let her be drawn to him.

The wedding's joyful chatter suddenly ceased. All eyes turned to the main gate where a party of a dozen Indians, led by Squanto and Hobbamock, appeared, their faces painted.

Mercy could not breathe. Were her worst fears about to be realized?

And then she relaxed. Amie was with them! And that was not war paint on their faces; it was celebration paint! They had come bearing gifts for the wedding—wild turkeys already plucked, colorfully painted clay pots with fascinating designs, a bear skin, and for the wedding couple two pairs of beautifully beaded moccasins.

The Pilgrims, as relieved as Mercy, welcomed the Indians warmly, who celebrated with them by performing the most intricate of dances.

Amie was not one of the dancers. She came over and stood by Mercy, as together they happily watched. Using the same sign language with which Mercy had explained the wedding, Amie said, "Your people," and indicated her left hand. Then she said, "My people," and indicated her right hand.

And she clasped the two hands together.

39

HIDDEN SECRETS

June was not always pleasant and mild, as Mercy remembered it being in Holland. Here, some days were stifling hot and humid, like this one. Pushing damp strands of hair back in place, she continued to harvest wild watercress along the bank of Towne Creek. But she wasn't complaining about the heat, not after the bone-chilling winter they'd all come through.

Ahead of her, under the welcome shade canopy of oak and maple trees, Loyal chased tiny dragonflies. Often Mercy would call her back, and each time the dog would come more reluctantly, until finally she simply refused to come back at all.

Mercy called to her again, trying to keep the frustration out of her voice, so as not to spook her. "Loyal? Come here, honey. Come on; it's all right."

No response.

"Loyal, this is no time for hide-and-seek." Her tone was angry now. "Now you come here, this instant!"

Mercy noticed that less and less sunlight was coming through the trees. It was getting close to sundown, and she was near the swamp. Underfoot it was marshy. Setting down her basket of watercress, she lifted her skirts with both hands, carefully stepping on firm clumps of ground. Where *was* that pesky dog?

Watching where she was putting her feet, she rounded a sycamore and froze. She was looking down at a moccasin!

Before she could respond, its owner stepped forward. Amie!

"Ah!" Mercy sighed in relief, "it's you."

"Shh!" Amie whispered, putting a finger to her lips. *"Kúkkita!"*

It was obvious what that word meant: "be still and listen."

Now Amie pointed, and through the tangled vines dangling from the tall cedar trees, Mercy could make out two figures on their knees beside a mound of earth. As she watched, her darkest fears were realized. It was the Billington brothers, both of them.

And they were digging at the sacred Indian burial mound—exactly what had so enraged Squanto, and what the Elders had expressly forbidden!

As she watched with growing horror, Francis and Jack pulled out an owl mask and a headdress, far more elaborate than anything King Massasoit had ever worn.

"*Chepasôtam,*" whispered Amie in awe. "Great Sachem." Then she slowly shook her head. "Very old things!"

As the boys stuffed their loot into sacks, Amie turned and looked at Mercy, alarm in her eyes. "This bring many warriors," she whispered. "Not just father's. Corbitant's. Iyanough's. Other chiefs. Warriors from all tribes kill all white men!"

Mercy paled. She was describing all-out war. Many would be killed, and it would not stop until one side or the other was defeated.

"*Musquàntum manit!*" whispered Amie sorrowfully.

"What?"

"Great Spirit angry," Amie softly declared. "Must tell father."

Shocked, Mercy put a hand on her arm. "We must stop those boys, make them put them back!"

Her friend shook her head. "Too late. Grave destroyed. Must give things back to father. Must rebury with honor!"

Before Mercy could argue, her friend leaped up and away into the forest, with Loyal, who had reappeared, running after her and barking.

Hearing the dog, the boys looked up. "We've been found out!" Francis yelled.

"Get her!" cried Jack, pointing at the fleeing Amie. They dropped their sacks and ran after her.

Mercy couldn't believe the evil in their hearts! "Oh, God!" she whispered, "Don't let them catch her!"

They separated, trying to cut her off. But they were no match for the swift-footed princess, who knew the trails through the swamp far better than they. In a few moments she had disappeared, even from Loyal.

Mercy decided she'd better get back to the plantation to tell Governor Bradford what had happened. With the Billingtons out of sight, she got up and did her best to retrace her steps.

"Mercy?" she heard Jack call behind her. "My, my, these woods are just full of surprises."

Hiking up her skirts, she started to run. And soon put her foot in a squishy deep hole, twisting her ankle.

Jack caught her then, holding her by the same arm he had not long ago taken her by as he forcibly escorted her through the wedding arch. Only this time there was nothing affectionate in the grip. It was mean and hard.

"You were spying on us!" he exclaimed. "Betrayer!"

She looked at him with a mixture of fear and fury, seeing in his face for the first time exactly what she had seen in his father's. And to think she'd once entertained the possibility of spending the rest of her life with him!

"*Me*, a betrayer?" she retorted. "You've betrayed the trust of the Indians *and* the Pilgrims!"

"And you'll be running back to tattletale on us!" His eyes narrowed, menacingly; and suddenly Mercy was afraid of him. Very afraid.

"Let go of me!" she demanded. "This instant!"

"I'm not your little dog, Mercy," he said with a cruel smile, tightening his grip on her arm. "I was going to marry you. But now I think I'll simply mourn you. Poor Mercy; she must have gotten lost in the swamp and drowned."

All at once, a piercing Indian war whoop—a real one—echoed through the swamp. There was no telling where it was coming from. And now it was followed by another and another.

Looking him in the eye and noting the fear she saw there, she said grimly, "Squanto told you they hated grave robbers. You're about to find out how much!"

"Francis!" he called out to his unseen brother. "Run for it!"

And with that he released Mercy and started following his own advice.

"What about me?" she called after him. "They're going to think I was helping you!"

"You should have thought of that earlier, Mercy girl!" he cried, without looking back.

"Come back here, you miserable coward!" But already he was out of sight.

Mercy looked around, and finding a thick tree limb on the ground, she picked it up. Any Indian who tried anything with her was at least going to get a good lump on the head for his trouble!

"You no hurt me?" murmured a soft voice behind her.

Amie! "Oh, thank God!"

Amie was silently laughing, her eyes dancing.

Then it dawned on Mercy why. "That war whoop—that was *you!* You had him, and me, so scared that . . ." words failed her.

Amie looked in the direction that Jack had taken and chuckled. "Big boy only little boy inside."

Both girls laughed. And at the sound of their voices, a frightened Loyal trotted up. She looked up at Mercy with her big brown eyes, as if to say she'd learned her lesson and would never wander off again!

"I forgive you, you little scamp!" said Mercy, hugging her.

Then she frowned; it was getting dark. "Where's Francis?"

"Other boy try to follow me," Amie replied, "but he much lost now."

What Mercy saw in her friend's face worried her. "Amie, are *we* lost?"

40

BLOOD SISTERS

Amie just smiled and shook her head. "No lost." Her smile disappeared as she glanced at the rapidly darkening sky. Pointing at the dense woods beyond the swamp, she added, "No go there, this night. We stay here."

Mercy realized that Francis had run off into those woods. Had he doubled back and made it home before dark? Was Jack even looking for him?

Her Indian friend made it clear they would have to stay where they were until sunrise. Reaching for Mercy's swollen ankle, she carefully examined it. Then, picking wintergreen leaves, she chewed them and applied the salve, which began to reduce the ankle's swelling.

Then she pointed to one of Mercy's petticoats, indicating that she wanted Mercy to give it to her. When she did, Amie tore it into strips and bound the ankle until it could give Mercy some support. She could not walk too far with it; but before Amie had tended it, she could not walk at all.

As night fell, the girls huddled together for warmth. Amie slept, but Mercy spent most of the night listening to the chirping of crickets and croaking of bullfrogs in the swamp. And swatting mosquitoes. She envied Amie, who slept like a babe in her mother's arms—an apt comparison: these woods were her native cradle.

Loyal lay down with her back nestled against Mercy's. But the faithful pet only dozed with one eye open, watching. Every now and then, her ears would perk up until she decided the strange noise was no threat, and she'd settle back down.

Suddenly her head jerked up, and her shoulders tensed. She growled.

"What is it, girl?" whispered Mercy nervously.

Silence. Then a spine-tingling howl echoed all around them.

In an instant Amie was up, bow in hand, an arrow notched on its string. *"Ontoquas!"*

"Wolves!" gasped Mercy. The thinnest beam of moonlight outlined a large, pale-furred creature almost hidden in the underbrush.

157

Amie was motionless, listening intently. Slowly she held up one finger and smiled grimly. There was only one of them. He would probably leave them alone. And if he didn't? The Indian girl seemed ready for him.

But neither of them was counting on the reaction of Loyal, who now ran at this intruder, barking furiously and determined to defend the girls.

Annoyed, the wolf turned his attention to the little spaniel.

"No! Loyal! Come back!" cried Mercy, knowing how one-sided any contest between them would be. She lunged for Loyal, but it was too late. Loyal had launched herself at the fearsome opponent, who took her in his strong jaws, crunched her, and tossed her skyward.

Loyal's bark turned into a scream of pain and fear. When she came down, she was too hurt to get away. She just whimpered and looked up at her destroyer helplessly, as he bent down, opening his jaws to finish her off.

Thunk! An arrow struck the wolf just behind the shoulder. Stunned, he staggered and toppled over, dead.

Mercy turned in awe to see Amie staring intently at their foe, another arrow at the ready, just in case.

When it became apparent they had nothing more to fear from the wolf, Amie turned her attention to their pathetically crippled defender, who tried to raise her head and couldn't. Gently she felt for broken bones, of which there were several. But the biggest concern was the deep gash the wolf had opened in her underbelly, which was now oozing blood.

Mercy wept. All the grief dammed up in her since her parents' death came flooding out. The tears came harder now, as she realized Loyal would not survive.

"Oh, Amie! We should put her out of her misery, shouldn't we? But I just can't!" She shook with sobs.

Amie did not answer. She pointed to Mercy's other petticoat and made a gesture for her to tear it into long strips. When Mercy did, Amie tenderly bound the dog's stomach. "I take *aunum* my village. We make her better."

"Oh, thank you!" cried Mercy. "Thank God for you!"

"Great Spirit—" Amie hesitated, then touched her heart. " Great Spirit love *aunum*."

"Yes!" cried Mercy, weeping. "Yes, He does!"

As the eastern sky began to lighten, Amie carried Loyal to the path by the creek, but it soon became apparent from the little dog's moans at each step that this mode of transportation was more than she could bear. So the Indian princess laid the animal down, took her flint knife and cut strips of birch bark, fashioning a crude sled. Then she took the rest of Mercy's petticoat and made a bed on the sled for Loyal, which she would pull, using the petticoat's lacing as a cord.

As Amie finished her task, she looked at Mercy, concerned. Something was troubling her, and it wasn't Loyal. "We no tell my father or your Governor about boys robbing sacred burial ground. It cause much war! Your people, my people—many die!"

Solemnly Mercy nodded. She could imagine many tribes attacking the common house. The Pilgrims would defend themselves as long as possible, but they would be overwhelmed and slaughtered.

"I go now," Amie said. "Take Loyal. But first. . . ." with the point of her flint knife she deliberately cut her own index finger. "Now you," she urged, offering Mercy the knife and pointing to her index finger.

Mercy realized what she was asking. She didn't want to do it, but she didn't want to *not* do it.

With a gulp she took the knife and cut her own finger.

Beaming, Amie took Mercy's bleeding finger and pressed it to her own, mingling their blood in the sight of the Great Spirit. "Now we *weetompas.*"

"Blood sisters?" guessed Mercy, smiling. "And sisters keep secrets!"

Amie nodded and smiled.

Then she held up a hand, signaling Mercy to remain quiet. She'd heard something.

What? Mercy strained to hear. Holding her breath, she tried to make her ears hear whatever Amie was hearing. Nothing. Frustrated, she was about to complain to her new sister, when finally she heard it, too.

Someone, afar off, was calling her name!

41

NOT THE WHOLE TRUTH

A search party! Mercy's heart jumped. They must have left the plantation at first light! They were calling her name and Francis's, over and over. . . . And only their names, which meant that Jack must have made it back. And abandoned not only her but his young brother, as well! What a spineless cur! What had she ever seen in him?

"I'm here!" Mercy called out to the searchers.

"Mercy? Thank heaven!" It was Captain Standish's voice. "Are you all right?"

"Twisted my ankle. Otherwise, fine."

In a moment the captain and Hobbamock came running up the trail, with six other men with them.

"Thank God, you're all right!" exclaimed Edward Winslow.

"Yes," added Jack, trying to sound as worried and relieved as the others.

"Have you seen Francis?" asked John Billington.

"Not since yesterday afternoon," answered Mercy truthfully. "He was running that way." She pointed to the dense forest beyond the swamp.

"How is your ankle?" asked Jack, as if he cared.

"Bearable, no thanks to you!" she whispered tartly. "She's the one who helped me."

She turned to point to Amie, but there was no one there! She and Loyal had slipped away.

"Mercy," said Captain Standish kindly, "we need to know what happened yesterday afternoon. Jack tells us that he and Francis were fishing for eels when you all were surprised by an Indian war party. But some of it, doesn't . . ." He didn't finish his sentence. "Can you tell us how *you* remember it?"

Jack caught her eyes and silently pleaded with her not to reveal what he and Francis had been doing.

She glared at him. Well, she would not reveal his grave robbing. But not to save his skin. To save *all* of their skins! Amie had warned her about what would happen if the Indians learned of the desecration of the Great Sachem's grave.

She turned to the captain. "I was gathering watercress along the creek. Loyal was with me, and she ran off. I went after her, into the swamp." She paused. "Then—"

Jack turned pale. Everyone's eyes were on Mercy, so they did not see him mouth the word to her, *Please!*

"Then I heard Indians whooping and turned to run. Just as I got to that path," she indicated the one they'd just come up, "I twisted my ankle. The Indians didn't find me, but Amie did. She bandaged my ankle and stayed with me during the night. She also saved my life and Loyal's."

She told them of the wolf's attack and about Amie killing it with an arrow to the heart.

"Where is she now?" asked Stephen Hopkins.

Mercy shrugged and raised her hands. "She left just as you arrived, and took poor Loyal with her."

Captain Standish frowned. "Something is not right about all this."

Hobbamock now turned to Jack. "You say you heard war cries. No Wampanoag on warpath here. We at peace with you."

"But they were there!" Jack insisted, digging himself in deeper. "And angry, too!"

Mercy looked away quickly, so no one would see her smile. Amie, her new sister, had been transformed into a war party of many braves!

"That's odd," said Stephen Hopkins thoughtfully. "If they were hunting you, they'd just sneak up and cut your throat before you knew it."

Hobbamock looked at Jack through eyes narrow as slits. "What you do to make Wampanoag angry at you?"

Jack shrugged, his face turning red. "Nothing."

"If not Wampanoag," Hobbamock persisted, "who?"

"How should I know!" retorted Jack, rattled.

"I think we've wasted enough time here," declared his father. "We have a missing boy out there—my son!"

Captain Standish ignored him. "You didn't actually *see* them; you only *heard* them, is that correct?" he asked Jack.

"I already told you!" the boy shouted. "There were at least ten, maybe fifteen!"

Hobbamock grunted in disgust. "I came near this place before now. I saw footprints—two, three people, no more."

Mercy looked at Jack. The boy was trembling.

All at once Hobbamock gave a bloodcurdling howl, which badly startled everyone. "Did the war cries sound like that?"

"Yes!" Jack exclaimed. "It sounded exactly like that!" He turned to the others. "Maybe now you'll believe me!"

Hobbamock shook his head. "That cry not Wampanoag."

Mercy looked at her Indian friend. Hobbamock knew the boy was lying, and she suspected he had a pretty good idea of what the Billington brothers had been up to. It was only a matter of time before Jack's lies would find him out.

He was in the stew, she thought, and Hobbamock was heating up the fire under him. One or two more questions, and the whole truth would come bubbling out. She half wanted it to; it would serve Jack right! But it would also destroy the friendship between the Pilgrims and the Indians, and might well end in war.

Then Stephen Hopkins deflected the direction of the interrogation. "Well, if they weren't Wampanoag, were they Nausets?"

"Yes, that's it!" cried Jack. "I knew I'd heard that yell before; I just got confused." He turned to Edward Winslow. "You remember, on First Encounter Beach? The Indians down there made war whoops just like that." And to emphasize his point, he made one himself, which did sound like Hobbamock's, and like the ones with which Jack used to entertain the little ones.

Captain Standish nodded. "If they're Nausets, they could be angry about the corn we took. Or angry about the braves kidnapped by Captain Hunt. Or just angry. Squanto says they're more warlike than the Wampanoag."

Now Billington had had enough. "If my boy has been taken by them, what are we doing, standing around, jawing? We need to get him back!"

Hobbamock looked at Captain Standish. "First, we go to see Massasoit. All Indians here listen to him."

Their military commander agreed.

John Billington did not agree. "No more talking with Indians! There's no time for that now! We must go get him back, right now!" He raised his musket. "Even if we have to kill them all!"

Drawing up to his full height, Miles Standish put his face right in front of Billington's. "There is one commander of this operation. Me. The men have elected me their captain. One more outburst like that, and I will have you taken back to the plantation and put in the stocks. Do you hear me?"

"You need me here!" replied Billington, not backing down.

"I do not need you so much that I cannot afford to be without you. Now do you accept my authority or not?"

Billington stared at him defiantly and said nothing.

"Very well," said the captain calmly to Edward Winslow and Stephen Hopkins. "Take him home and put him in the stocks."

"All right, all right!" exploded Billington. "I'll be quiet. But that's my son out there!"

The captain nodded. "And that is the only reason you are still here. But this is your final warning, understood?"

Billington nodded.

"What about Mercy?" asked Edward Winslow. "Should we not take her back to the plantation?"

Thinking quickly, Mercy begged, "Let me come with you. You will lose a man sending someone back with me, and I want to thank Amie and see if Loyal's all right."

"What about your ankle?" asked Stephen Hopkins.

"It's better," she insisted, "and Hobbamock can help me."

Captain Standish mulled it over. Then he agreed. "We would have to send Hobbamock or one of us back with you, and I cannot spare either. Besides, I have more confidence in your version of what happened," he said to Mercy, "than his." He nodded toward Jack. "And since the chief's daughter did spend the night looking after you and your dog, it might be wise to have you with us."

He turned to the men with him. "It is important, gentlemen, that we keep things between us and them on a friendly basis."

Indeed so, Mercy thought. Obviously Captain Standish had his own suspicions about what Francis and Jack had been up to—and what it might cost them should things go badly.

He smiled at Mercy. "Consider yourself our ambassador of good will."

She gravely nodded. The alternative was too horrible to contemplate: if the tribes united in battle against them, they might find themselves facing more war painted braves than they had musket balls.

42

THE RAID

After two hours of Hobbamock helping her down the trail toward Chief Massasoit's village, Mercy's ankle was throbbing. Each step brought a fresh stab of pain, but she was determined not to complain.

Sensing her pain, Hobbamock stopped to cut and trim a limb for her to lean on and had given her his moccasins, going barefoot himself. But he'd explained that they had to keep moving, if they were to reach the village by nightfall.

Suddenly there was movement up ahead on the trail. It was Samoset! Running toward them as hard as he could! Breathless, he gasped his message to Hobbamock, who translated it for Edward Winslow and Captain Standish.

A chief named Corbitant, a petty sachem whose tribe bordered the Narragansetts, had taken Chief Massasoit and Squanto hostage and was holding them in a village called Nemasket, not far from here. Samoset explained that Corbitant had long been jealous of Massasoit's position as chief of all the chiefs east of the Narragansetts and was looking to take his place. For the Pilgrims this would not be good. Corbitant hated white men, and was furious about the peace treaty Massasoit had entered into with the Pilgrims. The last time Samoset saw Squanto, Corbitant had been holding a knife to his chest and talking about killing the Englishmen's "tongue."

For a long time no one spoke. Then Edward Winslow turned to the captain. "We're going to have to help Massasoit and Squanto if we can. The cornerstone of our treaty is that we come to each other's aid in the event of an attack."

With Hobbamock translating, Captain Standish asked Samoset, "How many Indians are there?"

"Five, six."

Standish thought about that. "We don't have any more men than they," he mused. "But if we hit them at night, they would not know that." Mercy could see that a plan was forming in his head.

"Where exactly are they?" the captain asked Samoset.

"In wigwam, in middle of village."

"All of them?"

"No. One scout."

The captain frowned. "Can you and Hobbamock silence him? Don't kill him. We're not going to kill anyone tonight. Just make sure their scout does not sound the alarm."

The Indians conferred, then smiled. "We hit head and stuff animal skin in mouth!"

The captain chuckled. "That will do. When it's dark, we'll surround the village. At my command we'll start shouting and fire off empty muskets. That should do it."

He turned to Edward Winslow. "Then you and I with loaded muskets, and Hobbamock, will storm the wigwam."

"What about me?" demanded Mr. Billington. "I've been looking forward to bagging me one of those red devils, ever since we met them!"

Captain Standish regarded him with thinly veiled contempt. "Did I not just say, no one dies tonight? You will be out of the action, protecting Mercy." He nodded at Billington's musket. "Only if her life is threatened can you use that. But only then, understood?"

Billington nodded sullenly.

"When it's over, and it's safe for her to come, we'll call you."

Samoset and Hobbamock led them to within a mile of the village, then signaled them to wait for nightfall. "Sleep," Hobbamock suggested, as if anyone could.

When the woods had lost their color and then their shape, Samoset signaled that at last it was time to advance. Slowly, noiselessly they approached the village and then stopped. Hobbamock and Samoset slipped away, ahead of them. The rest of them waited.

There was a scuffle and a faint *thwock*—the sound, reasoned Mercy, of a rock hitting a skull. Then silence.

The silence was broken by a bird call, the agreed-upon signal that it was safe to move forward again.

When they could see the lights of the village, they stopped again. The dancing light from cooking fires revealed a number of brush and reed wigwams, but one of them was bigger than the rest.

Captain Standish nodded. This was the one they would storm. He pointed to John Howland and John Alden, silently sending them off to the left. Jack Billington and Stephen Hopkins he sent to the right. He, Hobbamock, and Winslow would stay where they were, moving slowly forward along the path.

He turned to Billington and drew an imaginary line across the path. He was not to cross that line!

As the men began to encircle the village, and the captain and Edward Winslow edged forward, Mercy's heart was beating so hard she thought it would jump out of her chest!

More silence.

Then suddenly Captain Standish cried, "Charge, men!"

Instantly all the men cried out encouragement to imaginary troops behind them. "Attack, men! Attack! Corbitant, we're coming for you!"

Ka-boom! Ka-boom! One by one, the muskets roared in the night!

In the big wigwam Mercy could hear Indians yelling, so panicked that they tried to burst out of the sides of the wigwam! They managed to find the entry and ran out into the night. Seconds later Hobbamock, followed by the captain and Winslow, muskets at the ready, rushed in!

Beside her, John Billington could stand it no longer. He ran forward, and seeing a dark form running away, aimed and fired his musket at it, cursing when the musket ball went crashing through the trees instead of through the back of a running brave.

Inside the wigwam she could see Edward Winslow and Captain Standish begin cutting the bonds holding Massasoit and Squanto. The captain called to Billington and her to join them; and when she entered the wigwam, she was relieved to see Amie's father and Squanto massaging their wrists, apparently unharmed.

Massasoit was smiling. He said something to Squanto, who also smiled and told the others what the chief had just said. "Corbitant not stop running till sun comes up!"

The chief extended his arm to Edward Winslow, who extended his own. The two men gripped each other's forearm. Chief Massasoit said something to Edward Winslow, who looked to Squanto for the translation.

"You and he are friends forever."

The chief nodded and said something else.

"This night, you," Squanto indicated that he meant all of them, "come to his home."

43

THE SWEAT LODGE

It took about one hour of marching through the woods at night, single file, following Chief Massasoit to his home village, for the excitement of the night raid to wear off. But wear off it did, and the second hour was painful for Mercy, as she limped along, leaning on the staff Hobbamock had cut for her.

Finally they reached the village, where they were greeted with great rejoicing. Massasoit, their beloved sachem, was back! And unharmed! His braves gathered happily around him. And here came Amie, running to her father, laughing and embracing him! Then she saw Mercy and did the same to her. "You stay my wigwam with my mother's mother and her sister."

So Mercy was led away to where she would spend what was left of the night with Amie's grandmother and great aunt. Scarcely had she laid her head down on the sleeping mat than she was fast asleep. If there were mosquitoes, she never knew.

In the morning Amie let her sleep. And she did, until her growling stomach woke her up. As she became aware of how hungry she was, Amie handed her a small piece of baked fish. "Father very sorry no food in village. He catch two fish—for all."

While Mercy was eating, Amie slipped out of the wigwam and in a moment returned with Loyal in her arms. The little spaniel still had Mercy's petticoat bandage around her middle and was very weak. But when she saw Mercy, she feebly struggled to get out of Amie's arms and go to her.

So the poor dog would not aggravate her wound, Mercy quickly got to her feet and went to her, putting her face close to the dog's. "My brave little protector," she cooed. "You attacked that big old wolf to save me. I'll never forget that, Loyal." She paused and then with a catch in her voice added, "But you must stay with Amie until you're better. We've got to get you well, because you're all the family I've got."

Then Amie had a surprise for her: a buckskin jerkin and pants, just like the ones she wore, and moccasins for her feet. Mercy hesitated and then accepted them with joy. When she had changed out of her Pilgrim attire and into her new clothes, she was amazed at their light weight, warmth, and softness, and the freedom they gave her.

A short while later Amie was showing her around the village when they came upon Edward Winslow and Stephen Hopkins, who were discussing their night as the guests of Amie's father. It was not a restful night, Mercy gathered, judging from the bug bites on their faces and forearms. "The big bites are mosquitoes," she said to them, smiling, "but what are those little ones?"

"Lice and fleas," replied Edward Winslow. "The sleeping mats were alive with them."

"Could you not sleep outside?"

"And refuse the sachem's hospitality? It would have insulted him," replied their governor's emissary. "So when he had all of us sleep at the other end of the sleeping platform that he and his wife were on, we had no choice."

"Nor could we complain," added Stephen Hopkins with a rueful smile, "when we were joined by two other braves we'd not met." He looked at Edward Winslow and added, "The worst part was when they sang themselves to sleep. It took forever, and of course we were wide awake after that."

The Pilgrims' emissary nodded. "And we were kept awake by another song, the song of the mosquito." He chuckled. "One more night of their hospitality and lack of food, and we'll be too weak to go anywhere."

Mercy frowned. "What about Francis? Is there any word of him?"

Edward Winslow spoke up. "Chief Massasoit told us that a hunting party from another tribe, far to the south of us, was seen in these woods. Deer must be exceedingly scarce this summer for them to leave their hunting grounds on the Cape."

Mercy's eyebrows raised. "You said, 'the Cape.' Were they Nausets?"

Edward Winslow nodded solemnly. "I'm afraid so."

"But they're the ones who attacked us on the beach! Jack told us the story."

Stephen Hopkins sighed. "That's not the worst part. Massasoit's scouts reported that they had a captive, a white boy. He was injured; his leg was splinted."

Mercy caught her breath. "Poor Francis!" All of the trouble the boy had caused was not as important as his safety.

At that moment Chief Massasoit came up to them, gesturing for them to come with him. Squanto, who was with him, explained. "Great chief want you in hot with him."

The Pilgrims stared at him, mouths open.

Squanto frowned, trying to think of how to better explain this. Then he shrugged and simply said, "You must come."

Everyone followed them to a man-made cave—a dugout space, covered with thatched branches in the base of a bluff. As they went inside, the Pilgrims were astonished. The interior was filled with steam, from water being poured over heated rocks. On logs sat five sweating and apparently naked braves. Now their chief started to remove his garments, indicating that the Pilgrims should do likewise.

Eyes widening, Mercy backed out of the sweat lodge and went looking for Amie who, giggling at her expression, took her by the arm to show her a collection of furs that would have made any European princess green with envy.

From the bath came sounds of protest as the Pilgrim men objected to taking off their clothes. The loudest, not surprisingly, were from John Billington, who suspected a trap. The savages wanted to get them defenseless, without their weapons or their clothes, he protested.

"You, me, hear," said Amie, smiling mischievously at her friend. And before Mercy could object, she led her to the top of the bluff, above the thatched roof of the sweat lodge. She pointed to a hole from which steam was escaping, and then to her ear.

Mercy nodded. She could hear the men talking, with Squanto interpreting. Edward Winslow was speaking of the Pilgrims' primary concern: an expedition from Plimoth to the Cape, to retrieve Francis from the Nausets.

Then Massasoit spoke of his primary concern: the restoration of his authority over Corbitant and the tribes to the east. That must take place now, before the harvest. In recent years, without the Patuxets to help them, the Wampanoag were not strong enough to stand up to the Narragansetts, who would raid their freshly harvested corn. Last year they took the island of Aquidneck, in Naragansett Bay, from Massasoit's domain; and he had been powerless to stop them.

Edward Winslow assured the chief of their loyalty. Had they not rescued him last night? They had many fire-sticks. (He was careful not to say how many, Mercy noted.) And they had several great fire-sticks, referring to their cannons, which the Indians had seen in the center of the plantation.

Their combined firepower would give even the Narragansetts reason to reconsider any raiding plans.

Then Winslow changed the subject back to Francis, "the younger son of that man," he said. (He must have pointed to John Billington.)

Amie's father replied that the Pilgrims had taken the Nausets' seed corn, without which they could not plant. It must be repaid.

"We most certainly will repay it," returned Winslow, "but we cannot do it now. We will have no corn until the harvest."

"No," responded the chief through Squanto, "too late." He would give them enough out of his own stock now to exchange for Francis. But after harvest it must be repaid.

Edward Winslow agreed. And now, he said, he had a great blessing for the chief. (Mercy knew what it was: a full-length bright red horse coat. She could hear the chief's loud expression of delight, as it was presented to him.) Also, there was a copper neck-chain that the chief would send along with any Indians that he wished the Pilgrims to receive and feed. The chain would be the sign that they were from Massasoit. The reason for this, Winslow explained to the chief, was that Indian visitors were constantly dropping in now, expecting to be fed. Like the Wampanoag, the Pilgrims put great value in hospitality, but feeding all visitors was wiping out their dwindling food supplies, which must last till the harvest.

The chief was pleased with this arrangement and declared, "Me, King James his man!"

All was agreed upon; all was peace and good will.

But then Mercy noticed someone running toward the lodge. It was Hobbamock, and in his hand he had a sack which she recognized. It was the sack into which Jack and Francis had stuffed the ceremonial headdress and the owl mask that they had stolen from the burial mound of the ancient sachem, the revered ancestor of many local chiefs!

Jack must have dropped it as he ran away from Amie's imaginary war party!

She buried her face in her hands. Everything was about to blow up!

44

THE EXPEDITION

Massasoit's roar of anger practically tumbled Mercy and Amie off the bluff! All the men in the sweat lodge were shouting at one another. No one was bothering to wait for Squanto or Hobbamock to translate; their meaning was perfectly clear. It was a good thing they didn't have their clothes on, Mercy thought, and had left their weapons outside, or someone could get seriously hurt!

When they finally calmed down, the peace and goodwill which had prevailed a short time before had pretty much gone up the smoke hole. The Pilgrims and Indians still needed each other just as much, but their mutual-assistance pact was now more grudging than friendly.

As the two girls listened and Amie whispered explanations to Mercy, it became apparent that Massasoit had immediately taken custody of Jack Billington and his father. The chief held the father directly responsible for the actions of his sons. Whatever fate befell the boys, the same was going to happen to their father. Massasoit would still lend the Pilgrims the seed corn to trade for the return of young Francis Billington, but he had no intention of turning the Billington men over to the Pilgrims unless they were completely successful in their bid to reconcile with the Nausets and make peace.

In that unlikely event, the sacred items that the boys had stolen from the ancient sachem's burial mound would be quietly reburied with no mention of it to the other tribes. For if they ever got wind of it, they would all unite against the Pilgrims and Massasoit, and massacre them all.

Mercy whispered to Amie, "What of Jack? If they're successful, will they give him back?"

Amie nodded, and explained that the Billington men would be turned over to the Pilgrims for appropriate disciplinary action. But if the expedition was not successful, then Massasoit's council would decide their fate, which in all probability would mean their deaths.

In a few minutes everyone was dressed, and the Pilgrims prepared to depart for home.

"Take care of Loyal," Mercy pleaded with Amie.

"She be fine," her new blood sister assured her. "You take care," she added, with a look of genuine concern.

Through Squanto, Edward Winslow informed Massasoit that he would make a complete report to Governor Bradford as soon as he reached the plantation. The governor would decide how much of a force to send to the Cape in the shallop. He extended his arm to Massasoit as a gesture of friendship.

The chief did not extend his.

When they arrived home, Governor Bradford and Elder Brewster met them at the gate. Everyone started talking at once, until the Governor raised a hand. "Friends, friends!" he pleaded. When they fell silent, he nodded to Edward Winslow and Captain Standish, and received a full account of their mission.

The four men conferred for a few moments, and then Governor Bradford clapped his hands together. He had made up his mind. Edward Winslow and Captain Standish would be in command of the shallop, he announced. They would take the seed corn that Chief Massasoit had so graciously provided. Squanto, their "tongue," would accompany them, as would the two Johns, Howland and Alden, and Stephen Hopkins.

Edward Winslow waited for him to name more men. When that didn't happen, he objected. "Governor, with all due respect, that's only five muskets." He hesitated. "Six, if we give one to Squanto and teach him how to use it."

"I know. But they're all we can spare. If the friendship between us and Massasoit breaks down any further, we're going to be in great peril here, as it is."

"But, sir, the Nausets were none too happy to see us last winter after we took their corn. And we did not know then that the despicable Captain Hunt had years ago carried off seven of their young braves."

The Governor nodded sympathetically but did not change his mind. "We'll be praying for you, Edward."

Mercy looked to Captain Standish, who until this moment had remained silent. No longer. "Governor, he's right." He paused. "And so are you. But it is a mistake to divide our forces when there are so few of us."

"What would you have us do, Miles?" the governor responded in exasperation. "Abandon Francis Billington? Abandon the peace process? Abandon John and Jack Billington? Hunker down here and await the attack that would surely come?"

He put a hand over his eyes as if to shield them from the sight he was seeing in his mind. "We might hold them off for a day or two. But in the end they would overwhelm us. We would be slaughtered, and our women and children would be taken."

Now Elder Brewster spoke. "We're forgetting something. We came here out of obedience to God. He has honored that obedience time and time again. He saved John Howland. He prevented the ship from sinking on the crossing. He sent Squanto to us, who gave us eels, taught us how to plant corn, and enabled us to live in peace with our neighbors."

In a sweeping gesture he took in all the land they had cleared and planted. "He is *continuing* to favor us, friends. Last night He enabled us to rescue Chief Massasoit without loss of life." He paused, appreciating the size of that miracle. *"No one was even hurt!"*

He now spoke to all of them, those who had just returned and those who had gathered behind the Governor. "The Lord has assured us in His Word that He will never leave or forsake us." One by one he looked them in the eye. "He will not abandon us now, any more than we will abandon Francis Billington."

"Amen," murmured Mercy, echoing what many were expressing.

It was settled. The rescue party would leave as soon as sufficient provisions could be stowed in the shallop.

Now Mercy asked if she might have a word in private with Elders Brewster, Bradford, and Winslow. When they were alone, she addressed them: "Sirs, you have all done your best to care for me after I was orphaned, and I am so grateful to you." She looked at each. "And I think I am beginning to see what God means to do here."

She looked down at her buckskin jerkin and pants. "There may be a way I can help. Let me go with the shallop. For one thing, Francis is hurt. He trusts me," she said with a rueful smile, "probably because I dared to discipline him. In fact, I may be the only one outside his family that he does trust. Let me go to care for him."

As she anticipated, Edward Winslow strongly objected. "The very idea! A girl on a life-and-death expedition? Never!"

But the governor and Elder Brewster, she noted, did not rule it out. They were waiting to hear what else she might have to say.

"There is a more important reason," she went on. "I ask you to consider this for a moment: What would it say to the Nausets if a girl," she threw a glance at Edward Winslow, "were to accompany such a mission. Would it not say: 'We come in peace. We are not coming to bring harm to anyone! This is not a war party! We are merely coming to repay a debt we owe. To ask forgiveness for what another captain in another time has done to you. To beg the return of a naughty child, to whom we will teach the error of his ways. And to bring lasting peace between two peoples, you and us.'"

The three men were silent.

Then William Bradford expressed what was on all of their hearts. "Mercy, I am going to allow you to do this. I believe God is speaking through you." He turned to the others. "If any harm befalls her, it will be on my hands and on no one else's."

Looking at Mercy, he smiled. "You'd best get to the shallop, Mercy Clifton."

"Yes, Governor!" she exclaimed, tears of joy springing to her eyes.

Leaving quickly before anyone could change his mind, she was careful not to limp.

45

"THESE MEN COME IN PEACE!"

Mercy took a deep breath of the fresh salt air and slowly let it out. Reaching over the side of the shallop, she idly splashed a hand in the warm water of the bay and smiled. She was enjoying this trip almost as much as if it were a pleasure outing. The sun was hot but not oppressively so. The wind was brisk but not so much that it whipped up large waves. Except for the low cloud bank ahead of them, it was a picture-perfect day.

Stretching and relaxing, she admired how skillfully John Alden and John Howland handled the shallop, shifting the sail from side to side as they tacked back and forth across the bay. They had to tack frequently now, as the wind had shifted to the southeast, exactly where they were headed. And it was picking up; there were larger waves now, some with little white caps on them. The shallop was beginning to rock.

Mercy shivered. The cloud bank had risen up to blot out the sun, and suddenly it was much colder. And now came the first fat drops of rain. Edward Winslow found the spare sail, which he stretched over all the passengers who were not actively sailing the boat. As Mercy huddled under it, the rain fell harder, quickly becoming so severe that the men decided they should beat into the natural harbor that had just appeared off their starboard bow. They would take refuge there until it passed.

As Alden and Howland jumped over the side to draw the shallop up onto the sandy beach, Mercy's eyes grew large. Behind them in the woods—was she seeing what she thought she was seeing? Forms were moving through the shadows of the oak trees that crowded the shore.

"Indians!" she cried, sounding the alarm. "Look there!" She pointed to a dense copse of trees not more than fifty yards from them. Others saw them as well, and now the men busied themselves getting their muskets ready to fire—not an easy task in the rain.

Hearing her cry, four figures emerged onto the beach and started walking toward them.

Up came the muskets, until Captain Standish called out, "Stand down, men. They're unarmed!"

It was true. Mercy could see that they carried no bows or arrows, no spears, not even knives, which did not fit with the stories she'd heard about the fiercest tribe on the cape.

"Are they Nausets?" she asked Squanto, who was getting out of the shallop.

"No," he responded, loud enough for Edward Winslow and Captain Standish to hear. "Cummaquid!" Then pointing to their leader, he added, "Chief Iyanough."

Hearing his name, their leader raised his hand, palm open to them signaling that they came in peace.

Edward Winslow and Captain Standish raised their hands in the same gesture. "Greetings!" said the Governor's emissary warmly, with Squanto translating.

As if on cue, the squall passed, and the sun reemerged. Everything seemed brighter and freshly washed.

Through numerous exchanges patiently translated by Squanto, they were able to establish that the Nausets, further down the Cape, did indeed have Francis. They had come by here the day before, carrying him on a traverse. They knew about the Pilgrims' fire-sticks—they all did. Everyone had heard what had happened to Corbitant. And tribes had been observing the shallop ever since it left Plimoth.

Looking carefully at those aboard the shallop, the chief's brows knitted together in puzzlement. "Why you bring squaw?" Squanto translated.

Slowly Chief Iyanough smiled, understanding, and said through Squanto, "She being here means you come in peace. Braves don't take young squaws to war. Squaws stay in village." Then he nodded and said something further to Squanto, who turned to Edward Winslow. "Chief said you are wise to bring young squaw with you."

Mercy beamed at Edward Winslow, who carefully avoided her gaze.

Winslow proceeded to secure a promise of long-term peace and mutual support between the Pilgrims and the Cummaquid, which would be sealed under the overall leadership of Massasoit, whose counsel Iyanough and the other eastern chiefs listened to.

Iyanough made it clear they were to be his guests that night. The next morning he would take them to the Nausets. His presence with them would be a further indication that they came in peace—necessary, because the Nausets were likely to start shooting arrows, even if they saw a young "squaw" with them.

As the shallop approached First Encounter Beach, Mercy thought it was providential that Iyanough was on board. Dozens of Indians were standing on the beach, many of them armed with bows and arrows. In the center of them stood a tall and regal figure, arms folded across his chest, an eagle feather stuck in his black hair.

But before the shallop could reach the shore, four dugout canoes paddled out toward them. And unlike the Cummaquid, these warriors were fairly bristling with bows, arrows, and spears.

Iyanough stood up in the bow of the shallop so the Nausets could see that he was with the Pilgrims. His presence did not seem to make a difference. In the two nearest canoes, warriors took arrows from their quivers and fitted them to their bowstrings. They meant to shoot first and ask questions later.

Iyanough appealed directly to his counterpart on the beach, Chief Aspinet. Squanto translated: "Hear me, my brother! These men come in peace!"

The Nausets did not lower their bows. Instead, they looked to their chief for the signal to loose their arrows.

Mercy held her breath. Miles Standish resolutely readied his musket. He took aim at the chief's canoe drawn up on the shore, distinguished from the others by a wolf's skull affixed to its bow.

Captain Standish's musket roared! The wolf's skull on the bow of the chief's canoe exploded, its pieces flying everywhere.

Looking at what was left of the wolf skull, Chief Aspinet called off his men.

They stopped paddling, lowered their bows, and let the shallop come to the beach. Mercy let out the breath she'd been holding.

When Winslow and the others had waded ashore through the light surf, Iyanough and Aspinet conferred. Then, through Squanto, Aspinet admitted to holding Francis. What were the Pilgrims willing to exchange for his release?

Edward Winslow had his men bring ashore the two large baskets of seed corn. "This is to replace the corn we took from you eight moons ago. We are sorry; we did not think it belonged to anyone. And we did not understand then how much you needed it to get through the winter. Please forgive us and accept this corn with our apologies."

Squanto translated, and Aspinet was silent. Then, through Squanto, he made his reply. "Not enough."

"But it's more corn than we took from you."

"Not enough."

From the bag that held knives and trinkets used for trading, Edward Winslow withdrew a knife. He handed it to Aspinet, who tested its sharpness with his thumb. The blade was sharp enough to draw blood. Impressed, he called to one of his warriors, who went away for a few moments and returned carrying Francis Billington, his leg splinted with a branch.

The boy was elated! They'd come to rescue him! Seeing Mercy, he called her name, and she smiled at him.

But Aspinet held up his hand. Through Squanto, he said again, "Not enough."

"All right," Edward Winslow said to Squanto. "Tell him that we will give him double this much corn. But he will have to wait for the rest until after our harvest. He paused. "And tell him he must give us something in addition to the boy."

After Squanto had relayed Winslow's words, Aspinet frowned, and asked "What?"

"Your promise that there will be a long peace between us," replied the Pilgrims' ambassador. "The Nausets and the Pilgrims must live together," he said, putting his hands together to illustrate this, "for many moons."

"How many?" asked Aspinet.

"Till your sons are grandfathers."

Aspinet considered this, then slowly he nodded. He waved to the warrior holding Francis to bring him to the Pilgrims.

Francis was handed over to Mercy and promptly threw his arms around her, hugging her tightly.

Edward Winslow extended his forearm to Chief Aspinet, as he once had with Massasoit. The chief was about to grip it, when a great howl erupted from the Indians gathered to watch. Astonished, Mercy stared at an ancient woman standing there, wailing at the top of her lungs, inconsolable.

Shaken, Chief Aspinet withdrew his forearm.

"What is it?" Winslow asked Squanto. "What troubles her so?"

"Ten years ago, seven Nauset men were taken away by the slave trader, Captain Hunt," Squanto told him, adding, "I remember them. They went across the sea with me."

"We have condemned what he did!" declared Edward Winslow. "Why is this woman so upset?"

"She is mother of three of them," Squanto translated. "Now in her old age she has no family to take care of her."

"And the chief?" asked Edward Winslow, fearing that the peace treaty which was almost a reality was about to evaporate.

"Chief will decide what he will do."

The next few moments were critical, Mercy realized. The fate of their mission now hung in the balance.

Suddenly she had an idea! To Squanto, she whispered, "Tell the chief your story!"

He did. He told Aspinet that he, too, had been taken by Captain Hunt at that time and had been sold into slavery with the rest. But monks in Spain had bought him, and taught him that their God was the same Great Spirit that the Patuxets and Nausets worshipped. He had obtained his freedom from the monks, gone back to England, and eventually come back across the ocean. He found that all his tribe had perished, but now he had a new life, helping these good people to survive.

"In conclusion," he said to Chief Aspinet, "they are men of their word. You can trust them."

Aspinet then put his hands together, as Edward Winslow had. "He said 'Until sons of our sons have sons of their own,'" relayed Squanto.

Edward Winslow nodded. "And we want you to come to Patuxet to meet with Massasoit and smoke the pipe of peace."

The chief nodded his assent and extended his forearm to Winslow.

46

SISTERS

Mercy shook her head in disgust. They'd not been home fifteen minutes, before Francis was strutting around on his injured leg like he was some kind of hero, instead of the one who had nearly provoked a war. Would he never learn? Would the Billingtons always be the plantation's greatest problem?

"He's changed, Mercy," said a kindly voice behind her. "He may not look it, but he has."

It was Elder Brewster, scratching his white beard and smiling. "And so have you. Pastor Robinson would be proud of you." He paused and added with a chuckle, "But for the sake of peace and harmony among us, it might be best if you took off your Indian garb now and went back to wearing what the other women wear."

She smiled sadly. She'd grown to like the freedom and warmth of her buckskin attire, which made her feel closer to her new Indian sister. It would be hard to go back to skirts and petticoats and clumpy shoes.

When she had put on her former garb, she went to the common house kitchen to work with Elizabeth and Priscilla and Desire. As always when they were working together, the young maidens of Plimoth Plantation had opinions to offer on everything. They began with Mercy's forefinger, which stung from the lye soap in the wash water. The tender scar tissue forming over the blood-covenant cut protected her finger far better than her heart, which was seared by the caustic words of Elizabeth Tilley.

"Weren't we sisters enough?" The jealous words had spilled from Elizabeth's lips as she scrubbed an iron skillet. "Whatever possessed you to do that bloodletting thing with that little savage? Why, she nearly cut your finger to the bone!"

Now it was Desire's turn. "She told us why she'd cut covenant with an Indian, remember?" She whacked a mat with a rug beater, sending a puff of dust in Mercy's direction. "She still wants to be the Princess of Plimoth Rock!"

Mercy closed her left hand into a fist and briefly contemplated doing something decidedly unladylike with it. But then she took a deep breath and calmed down. What she'd done was right, even if they never accepted it.

"And tramping through the woods like an Indian with my John Howland," Elizabeth was saying, "and Priscilla's John Alden! I'll bet she had them both helping her over every rock along the way."

"All right, that's enough!" declared Priscilla, returning with a load of laundry to wash. She wagged a finger at Elizabeth and Desire. "You two, quit it! You're so green with jealousy that the grass is pale next to you!"

Mercy had always been grateful for her level-headed friend, and never more than now.

"Thanks to Mercy, a great wrong will be set right, and Francis has been rescued," declared Priscilla, taking her by the elbow and raising her to her feet. "She's the most courageous woman I ever knew in my life! And just maybe, thanks to her, we'll be liberated from the limits of being the 'weaker sex.' We'll labor alongside our men and blaze new trails into the wilderness with them," she predicted. "And we'll win the hearts of our enemies, as Pastor Robinson called us to."

Mercy smiled for the first time since she'd come back from the Cape. And Priscilla hugged her tight. "I say there's room for another sister in our sisterhood, Mercy; and I'm glad you've given Amie that right. I, for one, look forward to thanking her for rescuing you."

"Hear, hear!" said someone, applauding and startling Priscilla from the dramatic pose she had struck, with one arm around her friend and the other raising a soup ladle heavenward.

It was Edward Winslow with Elder Brewster, leading Jack Billington and his father to the cornfields for a day of hard labor, the sort that the other men had been doing regularly.

As Elder Brewster led John Billington off, Edward Winslow took Jack Billington aside for a private word with Mercy. "Go ahead," he prodded him.

"Mercy Clifton, I have seen the error of my forward ways. Please forgive me for what I've done, that I may obtain your good graces, to abide in this plantation at peace with you. Otherwise, I shall be exiled and my father likewise."

Mercy nodded but could not bring herself to utter the words, "I forgive you." That was pushing things too far. And besides, she couldn't tell if he was sincere or had just been coached by Elder Brewster.

A nod was all she could give, but it seemed to be enough.

As the work party proceeded on down the path with scythe and sickle in hand, Priscilla concluded, "Be grateful, girls. Mercy has been relieved of the mistake of ever marrying the likes of him!"

But Mercy heard Desire mutter, "Good! Then he's all mine."

As usual, the shade of the dense forest along Towne Creek that led to the swamp was decidedly cooler than being out in the blazing August sun. Mercy, back in her buckskins for this special occasion, followed silently behind Squanto and just ahead of Governor Bradford, Elder Brewster, and Edward Winslow.

Bringing up the rear was Miles Standish, who looked almost naked without his musket. But there would be no need of weapons. Peace was the order of the day.

The small party arrived at the ancient burial site, just as another party of the same size did. Chief Massasoit led the other one, accompanied by Samoset, Hobbamock, several other tribal elders, and Amie.

The two groups came to a halt on either side of the ancient grave. At Massasoit's nod, Samoset knelt down and carefully unearthed the resting place of the Great Sachem, the ancestor of all the chiefs of the tribes in the territory. Then Hobbamock produced the owl mask and the full ceremonial headdress that the Billingtons had stolen. Massasoit himself stepped forward, knelt, and reburied them, after which Samoset covered over the grave.

Getting to his feet, the tribal chief looked down at the grave and spoke quietly, waiting for Squanto to translate each phrase.

"We ask that the Great Spirit forgive the English boys who disturbed this resting place. May the chief sleep in peace forever. And may our English friends respect this ground, as we respect the sleeping places of their tribe."

Now Elder Brewster stepped forward and opened the Bible in his hand to Genesis, chapter 3. "The Great Spirit says: thou shalt return unto the ground; for out of it thou wast taken; for thou art dust, and unto dust shalt thou return." Then he quoted from Matthew 19, "Honor thy father and thy mother" and "Thou shalt love thy neighbor as thyself."

On this point Governor Bradford had something to add. He spoke slowly, pausing between phrases to allow Squanto to translate. "It is not easy to love thy neighbor, especially when the neighbor has done great harm to what one holds dear. The words of the Great Spirit say that we must choose love, even when we want to take vengeance. Our brother," he looked at Massasoit, "has chosen love and not war. We are eternally grateful to him. And this matter will remain private between us forever."

The chief said nothing. He extended his right forearm, as did the governor. They gripped one another's arm.

But Governor Bradford was not finished. "Mercy and Amie, come forward."

The two girls, each in buckskins, stood before him.

"In large measure we owe the peace between our peoples, which has been reestablished today, to the courage and maturity of you two."

He turned to Mercy. "You were a diplomat of peace to the Cummaquid and the Nausets, and when you asked Squanto to tell Aspinet his story, you saved us from war. The entire plantation is grateful to you."

Now he addressed Massasoit's daughter. "Amie, after the young Billingtons robbed the chief's grave, your wisdom saved both your people and us much bloodshed. You have made your father proud. And for your courage in killing the wolf and caring for your new blood sister, we cannot thank you enough. We trust that the deepening friendship between you and Mercy will be symbolic of the closeness between our two peoples."

Amie and Mercy looked at each other and smiled. And with that the secret ceremony ended, and all returned to their homes.

47

WE GATHER TOGETHER

It was the morning of September 13, Anno Domini 1621, the day that all the chiefs were coming to Plimoth to take a dual oath of allegiance—to King James, and to their Sachem of sachems, Massasoit. And as always before a big event, there was food to prepare.

Governor Bradford had called on the women cooks of the plantation to use the last of their reserves, if necessary, to prepare a proper feast for their Indian guests. It might mean they would go a little hungry afterwards, but it was almost harvest time. Soon they'd no longer have to worry about having enough to eat.

Mercy was at the oven, baking bread, when Francis came up to her. He handed her a curious clay lump, dried and cracked from the sun, with a dip in the middle. "Here, Mercy, I made this for you at the creek."

"Um, what shall I use it for?" she asked with a smile, not recognizing what it was but not wanting to hurt his feelings.

"It's a honey holder," he said, a little hurt that it wasn't obvious.

"Oh! Sweet, like. . . ." She tried to think of something to say.

"Like you, Mercy. You forgive everybody. I nearly started a war because I wouldn't listen to you, and then you came and rescued me. You've cared for me, no matter how mean I was."

"That's because God cares about you, Francis. You're important to Him."

He nodded. "You and me are like brother and sister now."

"How do you figure that, young man?"

"Well, you're Amie's blood sister. And those Nausets said I was one of them, a real Indian!"

"Why, maybe you are, Francis. And without your doing what you did, this day might never have happened."

Mistress Brewster came by. "We have to hurry now, Mercy. Someone saw Aspinet's canoes coming, and Corbitant is already here."

In another hour the Pilgrim women had prepared their bread and vegetables, and nine of the chiefs were gathered on the open hill on the other side of Towne Creek. The day was glorious, sunny and breezy, as if God Himself were smiling down on them. Mercy was certain He was. She and Priscilla and Elizabeth stood watching with the other women and all of the men who weren't involved with the ceremony. The whole colony was watching.

Aspinet and Iyanough Mercy recognized, and Massasoit, of course. Corbitant, she knew by reputation. Four others she didn't know. And the last one had long hair and red paint on his cheeks; that could only be Canonicus, the leader of the Narragansetts. That he was here, she marveled, made this truly a once-in-a-lifetime event.

Each chief had two elders with him. The Pilgrims were represented by Governor Bradford, Elder Brewster, Edward Winslow, and Captain Standish. She was proud of their governor. With his dark-blue cape unfurling in the breeze, he looked positively noble!

All at once in her heart, she seemed to hear, *"Record it, child."* Her eyes widened. *This was the scene!* The one she was to capture on the blank page in Papa's Bible!

She ran into the common house, where the Bible was kept under Elder Brewster's pulpit. Carefully extracting the precious page, she borrowed a cutting board to put it on. Then she went to the Winslow house and took the three sharpened, charcoaled sticks that Jack had made for her to replace the ones lost in the fire, and hurried back to where she'd been watching.

Up on the hill the chiefs and the Pilgrim Elders were about to seal their peace treaty. Mercy quickly and lightly sketched each figure in. Later Amie could show her how to add colors made from berries.

She smiled. This was exactly the scene Papa would have wanted!

The ceremony began with each chief having something to say. Squanto, who was standing by Massasoit, translated for the benefit of the Englishmen.

"What are they saying?" asked Elizabeth.

"I don't know; I can't hear," replied Mercy. The wind is taking away their words." But it didn't matter. The significance and solemnity of the occasion needed no translation.

"Well, it must be good," Priscilla chimed in. "Look what they're doing!"

Just before she spoke, Massasoit had produced a long-necked pipe, packed with tobacco, and held it across his bare chest. Now he lit it from a smoldering piece of charcoal and then puffed on it. This was the pipe of peace, adorned with two eagle feathers. He passed it to the chief on his right, who also took a puff and passed it on.

When the pipe had gone to all the chiefs and back to Massasoit, they all hailed him as their leader.

Massasoit then passed the pipe to Governor Bradford, who took a puff himself to signify that the Pilgrims would live in peace with all the chiefs and their tribes.

After this, Bradford made a few remarks to the chiefs, translated by Squanto, and followed by a statement from Massasoit. The chiefs nodded solemnly. Later Mercy learned that the Governor had said that Indians and Pilgrims alike were all now joined together by peace treaty under King James. Massasoit had pronounced, "King James, we all his men!"

At that moment Miles Standish gave a signal, and one of the cannon roared a salute!

The chiefs jumped but soon realized that the cannon was not loaded with anything but powder. Mercy smiled to think that Captain Standish must have suggested this, a harmless but significant show of firepower. Its meaning had not been lost on Corbitant or Canonicus, who were now whispering together. Peace, she suspected, real peace, had never looked so good.

A month later the harvest was in, and so abundant that they scarcely had room to store it all! Everyone was happy, including Mercy. True, she had no young man interested in her; and true, her peas died on the vine, as Squanto had predicted. But Loyal, her four-footed family of one, was back with her and healthy as ever. And she loved living with the Brewsters. Governor Bradford had expanded her garden plot, and next year, with a little more watering and tender care, even her peas would come in!

So she did not mind the extra work involved in preparing for the three-day harvest festival that the Governor had decreed. Massasoit was invited, of course, and Amie would be coming. It was going to be a time of Thanksgiving!

Except, word had just reached them that Massasoit was bringing *ninety* men, women, and children with him! For three days of feasting? Dear Lord, what would become of their precious food reserves, so recently stored away to feed the colony during the coming winter?

She needn't have worried. Massasoit arrived a day early and quickly sent out a hunting party, which soon returned with five deer trussed up on poles, and twelve wild turkeys! Plus, a number of his squaws had brought dried summer berries for the Pilgrim women to bake into pies.

But what a lot of cooking to do! Huge steaming pots of lobsters, and quahog clams that Squanto fetched for them with the help of the children. Amie taught Mercy and her friends to make *nasaump*, a mush out of hominy kernels, onion, and cranberries, of which there was an abundant supply in the landscape surrounding them, floating red on watery bogs.

Mercy helped Susana Winslow cut up pumpkins until her hands were stained yellow-orange! Mistress Brewster made loaves of bread from them, with beaten eggs and pearl ash. They cooked up kettles of sweet molasses. Elizabeth stood next to them cutting apples for brewing into cider. They needed enough to satisfy everyone's thirst for several days and still fill barrels for the winter. And to that she added the last of their supply of cinnamon.

"What are you doing," demanded Priscilla, "emptying the last of that into cider?"

"This is a very special occasion!" retorted Elizabeth. "Give, and ye shall receive. We can expect that the first ship to come will be bringing cinnamon, along with all the other things we need."

At high noon the festival began. And the first event was the singing of an old hymn, much beloved by all the Pilgrims. As they harmonized, the Indians were bemused.

> *We gather together in joyful Thanksgiving,*
> *Rejoicing in goods which the ages have wrought,*
> *For life that enfolds us, and helps and heals and holds us,*
> *And leads beyond the goals which our forbears once sought!*
> *We sing of the freedoms, which martyrs and heroes*
> *Have won by their labor, their sorrow, their pain.*

Mercy's eyes filled. They'd not sung that hymn since they'd left Leiden. She leaned over to Mistress Brewster and thanked her again for taking her in. The ample woman embraced her new charge fondly.

There were bow-and-arrow shooting contests, relay races, and a musket demonstration. And always more to eat.

Mercy had one twinge, when in the midst of the festivities, Priscilla, all atwitter, whispered to her that John Alden had asked her to marry him. Mercy told her how happy she was for her, but when her friend went off to tell the others, she sighed. If God wanted her to marry, He'd better bring her someone.

But even if He didn't, she had finally made up her mind. She was not going back on the next ship. This was her home, forever. This was where God had planted her, and this was where she would stay.

48

SAIL, HO!

One morning several weeks after their Thanksgiving celebration, the cry they'd long been waiting for was finally heard! *"Sail, ho!"*

A ship was coming!

Mercy could see its sail poking over the horizon. With Loyal following behind her, she ran up to her prayer rock and sat down, hugging her knees while she watched it get larger.

Thoughts flooded into her mind. There would be cinnamon for Tilley and spices for all of them. There would be carpenter's tools, to replace the ones that had worn out. Hopefully, there would be new clothes for everyone because they had repaired their garments so often that even the patches had patches!

And maybe there would even be some luxury items, like—dare she think it—ink and paper?

And then she had a sad thought. Some of the letters they would be bringing would be to those who had passed away to heaven in the time after the *Mayflower* had carried the last news of them to Europe, six months ago.

A shadow fell across her. She looked up to see Governor Bradford standing beside her.

"You come here, too, sometimes, I see."

"Sometimes," she said, starting to get up to let him have the space to himself.

"No, Mercy, I want to talk to you, if you don't mind."

She shifted over, making room for him on her rock.

Together, they watched the sail grow larger until they could see the whole ship. The Governor had brought a brass spyglass with him, a gift from Master Jones. Now he stretched it out and focused on the newcomer. "Thank God, she's not French!" he said with relief. "That's the Union Jack flying from her mizzen." He continued to study her. "She's a merchant-man, like the *Mayflower*, only bigger. We'll go down in a few minutes to greet her."

Now he put down the glass and turned to Mercy. "Well, are you staying? Or going home?"

"You mean home—to Holland?"

He nodded.

"I *am* home, sir. This," her eyes swept the plantation, "is my home."

His eyes searched hers, and then he said, "I was hoping you'd say that, ever since we reburied the headdress and the mask. I knew then—and I think you knew it, too—that God had a special plan for you on this side of the ocean."

"Yes, sir. I'm not sure it was settled then. But that's when I began to think about it."

"And is it settled now?"

"Absolutely!"

From beneath his cloak he withdrew the ancient red-leather pouch. "I think you've seen this before."

"The Crimson Cross!" Mercy exclaimed.

"Here," he said simply. "Open it."

She looked at him inquiringly.

"Go ahead."

She opened the pouch and took out the gleaming silver cross with its five rubies. "Oh, it's so beautiful! The most beautiful thing in the plantation! Thank you for letting me look at it!"

"You can look at it any time you want, Mercy."

"What do you mean?"

"I'm giving it to you. The bearer of this cross is a person that God has called to a lifetime of serving Him. It may or may not be a service that is widely known, but it will be known in Heaven.

He looked out to sea. "I was about your age when it was given to me, and I was told that when the time came I would know the young person to whom I was to pass it." He smiled. "I do know; I've known for some time. But it had to wait until *you* knew that you would stay here."

Mercy was speechless.

"Since our Thanksgiving celebration with Massasoit, God has shown me something more about this cross. He has brought it to the New World so that, from now on, everyone who receives it will be called by Him to advance His plan for America. And, He will watch over and protect each one who has the cross."

He turned his gaze back to her. "You may not ever have all the things in life you want," he mused. "But you will always have this cross to remind you that God will never leave nor forsake you. In return, He expects you to give Him your utmost."

"Sir, I shall do my best to live a life worthy of this calling."

"I'm sure you will, Mercy," said the Governor.

She thought of something. "How will I know to whom I'm supposed to give it?"

"When the time comes, you'll know."

Governor Bradford got up and gave her a hand. "Come on, we have people to greet."

As they went down the hill, Mercy carefully tucked the red pouch in her most secure pocket.

By the time they reached the plantation's landing next to Plimoth Rock, the ship had dropped anchor close enough to read the name on her bow: *Fortune.* Mercy scooped up Loyal and held her tight in her arms, as more and more Pilgrims came down to the landing.

And here came the ship's longboat, with its first load of passengers.

Suddenly, as the longboat arrived, Loyal bounded out of her embrace.

"Loyal! Come back!" Mercy yelled after her.

But then she stopped. Loyal was running to someone at full speed, her little ears straight back. Who?

Mercy squinted. No! It couldn't be! She looked harder. *"It is!"* she exclaimed aloud.

It was her dear childhood friend, Edward Winslow's younger brother, John! She had no idea that he was coming!

Edward Winslow was as surprised as she was to see his younger brother. "John?" he called. "I can't believe it!"

The brothers embraced. Then John bent down to pick up Loyal, who had been jumping up and down against his knees.

Mercy stared at him. Either he was more handsome than she remembered, or he had grown more so in the past year. He was now quite dashing!

Edward took John by the arm and led him toward Mercy, saying, "Come, John, there's someone here who will be glad to see you."

As John came up to Mercy, Loyal leapt out of his arms into hers!

Smiling, John tilted his head and asked, "Have we not done this before?"

Mercy blushed, remembering the barge leaving Leiden.

John bowed low. "I am truly blessed to see you, Mercy! And, my goodness! You have become a beautiful woman!"

He offered her his arm. "Will you do me the honor of showing me the plantation?" Putting her arm in his, she realized that her heart was beating rapidly. And something else . . . she felt complete.

HISTORICAL NOTE

While we have a tale to tell, we have, as much as possible, stayed true to the history of the Pilgrims' voyage on the *Mayflower*, and their first year ashore, creating Plimoth Plantation (now Plymouth, Massachusetts). Mercy Clifton is fictional, but she is based on Mary Chilton, who was thirteen when she sailed on the *Mayflower* and would later marry Edward Winslow's younger brother, John. Chief Massasoit's daughter *was* named Amie, due, we suspect, to their contact with French fur traders. The Brewsters, of course, as well as the Bradfords, the Winslows, the Carvers, and the Hopkins were all true to life. The *Mayflower*'s master, Christopher Jones, proved to be quite helpful to the Pilgrims. And, thanks to the poet Henry Wadsworth Longfellow, the romance between John Alden and Priscilla Mullins is well-known to all.

The Billington men were a major problem from the beginning of the Plymouth Colony. John, the father, would eventually be hanged for murder. Francis did nearly sink the *Mayflower*, but it was his older brother, John (whom we call Jack), who got lost in the woods and was found by Indians. Although there is no record of the boys digging up an Indian burial mound, the Pilgrims would not have been surprised if they had.

Some of the details of Squanto's remarkable story are lost in the mists of history, but there is no question of the pivotal role he played in helping the Pilgrims survive that first terrible winter and in concluding the peace treaty between the Pilgrims and Massasoit. William Bradford called him "a godsend." One year later he would die of a fever on a Pilgrim fishing expedition to Cape Cod.

The Indians' use of English varied. During Squanto's nine-year stay in England, his English would have become fluent. Amie, however, would know only the small amount of English that Mercy and Squanto could teach her. Other Indians would speak only bits and pieces of broken English, picked up through their contact with English fishing expeditions.

John Goodman did bring his Bull Mastiff and his English Springer Spaniel, but no one knows their names, so we named them. And every ship needs a rat-catching cat, so Charlemagne insisted on being included in our story.

In 1620, while there were several tribes in the region, none occupied the land on which the Pilgrims settled. The Patuxets had lived there, but they had died a few years before of a mysterious plague. Massasoit, chief of the Wampanoag, was headquartered near present-day Swansea. He was also the Great Sachem over some lesser chiefs: Corbitant of the Nemaskets (near Middleborough); Iyanough of the Cummaquid (near Barnstable, on Cape Cod); and Aspinet of the Nausets (near Eastham, on Cape Cod).

The relationship between the Pilgrims and the Native Americans was indeed a friendly one for many years. The crucial peace treaty between the Pilgrims and Massasoit did occur in March 1621 and would last until after Massasoit's death in 1661.